Finding the Route 40 Phantom

S.Collin Ellsworth

DEDICATION

This book is a work of fiction   based from a legend of a town very dear to me. Only one character is based from a real person and deviates from actual events. She doesn't object. If she did, she'd haunt me. Instead, she guided me through the story.

CONTENTS

ACKNOWLEDGMENTS

Special thanks goes to the members of the Chanhassen Authors Collective and my family for all of their support.

PROLOUGE

Rain turned into sleet. Wet roads became slippery as ice. Erwin once drove through the mud in Germany during the Great War. As crazy as it seemed, he preferred the dirt in a war zone that an icy freeway. Crossing the Route 40 Bridge over the Englewood Dam would be treacherous.

Moments of crossing the bridge, Erwin saw a dark station wagon in his headlights. As Erwin caught up to the station wagon, he realizes that the car was parked in the middle of the bridge! Erwin pulled the horn.

The station wagon took off like a jackrabbit. Two hundred feet it jack-knifed. Erwin hit the brakes to avoid hitting the car. The truck missed crushing the station wagon by mere inches.

Erwin got out of his truck. He was going to give that crazy driver a piece of his mind. That guy nearing killed him and himself.

Erwin had his hand on the station wagon's driver side door when the inside of the car glowed green. Erwin stepped back. He wiped his eyes. The car shone green and a skeleton was driving the car! Erwin ran to his truck.

" Excuse me, Sir, is something wrong."

Erwin turned to find a skeleton man behind him!

He went into his cab and hid. He didn't come out until he heard the ghostly car speed away.

ALEXANDRA

My phone keeps beeping. I always have to check it in case it is my husband, Anthony, or my mother-in-law calling about some family emergency. Heck, I'd even take my nine-year-old daughter calling about the drama in the third grade. Instead, it's a bunch of texts from my younger sister, Shona: "Alex. Urgent. Call me quick."

The last time I answered one of Shona's "urgent" texts I received the news that another bookstore was in danger of closing in our hometown. A month later the store remains open. Whereas I support locally own bookstores, I don't call that a "need to drop everything" emergency. What we classify as an emergency is one of the many difference between my sister and me. Currently, the biggest gap between us is the amount of time on our hands. I currently hold two jobs. Shona just graduated from college during horrible economic times.

I put the phone in purse and walk into the office of the Englewood Herald. Most of my fellow reporters are on their tablets looking up videos of cute animals on Youtube except for our sports editor who is kept busy with the stats of the townships' high school sports, which take up an entire page.

Donna Clayborne, our events columnist, looks up from her video of yawning cats. "Wilson, Chip wants to see you in his office right away." Donna's eyes go back to the yawning Persian cat on her screen. I walk upstairs to the office that overlooked the reporters' desk. Inside sat our editor-in-chief, Chip Edmundson.

The Herald is housed in an old tiny textile factory. I have to climb metal steps to reach Chip's office. I can see his round face peering through the window overlooking the staff. When I first climbed the stairs for my job interview, I thought he was a guy with a God complex with his office set up like that. That couldn't be further from the truth. Ten years my senior, Chip is a boyish man with massive amounts of energy. If he had it his way, he'd be sitting down with the reporters. Rumor has it that the staff forced him upstairs because when he's got a big idea, he vocally paces the floor. I open the door to see Chip walking with a smile on his face. Today will be no exception.

"Hiya, Wilson, sit down!"

I sit down in the chair in front of Chip's table. Somehow, he sits too, yet he twiddles his thumbs.

"Wilson, I must say that was a lovely article you wrote about Lisa Hubbard's battle with breast cancer. I was amazed. I knew when I hired you that you would be good. After all, you do work for the Dayton Flyer…."
"I don't exactly write for the Flyer, Edmundson."

"Well, you have better things to write than your Hollywood sources for Flyer's entertainment column. I swear, Wilson, you had me crying as Lisa said goodbye to her mother. How you quoted her saying that she couldn't imagine burying her mother so in a way the cancer was a good thing…"

Chip wipes his eyes with his sleeve. "I was going to save it for next month since October is Breast Cancer Awareness month, but I am going to push it up sooner. Get an earlier kickoff."

"We could make this a weekly piece for October," I suggest. "I would love to interview survivors of Breast Cancer as well."
"Hmmm," Chip says wiping a large oil slick on his forehead with his sleeve. "The thing is that Lisa Hubbard's story was an Englewood story. I want to keep the Herald strictly Englewood. I got this great idea for the month of October."

I knew Lisa Hubbard couldn't be the only woman in Englewood ever diagnosed with Breast Cancer. One of the downfalls of working under Chip was that he manically moved from one idea to the next.

"What are you thinking?" I inquire.

"Englewood Mysteries!" Chip exclaims.

"Englewood mysteries?"
Chip jumps up from his desk. "Think about it! Halloween! Things are

spooky!"

"You want me to do a piece on cemeteries and haunted houses in the area?"

Chip laughs. "You think I am sending you ghost hunting, Alexandra? Not at all! In fact, I have two potential leads for you to follow. Are you ready to write them down?"

I pull out my pocket notepad and golf pencil from my back jeans pocket.

"Potential number one: in nineteen seventy-four, Doug Bolster, a mild-mannered man of thirty-four years old kisses his wife and two daughters goodbye and heads to his job at Huntington Bank. But he never showed up for work that day, nor any day after that. He vanished. To this day, no one knows where he is."

I quickly jotted, Doug Bolster, missing since 1974.

"Potential number two: in the early to mid-fifties a dark car sped past truckers on old Route 40. Suddenly the car would jack knife miles in front of the truck. Then the trucker would see a skeleton illuminated by an eerie green light sitting in the driver seat!"

"I thought you weren't going to send me on a ghost hunt, Chip?"

"Wilson! Don't be silly! Ghosts aren't real. However, a person impersonating a skeleton was; but no one knows who he is!"

I wrote down, Explore the effects of drinking and driving-oh wait, it's been done.

"You think you got something to work with, Wilson?" Chip asks gleefully.

"I'll see if I can interview some people and take it from there." Chip swing his elbow upwards. "That's the spirit, Wilson."

I walk down the stairs with the eyes of Shauna Cousins, our receptionist, giving me the icy glare.

"Your sister left you five messages in the ten minutes you were in

Edmonson's office. Kindly tell her that I am not your private operator. I work for a newspaper, not a hotline for WASPs to air their perceived problems."

"Sorry, Cousins," I say.

Shauna huffs and struts back to her desk.

My phone vibrates in my purse. Shauna eyes me again. "Take that outside, Wilson."

Donna leans over to my desk. "If you compliment her on her weave, maybe she'll let up on you."

"Maybe her problem is that it is sewed too tight on her scalp."

My phone vibrates. "Wilson! Take it out!" Shauna yells.

With a smile towards Shauna, I head out the back door.

"This better be good!" I hiss. "You pulled me out of work!"

"I have news of epic portions!" Shona whispers over the phone.

"Really? So why are you whispering?"

"So Pops doesn't hear me."

"You're at Pops'? What are you doing there?"

"He wanted Jo-Jo's room cleaned out. Mom isn't able to do it, so she sent me."

Jo-Jo was our maternal grandmother. She died this past July. She was an all right woman to me, tepid towards my sister, and could be downright nasty to my mother. The Lutheran community of Rochester, New York loved her. At her funeral, it took all the strength my mom had not to roll her eyes when an elder member of the congregation mentioned that Jo-Jo was a dear, loving woman.

"What did you find? A horde of empty cigarette cartons? Hardcore pornography? Letters from a lesbian lover?"
"Ewww."

"Come on, Shona. Gay is natural. Before you know it, Scientists may be studying whether it is genetic."

"I was referring to the cigarettes and porn you mentioned. Both disgusting."

I feel like lighting up a cancer stick from my emergency pack I stash in my desk. Being around the spirited Chip and my high energy sister drains my limited energy reserves. Yet, I am intrigued what Shona found in my seemingly perfect grandmother's closet. After a lifetime of indifference from my grandmother, Shona felt likewise about her. Whatever Shona found must be beyond newsworthy.

"Jo-Jo had a gay lover!" I chime, "It would be so like her to be secretly gay after telling Mom that she was an abomination for decades! I loved Jo-Jo and all, but the fact that she was a hypocrite never went pass me…"

"Alexandra!" Shona shouts, "Your theory doesn't hold up. Jo-Jo and Mom didn't share the same genetic material!"

My stomach burns as if it contained the fire which sizzled the incorrect pages of history as I knew it. I didn't need cigarettes; I needed TUMS.

"Mom was store bought?"

"Yes, she was adopted."

"Does Mom know she is adopted?"

"I haven't asked. I just found the adoption certificate that declares 'Baby Girl born on September 23rd, 1953 is now declared to be Susan Grace Richards' minutes ago."

"You're calling me about Mom possibly being adopted before you even ask her…or Pops even?"

"Well, the news wouldn't impact you that much?"

"Really…"

"Ohh, I got to go," Shona hush, "I hear Pops coming up the stairs." For the first time, Shona ends a call before I want her to. I don't know what to do besides stand in the paper's parking lot in disbelief.

My mom being adopted doesn't change things. My mom is still my mom. Jo-Jo and Pops are my grandparents. Biology didn't always determine family. I have to admit this wasn't the most earth-shattering news I ever received. As much as I rationalize it in my head, I can't carry on that life as I know it doesn't exist.

Thankfully, the Herald pays me a salary instead of an hourly wage. I go back to my desk and gather my things. I look up at Chip's window. He seems to be surrounded by faint smoke? Chip doesn't smoke.

I saluted Chip, so he thinks I am off to chase the next story. Chip salutes back with a smile. I head for the door to go home.

NATALIE 1952

"Geez, Mariola," I said as I enter the bathroom. "You sure are taking your sweet time!"

Mariola sat at the edge of my family's bathtub soaking up blood with toilet tissue. Three raging streaks ran down her shins.

"Jesus Christ, Mariola! What are you trying to do? Skin yourself alive?" I immediately took a beige towel from the towel rack and covered Mariola's skin, applying pressure over the gashes.

"I was just trying to shave my legs."

"Didn't your mother teach you to lightly drag the razor across your leg, so only the hairs get cut?"

"Women didn't shave their legs in the old country."

"Women don't shave their legs in Canada?"

"Women don't shave their legs in Sicily."

I let go of Mariola's leg and grab the bar of soap. I gently work a lather to rub on Mariola's other shin. I couldn't let my friend go with one hairy leg. Mariola placed the razor in my outstretch palm.

"What were you thinking hastily shaving your legs this morning?"

"It's too warm for wool stockings" Mariola answered. "Nylons would be much cooler, but they are so thin. My dark hair would show through them."

Mr. Whitman only ordered nylon for the pale folk of Englewood. I questioned where Mariola could find nylons tan enough for her skin tone. It didn't matter that day for Mariola sported thick red lines on her shin.

"I think my mom has a nice part of slacks. Maybe you can get by wearing them today."

"It's against the rules to wear pants at school."

"Boys wear them."

Mariola wrapped the towel covering her modesty tighter around her brassiere. "I would prefer not to start my senior year giving a reason for everyone to call me a boy as well."

"Well, my mother's slack wouldn't fit you well enough," I said. "She's about a half foot taller than you and me."

With that, I got an idea. I ran to my mother's room. In her closet was a floral print dress my uncle's wife made for her a couple of years ago. Mom only wore it once in to appease her family.

I ran down the stairs to the bathroom where I found Mariola bandaging gauze to her shin.

"Here, wear this!"

"That dress is for elderly ladies! You mother wouldn't be caught dead in that!"

That was true, but it was the only thing in my mom's closet that wasn't black. She eschewed any garment bearing color since the day my father arrived from Europe in a pine box.

"Well, unless you wish to explain your mutilated leg, you don't have much of an option," I pointed out. "The dress is long enough to cover the gash near your ankle."

"And my entire foot," Mariola replied.

"You can borrow the heels I wear to church."
Mariola dejectedly reached for the dress and went to our bedroom.

Mariola and I walked my little brother, Chester, to his school before we headed over to Randolph high school. Mariola kept tripping over the mother's dress. She was not used to the high heels I wore every Sunday. By the time we reached the school, the bottom of the dress was covered in shoe prints.

The late August heat purged my pores of their never ending supply of oil. There were ten minutes before we needed to be in homeroom.

"I need to go powder," I said.

Mariola followed me to the girl's room. She went into a stall while I went to the mirror. In walked Joretta Barr and her cohort, Mary Iris Stuart whose voice followed her from the halls.

"I don't see why you aren't concerned, Jo. Every guy in this school is going to go to Korea once they get their diplomas."
"I still don't see the point to your concern," Jo said, pulling out a color of lipstick that was too red to be allowed in school. "We saw this when we were children. The men go off marching into war, and they come marching back a year later."

I snapped my press powder, "Not everyone did."

Joretta gave me a snarky look. "Now who might you be?"

Mary Iris stood up to Joretta's ear on tip toes. "That's Dr. Studebaker's daughter, Natalie. Her father died when the Nazi's bombed England."

"Oh, yes," Joretta whispered before turning to me. "My sympathies for your lost, in fact, I know what it is like for you. I lost my father too."
I stood there silently willing my eyes not to roll. Joretta Barr lost her father to drinking five years ago. Ever since her mother was promoted from maid to the fiancé of Mr. Butterfeld, Englewood's richest banker, Joretta walked around town as if she was Miss America.

Joretta remained oblivious to my lack of receptiveness. She turned to Mary Iris.

"Now, the people we have to watch out for are the Cubans," Joretta said, "I heard Mr. Butterfeld talking to my mother this morning that an evil dictator has taken over."

Joretta's chatter ended with the flush of the toilet. Olive skinned and dark haired Mariola exited the stall. Joretta and Mary Iris stood wide-eyed for moments then started frantically whispering to each other.

"She's Canadian," I snapped, "Not Cuban."

"She must be an Eskimo," I heard Mary Iris whispered. "They are like the Indians we have here."

"Oh, you're right," Joretta cooed. "Mr. Butterfeld was talking about how churches are helping the government remove Indian children from their savage homes and sending them to proper white homes to learn American ways. Is she staying with you, Natalie?"

"She is but she is not…"

With that, Joretta shook Mariola's hand. "Welcome to Englewood! I'm Joretta Barr. If you need anything-anything at all in the way of Christian charity, you just let me know, okay?"

"Okay, Miss Barr."

"Oh, please, call me Miss Joretta," Joretta giggled.

Joretta and Mary Iris left the bathroom giggling as they left.

"You are never to add Miss to any of that rat's names!" I yelled. "She's not above you or me! She's not anything!"

"She was dressed mighty fancy," Mariola commented.

"How a person dress doesn't determine one's character!"

"Aye, Miss Natalie, I wish there was truth in that," Mariola sighed as she walked towards the bathroom door. "If it were otherwise, I would have proudly proclaimed I was a gypsy when she called me an Eskimo."

During my first two years at Randolph High School, I could be found alone reading a book by the tree. I didn't have much in the way of friends in Englewood. Kids my age baffled me. The boys walked around school saying, "I'm a jock. Bake me cookies, Girl."

The girls often responded in kind, "Sure, I'll bake you cookies," with a giggle from their lacquered pink lips.

Never did I hear, "Did you read the newspaper today?" or "What did you find interesting in our class discussion about current events?"

Square was what the others called me. Instead of spending time after school at Waltman's general store, spending my nonexistent allowance, I was at the library studying. I didn't waste my time primping for the farm boys of Englewood, Union, or Clayton. I intended to leave the three village township for a future. I was going to Ohio State University like my parents. My mother's boss promised he'd save back some of her wages for a college fund for her kids. There, I would learn to be an adult who did great things. If I happened to meet a man with the same ambitious, swell.

Although I had no interesting in conversing with the ninnies at Randolph High School, I did wish for a friend. The week after my junior year ended, my mother came home with Mariola. The band of gypsies she and her mother were traveling with got arrested for vagrancy. Mother's boss, Attorney Christopher Kristoff, was brought into the case as a public defendant. He urged my mom to take Mariola into our house while throughout the duration of the case. It would be a brief matter.

Unfortunately, Mariola's mother was found hung in her jail cell. The police never disclosed the circumstances.

Since her mother's death, Mariola lived with us. My mom managed to enroll her into Randolph High School in my class. Even though it was great to have a pal, I was sometimes baffled at Mariola quiet statements of wisdom. Sometimes at lunch, we just sat for the entire hour in silence.

That day, I did have something to say. "You don't have to call people our age Miss or Mr."
"I was told that was the proper way to address someone," Mariola said looking down.

"If you are a maid, maybe," I commented, "but here you are equal as anyone else."

"People called me ma'am today," Mariola replied, "that's a sign of respect."

I didn't have the heart to tell Mariola the reason she was called "ma'am" was because she looked like an elderly lady in that floral dress. "It sure is."

Lunch would be over in fifteen minutes. I had an errand to accomplish. "Come with me to the principal's office."

"Are we in trouble?"

"No. We just got something to do."

The Principal's secretary, Miss Bentley, was scribbling a memo as Mariola and I entered the office. She briefly lifted her eyes from her paper.

"Natalie Studebaker," Miss Bentley muttered, "Isn't it too early in the school year to be presenting grievances to Principal Chet."

"I bear no injuries," I said, "I just want to talk to Principal Chet."

"Principal Chet is not to be interrupted. He is currently on the phone long distance to Columbus. He hopes a college recruiter from Ohio State University will attend one of our football games in the fall. It's possible some students will receive scholarships as the result of his visit. If you don't have a significant grievance, then you need to leave."

"Thank you, Miss Bentley," I said.

"Why did you want to talk to Principal Chet?" Mariola asked as we shut the door to the Principal's office.

"I don't need to see him now," I answered. "I got the information I needed. If what Miss Bentley says is true I am going to Ohio State!"

"Aren't you already in Ohio?"

"The college, Mariola," I explained. "If I get to talk to the college recruiter, I don't have to see Mr. Benson, our guidance counselor and be handed this dribble."

Mariola took a pamphlet I had in my binder, "The Three 'A's' to Femininity," she read. "How to be Ambitious to take Action on Attracting a partner."

"I have more to do with my life than be pretty and run a house," I shout as the course bell rang.

ALEXANDRA

I am welcomed by the smells of Italian cooking. Despite giving me the common name of Wilson, my husband, Anthony, gave me an Italian-American mother-in-law who makes fantastic meals. It is among the many reasons she's allowed to live with us until she dies.

Nona is in the kitchen sautéing chicken and garlic. Sitting at our kitchen table making salad was our neighbor, Mother Hubbard. Like Nona, Mother Hubbard is of Italian heritage. She's over here for dinner a couple of times a week.

"Alex!" Mother Hubbard greeted, "How are you?"

"Good," I say kissing Mother Hubbard on both cheeks. "How are you?"

"Old," she chuckles.

I sit at the table and grab the vegetable peeler and a carrot from the table. Nona smacks me on the back. "No, you don't! You worked all day."

I shrug, "All I am doing here is sitting."

"After you worked! Besides, didn't you work at both jobs today?"

"I only ended up working a half shift at the Herald today."

"Still, you worked two jobs today. You don't need to cook. With Mother Hubbard here, I got everything under control."

I don't think Mother Hubbard should be using a vegetable peeler with her arthritis; however, if Nona catches me helping behind her back, she'll whack me again.

"Are Anthony and Natalia home?"

"Natalia didn't have much homework, so Anthony is having her ride her bike while he jogs next to her," Nona answers.

"Should Anthony really be jogging as much as he does?" asks Mother Hubbard.

"He's been doing it for the past nine years," Nona replies from the stove.

I go to the refrigerator and grab three bottles of water. Nona waves hers away. Back at the table I open one and place it in front of Mother Hubbard before opening my own.

"Chip loved my piece about Lisa," I mentioned. "In fact, he wants to move up the print date."

"Oh, he did!"

I could see a hint of joy before a cloud of sadness formed in her eye. Lisa was her youngest child and only daughter. She was only twenty-three when diagnosed. Lisa died twenty-five years ago, yet the pain never lessens. Mother Hubbard's son resides in Columbus but often joins his pastor wife in mission trips aboard. With her two grandchildren living out of town as well, Anthony and I became her honorary grandchildren. I love her as a granddaughter should.

"It was so easy to write about Lisa because I love you," I say. "I know that is why I did a great job on the article. Writing about Lisa made me feel like I finally had the chance to know her."

Mother Hubbard pats my hand.

"Chip says I could have a future as a feature writer at the Herald. I thought my article on Lisa could kick off a month long feature on women in the area who died or survived breast cancer; however, Chip is off to his latest idea."

"That's old Chip for you," Mother Hubbard chuckles, "What is he having you do?"

"Englewood mysteries," I answer, "He wants me to either look into the disappearance of Doug Bolster or discover the identity of some guy dressed in a skeleton costume who attempted to run truckers off the Englewood Dam in the nineteen fifties."

"The Route 40 Phantom? There isn't much of a story there."

"The missing man sounds interesting," Nona says from the stove. "Knowing Chip, you'll just have to write that one story, and he'll have you do something about Englewood dog owners throughout history."

"He wouldn't have me do something that lame."

"Didn't he have you write about the history of the vacant strip mall last spring?"

"That's because it used to be a functioning strip mall," I answer, "Chip intended the article to initiate a discussion about what to do with the property. It worked. It is now a gas station."

"I remember Dougie B.," says Mother Hubbard. "He used to deliver our newspaper. He had a twin sister named Darla. He married one of the Irving girls. Megan was her name. My husband was the city's detective at the time. It was the only case where not a lick of evidence surfaced. Poor Megan seemed to give up. She went back to South Dakota to live with her sister. It was such a mysterious case…"

Anthony and our daughter, Natalia come in. Anthony's black hair stands perfectly disheveled and slicked back with sweat. Natalia's braid clings to the back of her pink t-shirt. Nona takes the chicken off the stove.

"Both of you shower. We have company for dinner."

"No, we don't," Natalia whines, "It's just Mother Hubbard."

"Natalia, respect!" Anthony reprimands. "Go upstairs and do as you're told."

Natalia slumps upstairs. Anthony heads over to the refrigerator and drinks orange juice straight out of the carton. Nona hits him on the shoulder.

"What don't you practice what you preach?"

"What, Mom?"

"We have a guest for dinner. Quit acting like a Neanderthal!"

"Seriously, Mom, I am not a child anymore!" Anthony shouts as slumps upstairs as well.

Nona turns to me and Mother Hubbard. "An officer he may have been, but a gentleman, definitely not!"

****

"What did Shona want?" Anthony asks as he takes off his leg for bed.

"What?" I ask as I put a tank top over my head.

"She called the house ten times before Natalia and I went outside. She said she called your office and your cell, couldn't get a hold of you."

Sometimes our marital activities left me in a stupor. Tonight was no exception seeing how he caught me by surprise throwing me on the bedroom floor. I like it like that sometimes.

I rack my brain to remember if I had spoken to Shona. Suddenly today's conversation popped into my mind. "Oh, Shona discovered Mom was adopted today."

"What?!"

"Shona found an adoption certificate that listed Mom's name and birthdate on it."

I pull the covers over my shoulders. Anthony sits up.

"Well, why didn't you say something tonight?"

Going back to the normalcy of home helped me recover from the shock of the news. Our dinner conversation consisted of stories from Nona and Mother Hubbard of when they raised children. Most stories were funny enough to entertain Natalia for an hour. I felt no need to announce my mother's origins at the table especially since I didn't have answers to any questions.

"It was weird to hear at first," I say, "but I've quickly realize it doesn't change anything in my life. Jo-Jo and Pops were still my grandparents. If anything the news makes sense. Mom was a redhead born to brunettes. That genetic mystery is solved."

"You sure you're okay?"

"Anthony, I grew up for nineteen years believing my parents were heterosexual. It was a shock when they came out, but once it wore off I was cool."

"Tell that to your mother," Anthony muttered.

I turned off the lamp besides my bed. Anthony wrapped me in his muscular arms around me.

"Hey," Anthony whispered, "Mom saw a help wanted ad for part time work at Kroger's today. She's thinking about applying."

"She has a job."

Nona doesn't want for anything. With all she does for the house and caring for Natalia since she was a baby, she can buy whatever she wants for herself with our checkbook no questions asked.

"Well, Mom figures if she wasn't around, we could afford to have a second child. She hates being an additional mouth to feed if it means we can't have another kid."

"Who says anything about another kid?"

"Well, Natalia is almost ten. If you want our children to grow up in the house together, then we need to start thinking about getting pregnant again....Alex?"

"Isn't this a conversation a girl is supposed to start?"

"Aren't girls supposed to want guys who want kids?"

The last thing I want to do was to give anything serious thought. I kiss Anthony on the head and roll over.

NATALIE

Mariola and I went straight home to drop off our books and changes into our dungarees before we walked over to the elementary school to pick up Chester. Right when we turned into our street, Overlook Drive, Chester sped past us on his bike wearing a safari hat.

"Chester!" I called out, "What are you doing?"

Chester broke and looked back towards us. "I am riding over to Jimmy's."

"Are you and Jimmy planning on shooting lions?" I asked.

"I freckle!" Chester pouted. "I already promised Mom I'll be home in time for supper! Leave me alone!"

"When did you see Mom?" I shouted after him.

"She walked me home from school!" He shouted as he rode away.

My mother hadn't made it home before dinner in nine years. Something had to have been wrong. I started to sprint home.

"Wait, Natalie!" Mariola cried behind me. "I can't run in these shoes!"

I continued to run into the house. Instead of facing the unknown disaster, I found my mother in the kitchen by the stove. She had changed out of her black business dress into a house dress I haven't seen since my father left for Europe. Mariola panted behind me.

"Natalie Lauren Studebaker! The whole neighborhood could hear you shouting and clomping across the street like a horse! Was there a fire?"

"No, Mom!" I exclaimed, "Chester told me you were home and I just thought...."

My mother gave a no-nonsense smile. "Someone died? If that were the case, I wouldn't have allowed your brother to ride his bike to the Gordon's now, would I?"

Mariola walked to our bedroom. I stood in the kitchen watching my mother take out the frying pan. Her hair was still up in a chignon, and the string of pearls remained on her neck. Despite her old tattered apron, she resembled Maureen O'Hara, my favorite celebrity paper doll when I was a kid. I always thought my mother to be the most beautiful woman in Ohio, if not the world. As a kid I would gawk at her, wishing I would favor her instead of favoring my father as I did with my brown hair and glasses.

"If you are going to stand there, Natalie, you can at least shuck the corn or scrub the potatoes."

"Corn? Potatoes?"

"For supper," Mother answered. "I figured to celebrate the first day of school I could fry some chicken and serve it with baked potatoes and corn on the cob."

"We have Swanson chicken dinners," I said.

"For once, I want to feed my children properly. The first day of school only comes once a year. This year is your last. It warrants a celebration."

"I can help if you need me," Mariola said, entering the kitchen with her Dungarees and an old blouse.

"You can scrub the potatoes, Mariola," Mother replied. "Natalie, why don't you change into your work clothes before you shuck the corn?"

"Sure."

The stairs were next to the front door. From the frosted window, I saw a shadow. Suddenly there was a quick knock. The short knock and the slight frame of the shadow indicated it could be none other than Mrs. Metterschmidt on the other side. I hastily ran up the stairs.

"Natalie! Natalie Studebaker! If you are home, dear, answer the door!" I ran back down before Mrs. Metterschmidt felt incline to peer into our windows as she was known to do.

"Natalie, dear," Mrs. Metterschmidt greeted as I opened the door. "I am calling on behalf of the Englewood Friendly society."

As if there would be any other reason she would call. Busybodied Meredith Metterschmidt was not my mother's ideal guest for lunch or tea. Since my father's death, the Englewood Friendly Society took my family as one of the charitable cause. At first, they were a help when my mother faced the transition from wife to widow. The Friendly Society believed their support to be temporary. All the members expected my mom would transition from widow to someone's second wife within two years. Ten years later, the Friendly Society offered their services as a means to pry into our lives.

"I was at a luncheon at Mrs. Kaiser's home. We saw your mother enter your house then leave the house in different clothes. We stay awhile and saw her return to the house with Chester in tow."

"She walked him home from school," I explained with a roll of my eyes.

"Now, now," Mrs. Metterschmidt curtly replied, "as you know, your mother's boss, Mr. Kristoff has an important trial this month. He needs your mother's assistance. Yet, your mother took the afternoon off."

"She wants to make fried chicken for dinner," I retorted.

"As a mother should, yes, yes; however, Natalie, don't you find it peculiar that someone with your mother's, eh, work ethic would take an afternoon off from work?"

"Meredith." I heard my mother curtly greet Mrs. Metterschidmt behind me.

"Winifred! How are you?"

23

"I'm fine."

"Why that's a lovely dress you are wearing?"

"Want it is that you want?"

"Pardon."

"I've had this dress before Pearl Harbor. There is nothing special about it. You never come my home to simply pay me compliments. Now please quickly get to your hidden agenda. I have chicken frying. "

"Well, the ladies in the neighborhood find it strange that you are wearing beige instead of your typical Noir attire."

"I had chores to do. I wasn't going to ruin my business dresses with dust and flour."

"Quite true- now, I ran into Louisa Barr on the way. She said that her fiancé, Mr. Butterfeld, passed Mr. Kristoff's office on his way home for luncheon. There was mentioning of heated words."
Mrs. Metterschidmt's eye gave that gleam that indicated, "I know what you are up too." The thing was she knew nothing. As much as the ladies of Englewood believed in love everlasting, people never understood why my mother remained in mourning a decade after my father died. Some spread vile rumors that she was involved with her employer.

"As Mr. Kristoff's paralegal, I am not at liberty to confirmed or deny Louisa Barr's claim." My mother explained, "I am not to discuss matters of a case with anyone."

"I see," Mrs. Metterschidmt acknowledged in disappointment. "Well, I best be on my way. Winifred you should consider bringing that color into your wardrobe. It compliments you well."

"Thank you, Meredith," Mother remarked with a slam of the door. "Go upstairs," she ordered me. "Change and be down here to help me get dinner on the table by six."

My mother worked over forty hours a week doing legal research for Attorney Kristoff and was lucky to be home by eight some nights. Since the invention of the frozen dinner, Chester and I didn't eat a freshly prepared dinner after school. My brother and I stuffed our faces with chicken and corn straight from the market. Mother scold us for not making the bountiful feast last.

At the end of supper, Mother spoke, "Mariola, can you help Chester with his math homework?"

"Sure, Mrs. Studebaker."

"Natalie, I'll need your help in the kitchen."

I followed my mother to the kitchen sink.

"I should be the one helping Chester with his homework," I suggested,

"Mariola is terrible at math."

"So is Chester. They'll complement each other. Besides, it will give Mariola confidence in her abilities if she sees Chester succeed with her assistance."

Mother handed me a dish towel. She filled the sink with hot water and a squirt of dish soap. Usually, she would protect her hands with plastic gloves. That night, she took a glass and plunged it into the scalding water.

"I do have something I need to talk to you about. I had heated words with Mr. Kristoff today."

I took the glass she handed me. "About what?"

"Mr. Kristoff always told me that he would pay for my child's college education when it was discovered your father's insurance only paid for the house. I found out today that he thought Chester was my oldest."

I never met Mr. Kristoff in person. In some of the newspaper articles I have read of him, he came off as a little daffy. He lacked the attention to details that would able him to win a case on his own.

"Unfortunately, he doesn't believe girls should go to college. He told me that a woman's place is the kitchen; therefore, it is pointless to spend money on a woman's tuition so she can receive a degree she will never utilize."

"Mr. Kristoff hired you because you have a college degree!"

"A point I readily made," Mother said as she grabbed the frying pan from the stove. "He was quick to argue that the only reason I worked was that I was a widow."

"So he is aware that husbands die," I commented.

"He also stated Germany has learned their lesson and won't attempt to take over the world again; therefore, you shouldn't have to fear of becoming a war widow."

Mother vigorously scrubbed the congealed grease on the pan.

"What about Korea?" I asked, "Or Cuba?"

"Truman has managed to keep the war contained in Korea," Mother explained, "and we are not losing the war as we once feared two years ago. As for Cuba, the wealthy will just find an island without violence for their tropical vacation. Mr. Kristoff isn't foreseeing another world war."

"War is not the only thing that can kill a man," I said.

"It is a woman's responsibility to find a man who is good with finances to ensure her future existence," Mother mockingly quoted.

"So he is just like everyone else," I complained, "thinking that the only thing I can do is get married and have babies."

Mother continued to scrub the pan with her anger. Suddenly from the murky water she emerged a restored frying pan. Mother unplugged the kitchen sink. We watched the liquid tornado run down the drain.

"My father always told me that a man was only as good as his word. He kept his promised to send me to the university even though it killed him! I spent a decade winning cases for Mr. Kristoff when I really ought to have been here for you and Chester. I made my choice because I believed that I was ensuring your futures. Now, I lost moments in your childhood I can never get back and still no means to pay your tuition."

"I don't resent you for your choice," I murmured.

Mother wrapped me into an embrace. "Well, I am making a new

choice. Now, I will only work half my time. I will make the three of you breakfast. I will be home by the time you come home school and make your dinner every night."

With that, Mother dismissed me from my chores.

The Kaisers, who lived across the street, had a television. We only had a radio. Mother liked to spend the evening listening to classical music while as she worked on her needlepoint. For entertainment, Mariola and I would peer into the Kaiser's house with my father's old binoculars, to watch "I love Lucy" or "The Honeymooners" on their television. Without no sound, we had to rely on our maudlin ability to read lips.

"Mr. Kasier is blocking the screen with his fat bald head," I said. "I can't see what Lucy is saying."

"Whatever she is saying it is causing Ricky to say, 'Lucy, you have some serious splaining to do.'"

"Explaining," I corrected.

"Duck!"

Mariola and I crouch underneath the window.

"You saw Mrs. Kaiser?"

"Before she could see us," Mariola confirmed.

I let a sigh of relief. "One less visit from the Friendly society we have to endure."

Mariola and I slowly peered up to the window. Mrs. Kaisers had drawn the drapes. With school, tomorrow, Mariola and I went to bed.

"Natalie," Mariola whispered in the dark, "What do you suppose Lucy sounds like?"

"I don't know," I sighed.

"I bet she has a lovely voice," Mariola says.

"I suppose, "I yawned.

Seconds later, Mariola let out a snore. Last summer, she slept on a dirt floor of a tent. Now she slept in the guest bed in my room. I wished I was in her bed, being better off than I was in the past. I couldn't sleep with a head full of troubles.

Mariola had a sweet face when she slept. She slept with the peace of a child. She didn't worry about attending universities or obtaining a career after high school. I fell asleep wishing I had her sense of inner peace.

ALEXANDRA

Mother Hubbard told me that she last heard Doug Bolster's youngest daugh ter lived in Tipp City. With a bit of research, I found a Belinda Bolster indeed lived in the town. Instead of going into the Herald's office after working at the Flyer, I drove forty-five minutes East out to Tipp City.

Belinda Bolster's house is a cute cream color rambler with charcoal gray shutters. A black cat with a white tip tail sits at the front window. With the lawn and flowerbeds well kept, I figure that Ms. Bolster will be a kind elder women who would welcome an unexpected visitor.

A heavyset woman with short black hair wearing a large purple t-shirt and khaki shorts answers the door. She sizes me up. "What do you want?"

"Hi," I squeak, "I am looking for Belinda Bolster."

"As I said, 'what do you want?'"

Whenever I get nervous, I start rambling.

"I am with the Englewood Herald. I am doing a piece on mysteries of Englewood. Your father's disappearance came up as a potential section…"

"Let me stop you right there! I already told this Chippy guy who keeps calling me that there is no mystery."

"No mystery? You know what happened to your dad?"

Ms. Bolster snorts, "Nothing. It turns out I don't have a dad."

Ugh! It's happening again. Sometimes Chip sends me on assignments that sound like a promising story but what I end up doing is momentarily encroaching on someone's personal life. Cleary, the disappearance of Doug

Bolster, wasn't as a mystery to his family.

"I am sorry for your lost."

"There is no lost. I just have two moms. One lives in South Dakota, and the other resides in San Francisco with my Aunt Darla as her twin sister Darlene."

This was a better scenario than the domestic violence situation I was expecting.

"So he's living a happy life in California. Good for him."

"If you say so."

"Both of my parents are gay. They came out when I was nineteen…"

"Good for you!" Ms. Bolster exclaims as she slams the door in my face.

****

"Good for you!" wasn't the sentiment I received when my parents came out. I was nineteen. Shona was ten. My parents had spent over twenty years pretending to be heterosexual. Stunned by the revelation, I blurted out,

"Aren't you selfish? You aren't thinking about Shona!"
Needless to say, I rendered my family speechless that night. My parents finally got to announced, "We are gay. After all these years, we finally feel safe to reveal who we truly are."

What I heard was, "Shona, be prepared to be pushed into lockers." It was a reasonable fear. I witnessed a couple of kids at my school being shoved around due to the assumption of their homosexuality. Fortunately, my sister's generation outshined mine in generosity and global acceptance. Shona had a great group of friends who knew her parental situation. The one or two morons who teased her for having gay parents quickly found themselves suspended for harassment.

I have since explained my outburst blunder, but my mother has yet to let it go. No one let's go one a blessed gift. My anxiety driven outburst gave my mom the fodder she wanted to explain our strained relationship. To my mother, saying she didn't prefer me because I was a homophobe was more acceptable than saying she didn't prefer me because I wasn't her intellectual equal.

When I was born, my mother envisioned me taking advantage of the intellectual freedoms she was denied under the rule of the ever keeping up with appearance Jo-Jo. Without her watchful eye on my clothes, my demeanor, or my prospects for a future husband, I was to naturally gravitate to the open pages of Virginia Woolf and Sylvia Platt.

Mother didn't figure that the other contribution of my genetic material would come to play. My father had a slight learning disability, loved men, and was employed as the fine apparels manager at our local Bon-Ton. I inherited said learning disability and on a much smaller scale the love of men and clothes. What I inherited from my mother was the attribute that annoys her the most: the ability to live out of my mother's shadow.

Despite never sharing genetics with Jo-Jo, my mother inherited the delusion that if a daughter loved her mother, she would strive to be her exact copy. As I brought home the horror stories of R.L Stine and Christopher Pike as a teenager instead of a Bronte sister's book, I gain my mother's disapproval. I didn't mind. All of my friends had petty issues with their moms. I just chalked it up our strained relationship as a normal part of childhood.

My parents' separation was when the reality of our relationship became apparent. The moment they came out, my father was on the next bus to Manhattan where he became the boy-toy of a wealthy man. My mom remained in Rochester where she was an English professor at the University. Because I was legally an adult when my parents' divorced, Shona was the only focal point of the custody arrangements. Frankly, Dad didn't want a ten-year-old cramping his flamboyant lifestyle he had wanted to live since he was born. In Shona, who was reading Ernest Hemingway at the age of nine, Mother saw the daughter she failed to raise in me and insisted on being her sole guardian.

My plan was to stay out of my parents' way and go to college. I had applied at NYU, Penn State, and the University of New Hampshire. I got accepted to all three. One day while Shona and I were doing our homework among the cardboard boxes that held our former life, Mother burst in announcing, "Good news, Alexandra, you are now a student at University of Rochester!"

"I didn't know I applied?"

Mother shook her hand at me, "No worries. I took care of everything."

By that, I knew my mother embellished on my application. The University of Rochester was considered, "the ivy league school not in the ivy league." I did well at school, although I got held back in kindergarten. I wasn't into high school extra circular activities; therefore, I knew I didn't get in on my own merits.

"Shouldn't I get into a school more my speed?" I asked.

Instead of saying she believed in me she replied, "Alexandra, I just need you to go to a local school. I can't afford the moving cost. You'll get a faculty discount by enrolling into the University of Rochester that makes the tuition comparable to the schools you applied for."

"But am I…"

My mother interrupted me with an exasperated sigh. "You have caught up enough already. Now you just need to grow up and buckle down." Even though I sense my mother's disbelief in my cognitive abilities, I couldn't pass enrollment to an exceptional school. Despite my difficulties, I did enjoy learning. My taste started matured beyond the gossip of Hollywood and high school. I figured it would be fun to be in an environment that fostered intellectual conversation.

When Mother moved Shona and me into her lover's apartment, I quickly became disillusioned. Jolene gave up her wood crafting room so Shona and I could have a place to sleep. I accepted the arrangement initially thinking it was temporary.

"School starts tomorrow," I reminded my mother.

"And…"

"Well, isn't it funny I haven't received a dorm assignment?"

"You are not living in a dorm."

"What?"

"Seriously, Alexandra! The university is at capacity with incoming freshmen! All local students are encouraged to live at home."

32

"This isn't quite home to me. I thought…"

"Think about learning to adapt!"

That brief tiff set the tone for the rest of the semester. My mother often drove me to campus silently on the good days. Other days she lectured me on how I should write my paper or do my homework. I should have listened. That semester I got C's for writing my own ideas in papers rather than reciting my professors' opinions. In high school, writing original work was encouraged. At the University of Rochester, professors took your inability to be indoctrinated as an insult. Of course, those professors knew my mother and spun things out of proportion. Their conversations resulted in lengthy car trips back home:

"Seriously, Alexandra, you called Virginia Woolf out on her bipolar disorder!"

"Was it sage to mention the modern day film adaptation of 'Emma' is titled, 'Clueless,' Alexandra?"

"Really, Alexandra! The only contribution Mary Wollstonecraft made to literature was birthing Mary Shelley? If you are going by the merit that 'Frankenstein' is a classic movie, you are far below the par than I originally thought."

As a result, Mother didn't see fit to include me in her nightly walks with Jolene and Shona. She claimed it was so I could focus on my studies. That hurt. I always spent the night hanging with Shona growing up. We watched cartoons. I read out loud to her. We gaze out at stars. Before the divorce, I was Shona's primary caretaker. I'd pick her up from the neighbor's house after school, feed her dinner, and put her to bed. At the time, I thought it was due to my parents' jobs instead of them dating their forbidden lovers. Now that Mother was establishing a new family, she quickly reclaimed Shona.

Friends often served as a refuge in high school. After high school, the majority went to NYU. The rest left New York entirely. At first, I kept an open mind to make new ones. I quickly learned that the intellectual elite were just plain elitist. Whether enormous from Minnesota or skinny from Spokane, all the students at University of Rochester were looking for subordinates than friends.

"Right now, I don't have time to giggle and watch 'Friends,'" I often heard, "What I need is someone who will read my essay on being a reluctant feminist."

"No, I can't get coffee, well; actually, we can go if you are willing to read my script for the one-act play festival. Does the McDonald's playland set as heaven seem to be a far fetch concept?"

Everyone at the University of Rochester silently screamed, "Look at me! I am so smart and avant-garde!"

I could barely squeak, "You wanna get coffee?"

The first three months of college were lonely. Reading essays and scripts wasn't a good way to make friends, especially when you weren't smart enough to say the critical words that would get them to believe you were helping validate their testament of their genius. A call from my old friend, Heather, became the key to freeing me from my isolation.

"How's Ohio State?" I asked.

I expected Heather to complain that she was in the sticks. Her parents made her apply to their alma mater as a safety school when she applied for Yale.

"I love it here!"

"Really? It's not Yale."

For years, I saw Heather tact up pamphlets and flyers from Yale in her room. I stay at her house for a weekend to act as suicide watch after Yale sent her the small envelope instead of the welcome packet.

"Yale is not all it is cracked up to be," Heather replied. "My cousin who went there finally confided that she hated it. There was so much pressure to conform to her professor's views. When she got out, she had the same limited opportunities as anyone else."

"Sounds a lot like the University of Rochester," I replied.

"In Ohio, everyone has treated me like I am instantly their family. It's not like when my family moved to Rochester and had to wait two years for people to start warming up to me."

I have lived in Rochester my entire life. Some of my family members never warmed up to me.

"It's nice that they are friendly and all," I said, "however, it's like the Midwest, right? Aren't people in Middle America are narrow in their thinking?

"Whatever, Susan."

"Did you just call me by my mother's name?"

"Weren't you just acting like her?"

"No."

"Sure, there are people who hate gays here if that's what you were trying to ask. There are also people living in Rochester who hate gays. No matter where you go, there are diverse opinions. Some people have hateful ones."

I couldn't argue with that.

"Oh, I hate it here at the University of Rochester," I whined. "I feel so dumb whenever I go to class because I don't have the attention span to understand Virginia Woolf."

"I got a crazy idea!" Heather announced.

The last time Heather got a crazy idea I ended up swimming in my underwear at Niagara Falls…in January.

"Keep it to yourself."

"This is a good one," Heather said. "You should transfer over to Ohio State next semester."

"I can't. My family can't afford it. That is why Mother embellished on my University of Rochester application. She couldn't pay for me to move across the state to attend NYU. What makes you think she'd pay for out of state tuition?"

"Why don't you ask your dad?"

"What makes you think my dad could afford it?"

"Since when he has made many appearances in the Manhattan society columns," Heather replied.

The next day Heather emailed me links to the columns she mentioned. There was my father standing next to a millionaire who looked like Vincent Price. I immediately search "Vincent Price's" number.

"Hello, is Patrick McNally there? Can you tell him it's his daughter?"

Immediately I heard, "Peanut, what is going on? Is everything okay?"

With my father, I just found it best to blurt out what I wanted right away. He never liked it when people beat around the bush.

"I need money, so I can transfer to Ohio State University."

"Oh, Peanut, is living with your mother that draining on you? I should have known that was going to happen when she insisted you stay in Rochester. Oh, her damn pride!"

"What does that mean?"

"Oh, you know Jo-Jo. Ever since your mother and I have come out, she has been insisting our sinful ways are negatively impacting you and Shona. Your mother kept you in Rochester to demonstrate the three of you were a united front."

"How Jo-Jo of her," I responded.

"Sure is," Dad chuckled.

The next day, I got a notice from Western Union. Dad sent me the money I needed to move to Columbus. My application to OSU got accepted the next month.

The first holidays after a divorce are always awkward. Christmas after my semester at the University of Rochester became a barrel full. Even though she disapproved of her daughter's lifestyle, Jo-Jo insisted that the Richards' family Christmas still went on. Jo-Jo had enough social awareness to know shunning your child for being homosexual was unacceptable. Besides, if Jo-Jo shunned my mother, my mother couldn't hear her little quips.

My stomach was too full of nerves as I sat down at my grandparents' dining room table. Class at OSU began in two weeks, and I still hadn't broken the news of my college transfer to my mother. Smothered by my solipsism, I didn't notice the sardonic smirk on Jo-Jo's faces as she brought out the mash potatoes.

My mom also was oblivious to Jo-Jo's expression. As she carried the green bean casserole from the kitchen, she rattled on and on about the amusing sentences that read as she graded her students' papers.

"One student thought she could butter me up by writing, 'Expository Writing One is often required; however, it is a fun class to be forced to enroll in.' I'd be touched if she provided background to her statement. Ha! If one is going to praise expository writing, then she should add exposition to her paper."

Pops carved the roast goose after we said grace. As we passed our plates, Jo-Jo commented, "Anna called me today to wish me a Merry Christmas, Susan. Wasn't that sweet of her?"
Mother eyebrows shot up at the mentioned of her ex-mother-in-law. Shona and I shared quizzical expressions. Our grandmother didn't call us that day.

"Now you didn't think that we would stop being friends, did you?"

"No, Mom, I am not in the habit of thinking about who you befriend."

"Well, that's good. We both agreed not to blame the other for the selfish and immoral decisions you and Patrick made."

Mother drew a breath. "Mother, forgive me for not thinking that Patrick and my choice to be honest about who we love as licentious. I'll in kind forgive you for your intolerance for I know it is due to the ignorance of your generation."

Jo-Jo sat silently. Her smirk remained.

"Alex, your grandma Anna told me to tell you congratulation on your acceptance into Ohio State University. In fact, she and I have been talking about visiting you during your Spring Break. It would cut a trip for you and you wouldn't feel left behind on campus."

I felt the color drain from my face. Mother's fork full of green beans froze at her lips.

"What acceptance into Ohio State?"

"Didn't you hear?" Jo-Jo asked nonchalantly. "Patrick is paying Alexandra's tuition to Ohio State University. Well, actually Anna mentioned that Patrick's lover is paying her tuition. Either way, Alex is going to Ohio State."

"Patrick wouldn't make a decision to enroll our child into a school without my consent. I have custody."

"Of Shona," Jo-Jo corrected. "Alexandra here is an adult and has made the decision to go to Ohio. Really, Susan it is for the best. Alex is not happy living with you. Besides, living in the Midwest, she can make friends with people of intact families and learn family values through them."

All eyes gazed upon me. I sat wishing I'd liquefy and evaporate. Instead, I ran to the bathroom and dry heaved.

I thought I could escape to my room right away and lock myself there for the night. That may have been a possibility if I hadn't shared the room with Shona. When Shona came to bed that night, Mother followed her. I pretended to read the magazine I attempted to read when I retreated.

"Alexandra, Shona needs to go to bed. You'll need to go to the kitchen to read."

" I was about to…"

"Alexandra! The kitchen!"

I went into the kitchen to get myself some club soda to calm my stomach. Right as I poured it, I heard, "I paid for that!"

"I'm sorry. My stomach is upset."

"I would appreciate you taking care of your aliments on your own dime since you seem so keen to waste what I have given you!"

"It's not that...."

"I got you into a good school, Alexandra! I fretted every night about how to get you into U of R. I put my professional integrity on the line for you! Then you repay me by running away, allowing my smug mother to think she is right!"

Mother walked and took the glass of club soda out of my hands and poured it down the sink.

"University of Rochester is not cheap, Alexandra! Yet, writing checks there is an investment for your mind, your wellbeing, and your intellectual identity. Spending my money at Ohio State University is the club soda down the sink. All you'll become there is an inchoate."

Mother ran the tap, filling the glass. Before she took a sip, she muttered, "I bet you can't grasp what I am telling you."

"I would if you used proper grammar! Inchoate is an adjective, not a noun. Anyways, I will have no chance to form my own thoughts staying here with you telling me what to write, what to think, and what to be!"

Mother glared at me.

"Dad says that the only reason I am here is your lousy pride. As long as I remain in Rochester, you save face with Jo-Jo. Don't tell me that it is not true because you just insinuated that you know I am not smart enough to attend U of R! Why should I struggle to be something I'm not so you look good to the woman you hate?"

"Well, for nineteen years I pretended to be something I wasn't for your benefit. You can repay me in kind!"

"Quit being a martyr! I don't hate you for being gay! I hate you because you're a bitch!"

"Alexandra Nellie McNally! You have fifteen seconds to retract your statement!"

"Oh, you are so much like Jo-Jo, it is not even funny!"

"Get OUT!"

"What?"

"If you are going to continue to be an ungrateful bitch and disrespect me in my home, then you can get out!"

"Seriously?"

"Yes. By tomorrow morning, I want you gone."

Mother stomped out of the kitchen. I went to bed. There was no use in sleeping. She shouted the whole reenactment to Jolene. Shona wrapped a pillow around her head. "Thanks a heap, Alex!"

Heather's family took me in for the two weeks before driving us to Ohio State. My mother and I didn't talk the entire semester. Dad paid for summer classes to eliminate the need of going back to Rochester. Mother finally called me when Pops had emergency gall bladder surgery. Even now, we only call each other for life altering events, mainly births and death. The only reason Mother saw Natalia in the hospital when I gave birth was because Dayton was on the way to a Women in Leadership conference in Indianapolis. Beyond the rare events that called the Wilsons over to Rochester, Natalia doesn't see her grandmother.

I struggle with the way things are between my mother and me. I wish they were different. She'll never accept the way my life has fallen into place. I am not going to be sorry for having a loving family in the Midwest. So I live my life accepting that I will never have acceptance from her.

NATALIE

Mother strictly adhered to a new routine of being a part-time paralegal and full-time mother. Instead of hastily making toast before we ran off to school, Chester, Mariola, and I found Mother with a plate of toast along with heaping plates of bacon and eggs. We would run home to find Mother in the kitchen with a snack of freshly cut melons or sliced apples with peanut butter. She couldn't always make fried chicken, but the stew she would make with leftovers was better than any frozen dinner.

Unfortunately, Mother's new routine only lasted two weeks. One day after school, Mariola and I arrived home to find the house empty. There was no evidence that Mother came home after work. Chester's knapsack for school wasn't sitting by the door.

"Maybe she is standing in front of the school, talking like all the mothers tend to do around here," Mariola suggested.

"Unlikely" I replied, knowing my mom didn't have a thing in common with the ninny housewives of Englewood.

I opened the front door. Mrs. Gordon walked towards our house holding her son, Jimmy's hand and Chester's hand in the other. I ran out the door to meet them half way.

"Natalie, Darling, Is everything is alright?" asked Mrs. Gordon. "We waited for your mother for a half hour. She didn't come."

"I'm not sure," I hastily said taking Chester's hand.

"This school year has been peculiar," Mrs. Gordon continued. "The last couple of years I stayed with Chester until you were able to get out of school. Now this year, she is the first mother at the front of the school..." There was something peculiar about today. I certainly wasn't going to stand and indulge Mrs. Gordon in her need for gossip.

"Things are fine," I clipped as I dragged Chester down the street.

"Aww, Natalie! You are hurting me!" Chester said. "Why are you walking so fast? I want to go home with Jimmy, not you!"

Mariola stood by the door. I shrugged to her silent question of my mother's whereabouts.

"Go get your bike," I order Chester.

Chester ran past Mariola into the house. Seconds later he emerged from the door with his safari hat.

"Why are you wearing that?"

"I freckle!"

"We are going to Main Street! The entire town will see you looking ridiculous in that hat."

Chester hopped on his bike. "You know what looks ridiculous? Freckles!"

I motioned for Mariola to come outside. She locked the door and followed me onto our way to Main Street.

The three of us went down two blocks to Main Street. Mr. Kristoff's store was next to Carol's finery. A couple of ladies of Englewood were buying their feather hats for church. I pretended not to notice them looking out the window while praying they were only interested in Chester's silly hat.

Mr. Kristoff's loud voice vibrated the office as we walked in. "Mrs.

Studebaker, I hired you to research information for my cases. All I have received from you the last two week is obstinacy."

"You hired me on a part-time basis," my mother reminded. "For nearly a decade I have worked sixty hours a week. At the time, I thought I was working towards my child's education. Now that you have gone back on your word, I will work per our original arrangement."

Mr. Kristoff was a slight man with wild salt and pepper hair. He reminded me of a crazed Austrian composer instead of a lawyer. My mother was his height but due to having children had more girth. Standing next to each other, Mother was a boulder a fluster Mr. Kristoff couldn't move.

"I've apologized to you numerous times," Mr. Kristoff replied running his finger through his hair. "For some reason, I thought your oldest child was the boy. You know my stance on sending girls to college. Could they benefit from the education? Yes. However, most girls choose to devote their attention to boys than their studies. Sending girls to school is not a sound economic investment."

"My Natalie is devoted to books. She doesn't chase boys."

"Wait until she is away from your watchful eye," Mr. Kristoff bellowed.

"I beg your pardon, sir."

The stench of mold from the old law books stacked everywhere in Mr. Kristoff's office overcame us. Chester sneezed alerting the adults of our entrance. I took a handkerchief from my pocket to my nose. Mariola hiked her scarf up to cover hers.

"What is this?" Mr. Kristoff barked.

"Mr. Kristoff, let me introduce my children. The girl in the glasses is my daughter, Natalie. The boy is my son, Chester."

"Why is he wearing a safari hat?"

Mother spoke before Chester could protest freckle. "He must have been off to play lion hunting with his friend Jimmy Gordon when his sister brought him here."

43

"Who's the other girl?" Mr. Kristoff asked.

Mother walked over to us and put her hands around Mariola's shoulders.

"She is Mariola Chinnici," Mother explained, "the girl who you had me take into my home this past July."

"From the gypsy camp? I thought all of them left the area after serving their time for vagrancy."

"Her mother was the woman found dead in her cell."

"I remember," Mr. Kristoff gruffed. "I just thought you would have the sense to call Shady Acres."

"I couldn't take her to the orphanage. She will become of age in October. I couldn't bear the possibility of her ending back in the streets. At least with me she can finish school and gain proper employment next summer."

Mr. Kristoff rubbed his neck, "I am confused. You have an extra mouth to feed, and you are refusing extra hours. Word around here is that you aren't exactly receiving anything beneficial from the town's Friendly Society as of late."

"My diligent work for you has only made me a recipient of gossip. All falsehoods, however, I wish not to have working for you soil my virtue." Mr. Kristoff sat at his desk with his hand to his chin for awhile. Finally, he said, "I guess I do own you some compensation for your troubles. I'll add fifteen cents an hour to your wage starting tomorrow."

Mother clasped her hand to her heart. "Thank you, sir."

"However, I will expect the amount of diligence you brought forth over the past decade. I will have none of the obstinacies you have demonstrated this week."

"I will be here first thing tomorrow morning, Sir." Mother promised. I felt an explosion of air pop around me as Mother signed a new payment agreement. With that, my future was signed away.

We had enough leftover stew in the fridge to make a decent dinner along with oblong garlic rolls Mariola made. Mother talked the entire time gaily. Mariola responded with her sweet, "That's sounds neat, Mrs. Studebaker" and Chester responded with a loud "Golly!"

Mother insisted I help with the dishes that night. I told her I had too much homework to do. She insisted I do my reading in the kitchen.

"You've been quiet," She commented with her back towards me.

I grunted in response. I had a chapter in my Civics class to complete. My blood boiled as I tried to concentrate on the importance of citizenship. Like a steam from a kettle burst, "You didn't have to sell out and take the fifteen cents an hour!"

A dish clanked in the sink. "Sell out?"

"You could have insisted he pay the tuition money he promised you a decade ago!"

Mother turned with a dish towel to her hip. "So this is why you are so sulky? Well, I'd been a fool to turn down an extra fifteen cents an hour. It is a considerable amount of money."

"Too considerable," I replied. "If the town finds out about the raise in your wages, they are going to think Mr. Kristoff is buying your silence."

"I am his paralegal," Mother clipped. "The wages I earn buys my silence. Besides, it is rude to talk finances so that no one will know. I understand you feel cheated, Natalie. Had this raise come sooner, I would be able to save for your college tuition. This raise is fortuitous for our family."

"What is it that we need that we can't afford?" I asked.

Mother sat down at the table. "Natalie, there are months when I worried about being able to buy bread and butter for you and Chester. With the addition of Mariola to our household, food was getting spares in recent times. This raise means I don't have to worry about feeding the three of you."

I pointed out the back window. "We grow our vegetables. Mariola likes to bake bread. "

Mother shook her head. "We don't grow our clothes. You never cared to learn how to sew. I couldn't send you out in those asymmetrical sacks you made. Those ready wear dresses I order from the Sears-Roebucks catalog for you are not cheap! Despite the fact I pick the least expensive clothes on the page!"

Mother went back to the sink looking out the window. "I swear, we are the only family in America that still maintains a Victory garden. Having a flower garden for once would be nice. Maybe uproot the turnips and replace them with tulips. I could also give the three of you an allowance for once. You and Mariola could buy yourselves some records or whatever teenagers buy...."

Mother continued dreaming about what we could do with the extra fifteen cents an hour: A trip to Chicago, savings for a down payment of an automobile, maybe even a television. Each word was a dagger to my dream of getting out of Englewood.

ALEXANDRA

"Really, Alex, you went to a woman's house uninvited?"

I sit in Chip's office across from him at his desk. He looks a little perplex about my visit to Belinda Bolster, which surprises me because I have known him to use the same tactics to gain information for his articles.

Chip taps his pen at his desk. "Well, knowing Doug Bolster is living happily as a woman, we don't exactly have a mystery on our hands, do we?"

"We still have a story. October is a big month for the Gay, Lesbian, Bisexual, Transgender community. Maybe we can write about Doug Bolster experience as a transgender?"

"That would be a good story," Chip agreed. "The problem is Belinda Bolster slammed the door in your face. She won't be giving you her father's contact information."

"I suppose not," I sigh.

Chip jumps from his chair. "We still have an Englewood mystery! Alexandra Wilson, you are going crack the mystery of the Route 40 Phantom!"

Silently, I groan. Chip can't possibly think that a trucker's drunken illusion is a legitimate mystery!

"Who should I call? Jim Beam? Jack Daniels?"

"Neither! In fact, I know of a person you can talk to, Miss Irma Hoople!"

"What would she know?"

"Her father, Erwin Hoople, was one of the truck drivers who saw the Phantom. She knows his story. She is residing at Brookhaven nursing home. Visiting hours will start in an hour. Why don't you drive there, now? Get a jump start on the story?"

Chips practically push me out of the office and into my car.

Irma Hoople lives in an assisted living apartment, which I hope means she has the majority of her mental faculties. From what Chip told me, Ms. Hoople was a child when her father saw the phantom. How reliable of a source could she be?

I knock on her apartment door.

"Are you that woman from the Englewood Herald?" I hear from inside.

"Yes, Ms. Hoople! I'm Alexandra Wilson from the Herald. Chip Edmundson called about me coming over."

Looking from the corner of my right eye I see a face peering out the screen.

"You come right on in, Hon."

I walk in to find Irma Hoople sitting up against the arm of her couch with her legs stretch in front of her. Upon her lap is one of those tied together fleece blankets. She takes the glasses that lay on her lap and puts them on her face. She reaches her hand out to me.

"Thank you, Ms. Wilson, for coming over!"

"Please to make your acquaintance, Ms. Hoople."

Ms. Hoople points to the kitchen. "I don't mean to sound inhospitable, but if you want some tea while you are here, you will need to get a cup from the cupboard. Actually, if you can refill the electric teapot, that would be lovely."

I unplug the teapot from the end table behind Ms. Hoople and take it to the kitchen sink.

"My arthritis flared up something fierce yesterday. I spent the entire day sitting on this couch alternating between watching episodes of 'Gilmore Girls' and reading chapters from a Jodi Picoult novel. I finished an entire season and the whole book."

"A day of television and reading sounds like a good day to me," I call out over the noise of the kitchen faucet running.

"It is good for only a day," Ms. Hoople replies. "I don't know how old people survived without Amazon. My nephew's son insisted I signed up for it so I could instantly get books and movies. Now, I never believe one should obtain entertainment so quickly. My father told me to work for everything. I use to think getting things from the internet was spoiling society. Now I'm grateful for the internet. It's my books and TV shows that distract me while my joints flare up."

I bring back the electric tea kettle to Ms. Hoople and plug it into the outlet next to the end table. Returning to the kitchen, I grab two mugs.

"I am thankful I had enough of a reprieve to take a shower and change clothes this morning. The joint pain is getting so bad; it is hard to walk to the bathroom. I just need to come to terms that it is my time to move into a room at the main building. I just hate to lose my view."

Ms. Hoople draws one of the sheer white curtains to reveal a white gazebo. Two red cardinals are flying around it.

"It is beautiful," I comment.

"It is one of my joys. It's the little things in life, they always say."

49

Ms. Hoople pushes a caddy towards me that contains an assortment of teabags and painkillers. I select peppermint tea. She pulls a jasmine blended green teabag. I pour the water into our mugs.

As we wait for our tea to steep, Ms. Hoople says, "So Chip wants you to write about the Route 40 Phantom. I haven't thought of him for years. I don't believe it is going to be much of a story for you. Whoever it was probably left town a long time ago after the thrill of rattling the local drivers was gone."

I got out my notepad from my back pocket. "Do you know how long the phantom was active?"

"My father sighted him first in September 1951. Roy Fitzwater was the first published encounter with the Phantom, but it was my dad encounter that legitimized Roy Fitzwater's claim. My father just wanted to sweep it under the rug. He was afraid the phantom sighting was proof of losing his eyesight. He was fifty-one at the time. Most of his friends only had a wife to support because the kids left the house. My father had a five-year-old in the house. That was me.

"Now my father was supposed to be a minister. When The United States entered the war in 1917, he enlisted. He might have fudged his age on his application for he was only seventeen at the time. He believed that God called him to protect his country so he fought in Europe where the British allies let him drive their tank. He came home with a love for operating heavy machinery. He believed God's calling was to continue to serve his country by delivering equipment to different army bases which he did until after World War Two.

"My grandfather was a member of the Anti-Saloon League which championed prohibition. My father was his biggest supporter. That didn't go well with my mother's family. Her father owned a saloon. I am unsure how my parents met or how they came together. All I can figure is that they had another mutual activity I don't want to think about in regards to them. Anyways, they were married in 1921 and had three boys. All of my brothers fought in World War Two and came back alive. The youngest of my older brothers was the last to return. When he did, my parents celebrated. I was born nine months later. My father started driving for an appliance company around that time.

"Now you know my dad was not a drunk. He feared that he would be accused as one if word got out he saw the phantom. Young men wanted his job and his employers wanted to give it to them; but, back in those days, loyalty to a company and experience meant something. Still, there were always loopholes."

"You said that you were five at the time your father saw the phantom, Ms. Hoople. Did he tell you about his phantom sighting that year or did he wait until you were older and the Phantom had become a legend?"

"My father was coming home late that night was my first vivid memory of what I dub as the 'hush-hushes.' I spent many a night sneaking at the top of the stairway listening to my parents' whispered conversation. Most were about my brother, Michael, the youngest son. He was an alcoholic. The Phantom was the event that started my habit of lurking at the stairwell.

"It was the phone that woke me. Then I heard the patter of my mother's feet. I knew something was wrong. At the age of five, I wasn't allowed to be out of bed until my mother woke me up the next morning. I remember seeing the moon shining through my bedroom window and knowing it meant it was still night.

"My parents were very strict; therefore, I learned how to sneak quietly around at a young age to decrease the amount of trouble I got into. I opened the door a crack and saw Mother's shadow from the kerosene lamp talking on the phone. Suddenly she ran upstairs screaming at Michael to wake up. Suddenly, Michael ran down the hallway while putting on his pants. I giggled. My mother was screaming directives as Michael bolted out the door to hear me. The house became silent, and I ran back into bed before my mother checked up on me.

"Right when I was about to drift off, I hear the front door open. I snuck back to the stairs to peer into the living room from the corner. I saw my mother steady my father on an old plush chair. As a child, I always revered my dad as rather stalwart. That night, he was pale with fright. He kept muttering that he saw a demon before he abruptly began to rant that the devil had unleashed his minions! Hell was coming to earth!

"Michael entered the house with a police deputy. The name eludes me right now. I should know it. He was an officer here forever. I use to take care of his kids during church functions. Their names were Marcus and Lisa; I remember that."

"I know who you are talking about," I say after hearing the name Mother

Hubbard's children. "I live across the street from his widow. Hubbard is her name. I wrote an article about Lisa's breast cancer that will print next month."

"Yes, I remember now, McKinley Hubbard was his name. He was five years younger than Michael. It was a shame about little Lisa. She was a sweetheart as a child.

"Anyways, Deputy Hubbard, as he was called back then, followed Michael in the house. As he did so, Father shouted, 'He believes me! He believes me! He has seen it himself! The skeleton with the green fire surrounding him in a car, the devil exists!'

"I don't remember what Hubbard said to my mother and Michael. Whatever it was, he convinced my mother my father had all his faculties. Someone was playing a prank he claimed. Hubbard left, my family headed upstairs, and I ran to my room before any knew I saw anything. No one spoke of my father's phantom sighting until his death in sixty-one."

"How'd your father died?"

"Heart attack," Ms. Hoople answered. "He lived the trucker lifestyle the later part of his life by eating at greasy truck stops two meals a day."

"Did your father appear different after he saw the phantom?"

"He seemed rattled for a week. Soon, the phantom sighting was ancient history. My parents had different things to deal with, such as Michael's alcoholism. Some say Michael was who drove my father to his grave. As I told you, I didn't have much of a story about the phantom."

Snapping my notebook shut, I say "You have given me more than I hoped to get. Thank you for giving me your time, Ms. Hoople."

Ms. Hoople reaches out to clasp my hand. I can tell she is straining her joints to give my hand a significant squeeze. "The pleasure was all mines, dear. Thank you for visiting a lonely old woman. Now I hope you don't mind seeing yourself out. I don't have much strength to walk."

Ms. Hoople's couch seems plush, but I know everyone rest better in bed.

"Would you like me to help you to your room?"

Ms. Hoople looks at her phone for the time. "It's early, but my sleep on the couch last night was intermittent. It's best I get some solid hours of sleep."

I assist Ms. Hoople to her room and also fetch her some pain reliever with a glass of water.

"You are so sweet helping a total stranger to her bed."

"You shared your childhood with me," I reply, "that doesn't make you much of a stranger."

Ms. Hoople closes her eyes with a small smile. I almost urge to kiss her on the cheek like a grandchild would. I have to remember I just met the woman hours ago.

A frame photograph of a longhaired woman giving a peace sign caught my eye. It's the twinkle in her eye that captures my attention, not the fact that she is bare-chested underneath her hair. I pick it up from the glass night table. Its absence notifies Ms. Hoople with a "ping".

"That was me at Woodstock," Ms. Hoople explains.

"You went to Woodstock? Awesome."

"I got swept up in the sixties. In the end, it left me childless with gonorrhea. Might as well, the world never has become the peaceful world we strive for our children."

"That would be an interesting story," I say, "well, not the fact you got gonorrhea. But you must have seen many fascinating things at Woodstock. Maybe one day when you have more energy, you can tell me some."

"I would love to, Dearie. Now you have yourself a good day."

I always loved stories. That is why I work for the Herald. It gives me a chance to learn everyone's stories. People don't gather and tell stories like the adults of my childhood. Instead, everyone focuses on their smart phones and tablets, even in social settings. I had to feel sorry for half of the children at Natalia's soccer game that evening. Their parents rather feed their addiction to Candy Crush Saga than watch the kids play.

At times, it is hard for me to want to concentrate on Natalia's game. Because I am married to the "sexy coach", a group of single moms deemed me the enemy and always make it a point to sit directly behind me so I can hear their suggestive comments about my husband.

I arrive to the game late from Irma Hoople's place. The only seat open on the bleachers is directly in front of the single moms. With a sigh, I start heading over to the suspiciously available seat. My phone begins to ring. Shona's picture pops up.

"What's up, Shon?"

"Alex! You will never guess what I found out about Mom?"

I am still coming to grips with my mother's adoption and annoyed with Shona's obsession over it. As normal, I gave Shona's a dose of my dry humor.

"Her birth parents are Appalachian hillbillies? It would be ironic her birth family were red necks. Maybe that explains the red hair."

"Close enough," Shona remarks. "She was born at Good Samaritan Hospital. You remember the place, don't you?"

No one forgets the place where they spent twenty-two hours in labor. "She was born here in Dayton?"

"Yup, same hospital as Natalia."

"How did you find that out?"

"I requested a copy of her birth certificate," Shona answers. "Her last name and mother's name were whited out. The father's name is blank. Gosh, I would never have thought that Mom was born in the same hospital as Natalia! I figured she was born somewhere in New York.

"Oh, this is rich," I laugh, "after her calling me inferior for moving to Ohio…."

"Alex heads up!" Anthony cries.

Too late. The soccer ball hits me on the side of the face, causing me to drop the phone. Anthony runs over to me.

"Oh, Natalia. Your parents are going to kiss."

Anthony turns me towards the soccer players before he dramatically kisses my cheek.
"Ewww," scream Natalia's teammates.

Anthony picks up my phone, "She'll call you later, Shona."

Anthony leads me over to the sidelines as the game resumes and sits me down on the towel. I turn to the bleachers and wink. I don't think the gaggle of single mothers needs further suggestion about what I am going to do to their dream boat tonight.

NATALIE

Within a week of Mother's raise, the Montgomery Ward's packages started coming. Each one contained a new day dress for Mariola. I couldn't stand to be in near the front door when they arrived. Each delivery played the same scene:

My mother would say, "I know it isn't much, but it is better than the second-hand dresses donated from the church. You deserve more than rags."

Mariola would always coo, "It is exquisite, Mrs. Studebaker! I would never have dreamed of having anything so lovely."

I knew my feelings were selfish; yet, no matter how hard I tried rationalizing my thoughts my heart remained the same. Sure, I only had one dead parent while Mariola had two. I still had a roof over my head. Mariola lost her house in Canada. Chester even told me that Mariola's father was arrested by the Canadian government and put into a death camp because he was Italian-just like what Hitler did to the European Jews. Chester had a tendency to exaggerate. I never heard of any death camps in North America.

What was worse is that Mariola noticed I was in a funk and kept insisting on cheering me up.

"I asked your mother for our allowances before we left," Mariola said one morning in as we entered the school bathroom. "We should go to Whitman's general store after school."

"I don't need anything," I replied.

"We can get a soda? Everyone can always use a bottle of cola."

Mary Iris Stuart was leaning against the sink reading the newspaper. "Hey, Jo! The Phantom struck again!"

Joretta Barr exited the stall as the flushing toilet trumpeted her fanfare. "Oh pooh," she said as she turned on the sink, "Seriously, Mary Iris, I can't understand why you pay any mind to the Route 40 Phantom. Everyone knows ghost don't exist."

"I believe in crazy people," Mary Iris said. "Read this."

Joretta took the paper. Mariola eyes widen. I went into the stall to avoid the nonsense.

"What crazy person are you talking about?" I heard Mariola asked from the other side of the stall door.

"For the past year, there has been a man dressing up as a skeleton and trying to drive people off of Route 40," Mary Iris answered.

"Why would he do that?"

"Some people say it is because he is trying to steal from the trucks he's spooked. Other people say that he is trying to kill someone by pushing them off the road into the Englewood Dam."

"Well, it's nothing I am paying head to," Joretta remarked. "I'll tell you what I am occupied with: Miss Bentley being all in a tizzy over the recruiter from Ohio State University coming to the school in October. She practically sobbed to my mother at church on Sunday going on and on about the needed preparations. Of course, Mother offered my assistance. If it weren't to send one of our boys to OSU, I wouldn't be as happy to help. As beautiful as Miss Bentley is, there are reasons she can't secure a husband."

"What is she having you do?" Mary Iris asked.

"I'll find out this afternoon," Joretta answered. "Um, Mary Ella is it?"

"Mariola," I heard my friend reply.

"That navy is a brave choice for you. Most girls with an olive complexion would be afraid the color would wash them out."
I waited until a closing bathroom door followed Joretta's and Mary Iris's footstep. Mariola smoothed the skirt to her navy and gray checked dress.

"Did you hear that, Natalie?" Mariola asked.

"You shouldn't care for Joretta Barr's opinions, Mariola. She is just....."

"I am not talking about what she said about my dress! Joretta said the college recruiter is coming to our school! It's your chance for a scholarship!"

"I was listening. Joretta also said that Miss Bentley is handling the details of his visit."

"For Principal Chet," Mariola replied. "You need to talk to him, not Miss Bentley."

"There is no talking to him without talking to Miss Bentley. She can be very particular about who gets to visit him. One time last year she wouldn't let me see him because I didn't properly press my skirt."

"Then tonight, we'll press your skirt!"

The moment we got home with Chester in tow, Mariola and I pressed my red circle skirt with black embroidery and my black twin set. Mariola wrapped my hair up in ringlets that night.

Mother left for work when the sun came up. The moment she left, I snuck into her boudoir and applied her makeup to my face. I even pinched a string of pearls from her jewelry box.

Before homeroom, Mariola and I headed to Principal Chet's office. She remained outside as I walked in.

Miss Bentley sat at her desk typing vigorously. If she wasn't bent at such an awkward position, she would have looked lovely in her lavender twin set.

Miss Bentley stopped typing upon my approach to her desk. She greeted me with a quizzical expression.

"My, my, Natalie Studebaker, why aren't you done up nicely for once?"

"Hello, Miss Bentley," I choke out, "I would like to make an appointment to see Principal Chet."

"He's very busy, Miss Studebaker, to give audience to petty grievances."

"It's not a petty complaint, Miss Bentley. I just need to see him before the month's out."

"Miss Studebaker, Principal Chet has many preparations for an important guest coming at the beginning of next month. Whatever business you have to take to him will have to wait until the end of the month."

"It is in regards to Principal Chet's guest, ma'am."

"You can't be talking about the college recruiter from Ohio State University."

"I am. I heard that the college recruiter will give out scholarships. I would like to make arrangements with Principal Chet to meet with the recruiter while he is visiting....."

I stopped speaking when I saw Miss Bentley's mouth twist into that smug smile she often gave. This time, it was pair with her resting her face in her palm pretending to be in deep thought.

"The problem is Miss Studebaker, I don't know which position you would be better suited for: linebacker or wide receiver. Too late to contemplate that now. Football tryouts were in August."

"He's recruiting football players? But scholarships are supposed to be for scholars."

"Football is what brings money to the school," Miss Bentley curtly explained. "Ohio State has heard how well our boys play football that they are willing to send one to their college free of cost. This is a big deal considering many of our poor boys have to work on their family farms after school. This is an opportunity to give one of our players a better life. That is why Principal Chet has no time for you this month."

"Very well," I said as I turned towards the door.

From behind Miss Bentley said, "I don't know what made you consider your appearance this morning, Miss Studebaker, but I suggest you consider it every morning. Your prospects will become plentiful."

"Oh, Miss Bentley," I replied, "Joretta Barr has told me otherwise, at least in the regards to you."

That night we had dinner late so Mother could eat with us. Mariola made fried potatoes and onions prepped in butter with a pinch of every herb in Mother's spice cabinet.

"Mm, Mariola, I know I should give you a break from cooking this weekend, but these potatoes would be good with my pot roast on Sunday."

"Is Uncle Walter visiting on Sunday?" Chester asked.

"No, Chester. Before your father left for Europe, I would make a pot roast every Sunday. Do you remember, Natalie?"

"Vaguely," I answered.

"Come now, you were eight when he left. It wasn't too long ago."

Life with my father alive seemed like another lifetime. I didn't want to discuss him or anything else. I put a forkful of potatoes in my mouth to avoid my mother's attempt to rope me into a conversation.

"Natalie, care to tell us what has brought you to the table so sour, honey?" Mother asked.

"Is it because the college recruiter is only going to give money to a football player?" Mariola asked.

Growing up with gypsies, Mariola couldn't tell what topics of conversation were private and which ones weren't. Shooting her a look only picked my mother's interest.

"College Recruiter?" Mother asked. "I heard rumors around town that Principal Chet was trying to get someone from Ohio State University to recruit one of our boys."

"Football players don't deserve to go to college for free!" I blurt. "Those who play for our school pay the smart boys to do their homework. The teachers know about it but don't care!"

"Still, it is an excellent opportunity for an Englewood's son. Boys who don't have a family farm to turn to after graduation are going to Korea. If a local boy can receive a better fate….."

Mother was interrupted by a loud knock.

"Now, who can it that be at this hour?"

Mother got up from the table to the front door. Mariola, Chester, and I peered from the dining room. A delivery man tipped his hat to Mother as she opened the door.

"Good Evening, Mrs. Studebaker," the delivery man greeted, "I bring you an urgent delivery from BHA."

"Better Home Appliances?" Mother replied, "But I haven't ordered anything."

Like magic, the delivery man presented Mother with a correspondence card. Mother read it and almost fainted. Mariola and I ran out to the entryway before she swooned.

"Mother what it is?"

"It's…wonderful."

I took the card from Mother's hand as the delivery man wheeled in a box into our living room.

"Dear Mrs. Studebaker," I read, "Two issues have presented themselves this month. One, you see me as going back on my word once it was brought to light that it was your daughter you wish to send to college. Two, Mrs. Kaiser has called to my office twice to have me advise you to have your girls stop peering into their house to watch their television. I believe this to be the solution to both issues. Sincerely, Christopher Kristoff Esquire."

Suddenly Lucille Ball's face popped into our living room on our newly install television set whining, "Oh Rickkkky!"

"That can't be how Lucy sounds," Mariola said. "Are you sure that thing isn't broken?"

The delivery man tipped his hat to Mariola, " I assure you, Miss, that is

Lucy's voice coming in as clear as a bell."

With that, the delivery man left our house tipping his hat to each of us.

Mother had to shoo Chester and Mariola off the couch and up to bed at nine o'clock that night. I read my civics book in my room with the intent to have its propaganda put me to sleep. At eleven o'clock I heard stirring in the kitchen. I went downstairs to find Mother making coffee.

"Darling," she greeted when she saw me, "why aren't you in bed?"

"I was studying."

"Shouldn't you be sleeping now?" Mother asked, "If you don't you'll fall asleep in class."

"You aren't afraid to sleep in court. Otherwise, you will be in bed now too."

"Oh, I made the stupid decision to watch the news on WHIO. Now, I have to review these briefings before I come into Mr. Kristoff's office. He may take the television away if he thinks it is causing me not to get my work done."

"He had no business giving you that television," I muttered.

"What was that, Natalie Lauren?" Mother asked.

"Everyone in the neighborhood had to have noticed the delivery man coming to our house late at night. Everyone is going to talk."

My mother knew me all too well.

"Natalie, come now. I know you are disappointed that Mr. Kristoff isn't sending you to Ohio State, but you have to admit it was kind of him to buy us a television set with the money he set back to honor his word."

"How can you be so blind? He still has gone back on his word! The television is only a bribe to get you to see otherwise!"

"Which we wouldn't have if you and Mariola haven't spied on the Kaisers while they were watching their television!" Mother exclaimed, "Seriously Natalie, you and Mariola could be arrested for peeping if the Kaisers became sick of you two peering into their windows. Mr. Kristoff is very practical. If this how he wishes to pay off his promise, then so be it. He doesn't have to."

"Anyways," Mother continued as she poured herself some coffee, "this is the first appliance we have received since we got the refrigerator. The only reason Uncle Walter bought us that is because Chester almost froze to death in the ice box when you forgot him during your game of hide and sneak."

"That was a few years ago," I replied.

"Still, your sense of responsibility has not matured," Mother commented. "I have lost all my sympathy for you Natalie because of your attitude. All you have done these past few weeks is sulk. Mariola is the person helping me clean, cook, and take care of Chester. You have yet to contribute to this household. You have to work for things, including your right to go to college."

"Fine," I blurt, "I will go get a job!"

Most mothers would be astonished at their daughters for suggesting to do anything other than housework. My mom wasn't most mothers.

"That is not a bad idea. You won't be able to save for admission in the fall, but if you work hard, you might be able to attend the following year. You'll be attending with added skills to help yourself on your own. Very well, Natalie, Mariola will pick up Chester from school tomorrow. You go around town and find yourself a job."

ALEXANDRA

So what are we doing here?" Anthony asks as we sit in our parked car at the Englewood reserved.

"To see what could cause drivers to think a skeleton was driving down the road," I answer looking towards the Englewood Dam. "It had to be a moon shadow or a busted street light."

Anthony leans back and sighs, "Sounds like you are reaching."

I am. There haven't been any new names popping up since my interview with Irma Hoople. The story is going nowhere. Instead of moving to a new idea like I hope, Chip is hounding me for my first draft. My career could very well end with one good story when my shotty phantom piece follows my article on Lisa Hubbard.

"When most women beg their husbands for date nights, they suggest dinner and a movie."

"I took you to dinner," I say, "We have seen every movie based on a comic book that is out, and you don't want to see movies that won't have any explosion or naked boobs ."

"I like intelligent films," Anthony says, "I just don't see the point of watching everyone talk all points of a discussion to death. If I want to do that, I'd Skyped with Shona."

I roll my eyes. If it were allowed to speak ill of the dead, I'd give Anthony a few words about what I thought about his sister, Angie.

Siblings are on Anthony's mind. They don't belong to him or me; they should belong to our daughter. Anthony's finger finds my boob. He begins to stroke me.

"Mom is going to be home late, and Natalia is sleeping over at her friend, Julia's house tonight. Why don't we go home and you can finally let loose?"

I stifle a groan. Ever since Anthony declared his want for more children, I lost my drive to get frisky. In the few times we attempted since, I lost my desire due to images of Nona bringing out her rosary and praying for an egg to implant in my womb.

Suddenly Anthony vaults himself into the backseat. He starts twisting his leg off.

"What are you doing?" I ask.

"Ending this decade-long rut," Anthony answers. "I realized that we have only done it in our bed since we have been married. We never got to be teenagers together."

"That's because we were in our twenties when we met."

"Therefore, we never had the need to get creative in finding sexual location," Anthony replies, "but we are here, alone. With my left leg blown off, it will be easier having sex in the car than it was in I was younger."

With one more pat on the seat next to him, Anthony has me vaulting over to the backseat, without my pants.

****

One thing we will never tell Natalia about how we got together is that originally, Anthony and I were a one night stand. I won't be telling her about the boyfriend I had at the time either. I'll just have her believe I was a virgin when Anthony and I met. I might as well have been.

I moved to Columbus to escape my mother, but I didn't want to deny having one. I wouldn't be with a person who would cause me to hide the fact I had gay parents. In my sophomore year, I met Rand- short for Randolph. He was a colleague at the campus newspaper. His aunt was a Democratic Senator; therefore, his family loved gays and hated the military.

My relationship with Rand was nothing to write home about. It was spending the afternoons writing the school newspaper, eating dinner as I drown out the sound of his worldviews with a bottle of wine, and a round of maudlin sex. Looking back at our relationship, I was a little girl playing grown up. The only thing I knew about love was that I was straight, and Rand with his sandy brown ponytail and high cheek bones was handsome enough to ignite my loins.

By senior year, I had tire attending political dinners and keynote lectures. One night I reluctantly allowed Heather to drag me to Gamma Nu fraternity house to chase Jeremy Booth because I didn't want to hear Rand preach the same old speech at a "peace rally."

Jeremy had five girls in his room when we got there. Each girl subtly shoved each other to get a seat closer to him. Anthony sat in a chair closest to the door. That day he wore his Air Force dress blues. I felt his eyes lock on me the moment Heather and I arrived.

Heather shimmied her way on the couch between Jeremy and a girl from the Zeta Iota sorority. For ten minutes I stood in the doorway watching everyone else watch a raunchy comedy on Jeremy's television.

Anthony got up from his chair. He pulled a business card from his coat. Handing it to Jeremy, he said, "Call me when you are ready to deal."

Anthony motioned me to the chair he vacated then left. There I was alone with Heather in her pleather pants and tight sweater among the scantling clad sorority girls. Jeremy, who was conventionally handsome with his wavy brown hair and his popped polo collar, sat glassy eyed.

"Which one of you bitches is going to get me a beer and show me your tits?"

As the Zeta Iota walked up to him pushing down a strapped to her tank top, I got up.

"Catch you later, Heather."

"You're no fun, Alex," Heather called behind me as I exited.

I walked down the stairs where Anthony was mingling with the Gamma Nu boys.

"So tell me, did you ever kill anyone?" asked a chubby brother with a beer in his hand.

"Possibly."

"Did you shoot a towel head?" asked a brother with horrible acne with a beer in his hand.

"Not directly. I am with the Air Force. I engaged in air warfare."

"How was the Iraqi snatch?" a short brother attempting to look like Eminem holding-you guessed it-a beer in his hand.

"I find that question disrespectful. I do not engage in sexual assault."

"He didn't mean it," said the chubby guy. "We have nothing but mad respect for you, Man. You have to let me get you a beer."

"I can't drink in uniform."

Anthony's eyes locked on me again when I reached the bottom of the staircase. I continued to walk out of the house.

"You walking?" I heard behind me.

I turned to see Anthony following me out.

"I only live three blocks up from here."

"I'll give you a ride."

"It's not that far. I'll be fine."

"I use to work campus police when in college. If I got a quarter for every assaulted girl who initially walked home with that notion, I'd be miserably wealthy."

With anyone else, I would have retorted that getting in a car with a stranger would be a sure fire way of becoming assaulted. I felt a sense of safety with Anthony that I couldn't explain that day. I entered the car with no reservations.

When he pulled up to my apartment, I figured I should be hospitable.

"Can I offer you a drink?"

"I have to drive over an hour to Springfield."

"I have coffee," I suggested. "I am told the drive south of Columbus is boring. You'll need to stay awake."

Anthony turned off the ignition. "Sure."

In my apartment, I pulled out the five one pound bags of coffee from the cupboard. Anthony's eyebrows arched.

"Colombian, French Roast, Sumatra? What's with all the coffee?"

"My roommate often chides me for spending half our grocery budget on coffee," I said. "However, it is an occupational necessity. I have French Vanilla and Chocolate Macadamia Nut as well. Pick whichever one you want. I'll drink whatever you choose."

"Doesn't matter, you can choose."

I poured the French Vanilla coffee into a filter. While the coffee brewed, Anthony walked around my small kitchen looking at photographs on the refrigerator before finding the latest copy of the campus paper on the small kitchen table.

"Is this occupation that requires massive caffeine intake?"

"It is. I write the weekly spotlight section for professors and students."

Anthony turned to the second to the last page. I poured the coffee as he read my small paragraphs.

"Cream or sugar?"

"No."

I handed Anthony his mug. He placed it on the table as he continued reading.

"They need to get you a bigger section that three paragraphs for each person. The professor who scaled the Berlin wall and the student whose family got forced out of Bosnia deserve larger section that the crap printed on the front."

Anthony lifted up Rand's latest article, "Soldiers Unrightfully Demand More Funding."

"That's Rand being Rand," I replied. "Being vocal about hating the war and George Bush is how he attracts the stupid freshman and sophomore girls. They think he is 'compassionate' and 'worldly.' He is probably at the rally downtown wooing them out of their pants."

"You share his sentiments?"

"Nobody likes war," I said, "But shouting hate remarks about the soldiers isn't going to change the fact that the US is in one."

We sat down at the table. Anthony flipped through the paper. I think I heard him mutter that my articles were the only ones worth reading.

"I overheard you talking to the Gamma Nus that you fought in Iraq."

"Yes. I was deployed with Jacob Booth, Jeremy's brother."

Anthony avoided eye contact as he said Jacob's name. I knew what it meant.

"You were here to tell Jeremy of his brother's death....I'm so sorry."

Anthony sighed. "Jacob was my best friend. I figured I owned it to him to inform his brother personally. The kid isn't handling it well. Not that I should say anything. Booze and women don't do what you think they would. Nothing does."

"I suppose you are not at liberty to say what happened?"

"Speeding down a highway while not wearing his seatbelt," Anthony said with the mug to his lips. "We've been stateside a few months."

Anthony took a long sip. I sat with my mug in the cup of my hands now knowing what to say. I wanted to comfort the stranger sitting at my kitchen table but with what words? I twirled a curl with my finger; it was what I did when I felt too stupid to say something.

Anthony put the cup down and ran his hand over his buzzed head.

"I have lost three buddies this year. They all died stateside. You have to understand when you get back from war without crutches and all your limbs; you start thinking you are invincible. God, I went cliff jumping last month after burying a friend who died trying to scale a building like he was a ninja in 'Crouching Tiger, Hidden Dragon'. Sounds insane, I know…"

"Yeah," I agreed.

Anthony looked at me with an arched eyebrow. That was the moment I fell in love with his eyes. They were magnetic, drawing me into his soul. I kept that crappy poetry in my head.

"I'm sorry for your friend," I whispered.

Anthony wrapped a curl around his finger.

"I'm sorry they give the best article space to your dumbass boyfriend."

"I didn't say he was my boyfriend."

Anthony shrugged. "There was bitterness in your voice. Besides, you knew too much about him."

As the night wore on, Anthony and I knew too much about each other. We knew each other's favorite color-his blue, mine red. His mother's maiden name was Ventimiglia. He too had a younger sister. He grew up in Anaheim, California. The Air Force stationed him at Wright-Patterson Air Base in Springfield. When I said my parents were gay, his response was, "My parents are straight, but my family is not narrow!"

He knew more about me than Heather that night. How could I not sleep with him?

Looking back, the sex that night was probably our worst; yet, at the time, it was the best I ever had. We didn't sleep until four that morning. When he left minutes before noon, there was the awkward sadness. We had fun. We enjoyed each other. We both know we would never fit into the other's life. There was no point in forcing a relationship. I had to accept that Anthony was the one great night of passion every girl has.

He walked out of my apartment with a parting kiss that left me in a fog until Heather chimed behind me, "Alex, you dog!"

Didn't know she came home. Didn't think she should talk. To avoid her, I went to my room and sat at my computer to make a one night stand meaningful.

"This is crap, Alex!"

Rand flung my article at me from his editor desk. I straighten myself up in my chair.

"I respectfully disagree. This is the emotional gamut of war."

"Gamut?"

"Invincibility and fragility all are in this article as well as pride and regret. Greif yet a celebration of a life bravely lived! Jacob Booth was a genuine depiction of war! Wouldn't it be nice if we printed a feature about the war that people actually would want to read?"

Rand arched an eyebrow. Unlike Anthony, Rand looked mean. I wasn't to be deterred by menacing glances.

"Don't say this has nothing to do with OSU! Jacob Booth was an alumnus. His younger brother, Jeremy is a junior here. This is THE war story of OSU! You have to print this."

Rand pretended to scan my story.

"The way you constantly quote an Anthony Wilson, I could have sworn you slept with him."

I gave an exasperated sigh, "Is that why you aren't printing my article? Because you know you don't measure to his seven to eight inches?"

I paid for that remark. The following morning Rand sent me an email stating that a person of low moral character had no place in his bed-or his paper. That wasn't the greatest indignity I endure that week. As a parting gift, Rand printed my article on the front page. He created the headline:

How I sold my soul by sleeping with the devil for a good war story.
Seven inches of an emotional gamut by Alexandra McNally.

Needless to say, I stayed in my apartment the majority of the week only attending the classes where the professors took attendance. The Friday following my article, I left to attend my Media Law and Ethics class. Standing in front of my building was Anthony Wilson reading the latest edition of the campus newspaper while leaning against his car.

"Excellent story," he commented without so much of a hello. "The headline is misleading. I am at least eight inches long."

"The headline was the only thing I didn't write."

"Whatever it takes to get your rightful place on the front page," Anthony said, "You have this way of capturing Jacob's humanity in your article. He wasn't a statistic. You just….Okay, you're good. Mail me your next article."

"That was my last."

"Really?"

"You don't cheat on the editor in chief and expect to keep your job."

"So you're single?"

"Never been married; therefore, always have been."

Anthony opened the passenger seat to his car.

"You are in a need of a vacation. I am in need of company to Springfield. Why do you get in?"

"I can't," I answered."

The smirk on Anthony's face disappeared, "Ohh, okay…"

"It's that I don't have clean underwear or a toothbrush packed in here. I find them necessary to have them on any road trip. You know, just in case."

Anthony's smirk magically reappeared.

"Good idea, drop off your books and pack that bag with underwear. While you are at if, can you brew some of that coffee, only if you have to-go mugs."

"Sure!"

Like a little girl running to the carnival, I ran to my apartment and hastily stuffed my bag with whatever clothes and toiletries would fit. I should have left the clothes at home. I spent my weekend at Wright-Patterson airbase naked in Anthony's bed.

****

It is hard to determine what I like best about sex, the actual act or afterwards where we fall into each other as I bask in the afterglow. Anthony's head rests on my chest. My head rests against the door. I close my eyes to shut everything out and focus on the pressure of Anthony's body upon mine.

Suddenly, my closed eyelids illuminate with light.

"What the?" Anthony shouts quickly followed by "Alex, get your pants on! The cops are here!"

"Huh?"

The lights die down. Anthony zips his pants and peers through the fogged window.

"Ah, great it's Lincoln."

"Hubbard?"

"I don't know anyone else named Lincoln."

There's a tap at the window. After we fasten our pants, Anthony lowers the window. Sure enough, the round mocha head of Mother Hubbard's grandson, Lincoln, appears.

"Anthony. Alex. What are you fools doing here?"

"Alex is working on a story. What are you doing?"

"I'm working."

"Don't you work in Columbus?" I ask.

Lincoln points to his state police badge indicating that his jurisdiction is anywhere within the Ohio state lines. He leans into our car and chuckles.

"We didn't know you were visiting the area tonight," I mentioned.

"It was one of those spur of the moment visits. On my last shift,

I pulled over a punk for speeding, and he ends up having a warrant for his arrest in Cincinnati. It was the last two hours of my shift. By the time I dropped the punk off at the Cincinnati jail, my shift is over. I was barely making the hour drive to Nana's."

"I bet she made you an excellent breakfast when you woke up."

"Yup, with honey do."

"I thought she hated melon," Anthony says.

"Not honeydew, honey do. After I had my sausage and eggs it was nothing but, 'Lincoln Honey, do this for me please' and 'Lincoln honey, do that for me please'. She is so bent out of shape with Janelle arriving on Monday. I'd say have Janelle do all the work once she moves in. Still, I can't say no to my nana."

"Janelle is moving in?" I ask, referring to Lincoln's twin sister.

"Yup," he answers as he reads a pad of paper, "She's done with her residency in Michigan and starts a job at Good Samaritan hospital. She will be living with Nana for awhile."

"What are you looking at?" Anthony asks Lincoln.

"I am going to have to write you two for fornication. Yet, I am kind of embarrassed to do so since I know you both."

"What? Can't you give us a pass? You know, the Italian code."

"Italian code?" Lincoln replies pointing to his face. "Do I look Italian to you?"

"You're the same amount of Italian as my daughter, and she is no less of an Italian than anyone else."

Lincoln chuckles, "You need to go back to school for math as well as civics, Fool. I can't write you up for fornication. You're married! I can't write you up for being stupid either although I should. You can now, laugh, Alex."

Releasing my bottom lip I whine, "I can't. I bit too hard."

Lincoln laughs out loud.

"Hey, are you going to join us for the game tomorrow?" I ask.

"No, I have to work the highways near the University tomorrow just like every other football Saturday. Enjoy the lasagna tomorrow. I wasn't going to leave until Nana gave me a piece. It is good! You two get home safe and have a good night."

"You too!" I chime.

Anthony shoots me a look.

I shrug "Isn't it nice when Lincoln comes to town?"

As a state, Ohio doesn't have a professional football team. The state rallies around the Ohio State Buckeyes every Saturday, didn't matter if it was a person's alma mater. The houses on Overlook Drive took turns inviting neighbors to come over and watch the game every week during football season. This week Mother Hubbard was hosting. Nona made cannoli to go with Mother Hubbard's lasagna.

The moment the neighbors arrive, the men sit in front of the television, the children play in the yard or the basement, and the women congregate in the kitchen. I sit around Mother Hubbard's counter picking the croutons from the Cesar salad Shelley Hughes made. The kids momentarily blind us during their game of flashlight tag.

"I heard Janelle is moving in with you on Monday, Mother," I say.

"Aww, Lincoln found you."

"What were you doing at the Dam?" Nona asks.

Anthony and I decided not to tell Nona about our trip to the Englewood Preserve when we came home. "How do you know we were at the Dam?"

"Lincoln has his way," Mother Hubbard replies.

Figures. Nona must have visited Mother Hubbard before Lincoln left and encouraged him to track us on our phone's GPS. I didn't think that was legal.

"I am reaching for a lead to the Route 40 Phantom piece Chip has me working on."

"The Route 40 Phantom?" Shelley pipes up, "That's a name you don't hear much about?"

"Yeah," says Lynn Keegan, "My grandparents told me the stories when I was a kid. They never knew who it was."

"Oh come on," Mother Hubbard remarks, "everyone in town knew it was Heinrich Adolphson. His family owned a car repair shop. The land later became the place for the empty strip mall until the gas station bought it."

"Excuse me," I say.

I pull my phone out of my pocket as I walk into the hallway. I click Chip's number on my contacts.

"Hey, Chip, I may have a lead. Can you find sources to help me locate a Heinrich Adolphson?"

NATALIE

I started my job search the next afternoon. Every store owners dismissed me. Many advised they thought my proper place was to help my mother at home. Still, every night I tied my hair with rags for curls after pressing my skirt in hopes of gaining some employment the next afternoon.

I exhausted my options in Englewood proper after three days. On Friday, I started walking elsewhere. I was desperate to be hired on as a farm hand even though I knew nothing about tending to animals or the land. My mother's long face when I returned home unemployed became disheartening.

My saddle shoes were unsuitable for walking long distances. I felt blisters forming on the sides of my feet from the friction of skin against the leather. A discarded tire became my respite. I sat down dejected.

Every store and every office had a beautiful blonde, creamy skin girl with pink lacquered lips holding my desired position. Many had weddings planned for the following summer, so their employers encouraged me to inquire after I graduated. Being short, near-sighted, with dirt-colored hair; I was realistic about those prospects panning out once I was in competition with every other girl I graduated with in my class.

I leaned back looking to the sky in an attempt to look for guidance. My back hit a jagged piece of wood. Turning around, I saw painted words, "Help Wanted."

Above the sign, I saw what appeared to be a remnant of a Hooverville shanty on the horizon. I walked down a path that littered with broken cars. At the end of stood the open air shack with a blue Cadillac parked in front. A figure bent under the hood while two legs protruded from underneath.

"Excuse me?" I said meekly.

From the hood of the car, a man with coal black hair and oil on his pale skin poked his head out.

"Hey, Heinrich, it's a dame!"

Sliding from the hood came out a slender man with yellow hair. Like his buddy, he had his coveralls pushed down to his waist. One look at me caused him to pull his coveralls up. His dark hair friend stared at me slacked jaw. Heinrich swatted him in the stomach.

"A dame? Who the hell still talks like that?"

"Uff," was all the reply the dark haired boy could manage hunched over.

"Cover yourself up, Rooney! There's a lady in front of us."

Rooney clumsily put his arms into his sleeve as Heinrich zipped his coveralls.

"Excuse my friend, Miss; he has no manners. I'm Heinrich Adolphson, and this is my establishment. What brings you here?"

"Hello, Mr. Adolphson, my name is Natalie Studebaker. I saw your sign out front about your need to hire, and I am in need of employment."

Rooney laughed, "What are you? Avon calling?"

"I'm not selling anything."

"Get back to the engine, Rooney."

"Ahh, man," Rooney whined as he turned to the Cadillac.

Heinrich looked over at me, "My friend has a point. You appear to be more suited for employment downtown."

"The businesses in downtown don't seem to think so," I replied,

"All of their owners turned me away."

"Why do you want a job?"

"I don't see how that is your business."

Heinrich snorted. "If I am hiring you, it is my right to know. I got enough trouble. I shouldn't be inviting anymore in."

"I want to go to college. That costs money."

"Is that your only reason?"

"Yes, sir."

"You still in school?"

"I graduate in June."

"What sort of work you think is available here? You don't look like the set that has touched a tool in her life."

"I was walking this road to be a farm hand. I am willing to learn anything."

"Follow me."

Heinrich led me to an enclosed area in the shelter littered with papers and receipts.

"This is what my daddy left me. I can't make heads or tails of it. You're a female. Females like to organize. If you can neaten up this mess, the jobs yours, but I can only pay you the seventy-five cents I am required to pay you by law."

Most women downtown made sixty-four cents an hour. Seventy-five cents an hour was the male wage. I had to accept before Heinrich Adolphson realized his mistake.

"I can start Monday after school."

"Deal. Do you have any pants?"

"I have a pair of Dungarees."

"Best to wear those instead of your skirt, It gets dusty in here."

With a shake of the hand, I became Heinrich Adolphson's employee.

Chester had an earache that night. Mariola tended to him until Mother returned home. I came home and dined on a meal of chicken broth and sandwiches. Every one of the household went to bed before ten o'clock with the intention of sleeping in on Saturday.

"Winifred! Winifred Studebaker! Please open up!"

Mariola turned on the lamp. I grabbed my glasses from the nightstand. My clock read it was one in the morning. Mariola and I met Mother in the hall in our dressing downs.

Mother stomped down the stairs, "Of all the pathetic nerve!

This is a new low for...."

"Meredith Metterschmidt," Mother greeted as she opened the door, "this is quite a surprise."

"Winifred, Darling, I am calling on behalf of the Englewood Friendly Society."

Mrs. Metterschmidt walked into our house without an invitation. She stood in our foyer in a navy evening dress and bolero with an ostrich feather hat perched on her head.

"Excuse our state of dress," Mother replied. "We were not expecting company at this hour."

"I suppose not," Mrs. Metterschmidt answered.

"Let us go to the kitchen," Mother suggested. "I'll make some tea and you can tell me all about the poor woman's situation."

"The poor woman?"

"Why yes," answered Mother. "The only rational reason for the Friendly Society to call at this hour is that the Friendly Society has taken upon a battered woman. Is it Donna Bell? Did the drunken louse she married go too far this time?"

"No, Mrs. Bell is fine as far as I know. She is none of your concern. I am here to check up on things."

"Would you like to see the man I have in my bed?"

Mrs. Metterschmidt's eyebrows shot up.
Mother turned on the light to the stairway. "Follow me."
Mariola and I remained at the foot of the stairs. We listened to the clacking of Mrs. Metterschmidt's heels down the stairs. Suddenly a loud shriek pierced through the house.

"Not Mrs. Metterschmidt! I hate Mrs. Metterschmidt! Tell her to leave, Ma!"

Mrs. Metterschmidt flew down the stairs. Mother softly ran behind her.

"I'm afraid you'll have to excuse Chester. He has a horrible ear infection. He's been a handful. I figured it was best he slept in my room so I could more readily tend to him if he cried."

"I see. Be sure to call Dr. Woodruff tomorrow."

"Ah, Meredith, have you forgotten I assisted Dr. Studebaker for ten years? I know a thing or two about treating an ear infection. Now, please excuse me as I go to the kitchen. I think it is too late for a cab service to be in operation, but I know the police would be readily available.

"The police! Now, what would I need the police for?" With her back turned to Mrs. Metterschmidt, Mother smiled momentarily.

"Clearly, you have a little too much to drink at the Supper Club tonight."

"I have not!"

"Now, now, Meredith, it is nothing to be embarrassed about. It is Friday night after all. I understand how it is, you and the ladies toasting with your husbands..."

"I assure you Mr. Metterschmidt and I run a temperance house!"

"Oh dear, I'm afraid I am at a lost for the purpose of your call, Meredith. Why would anyone in their right mind call in the middle of the night if it is not an emergency?"

Mrs. Metterschmidt walked to the front door in a huff.

"I bid you a goodnight, Winifred! You too, Natalie, and you as well, Gypsy."

"Mariola!" my friend shouted back as the door slammed after Mrs. Metterschmidt.

Mother walked to the kitchen and flipped the light switch on. Mariola was quick to follow her. I peered at the front window. Mrs. Metterschmidt stood at Mrs. Kaiser's front stoop. Mrs. Kaiser stood at her doorway dressed in a brown evening dress. Mrs. Metterschmidt pointed to our house. I stepped away. It was best not to speculate their conversation.

As I walked to the kitchen, a reflection of the moon's shadow caught my eye. It shone through the green glass vase on top of the new television covered with a white lace tablecloth.

"Why is the television covered?" I asked as I entered the kitchen.

"Your aunt Victoria left me so many lovely things," Mother muttered as the tea kettle whistle, "it's a pity I don't display them."

"Who is Victoria?" Mariola asked.

Mother poured the hot water into three mugs.

"She was my sister. She became ill three months before her wedding. Scarlet fever killed people in those days. My parents gave me everything in her hope chest when she died."

"I'm sorry to hear that, Mrs. Studebaker."

"Mariola, for the last time, call me Winifred!"

"Why is Aunt Victoria's table cloth covering the television?"

"For tonight!," Mother exclaimed as she placed mugs on the kitchen table.

"Tonight?"

"Or whichever night the Friendly Society chose to make their 'Friendly' visit," Mother explained. "I have been waiting for them since Edith Kaiser saw the BHA delivery truck in front of the house. Louisa Barr told me of these visits in the earlier times of her employment to Mr.Butterfeld. They come at midnight to see if there is a man in your bed. Mrs. Barr was lucky that the man in her bed could bankrupt the businesses belonging to the husbands of the Friendly Society if he chooses to do so."
"

So you knew this was coming when you accepted the television."

"Natalie, the Friendly Society would find a reason to intrude on our business whether we have the television or not. Covering a television is easy. I also don't have to worry about the possibility of you and Mariola being arrested for voyeurism because you are peering at the Kaiser's house watching Ricky screaming to Lucy that she has 'some serious splaining to do.'"

"That's exactly what Ricky Ricardo says on the television," Mariola grinned.

"I'm just surprised Mrs. Metterschmidt or Mrs. Kaiser haven't paid a call sooner," Mother continued. "Yet, it makes sense that Mrs. Metterschmidt waited until Friday night after their evening at Supper Club."

"You sure were one step ahead of them, Winifred," Mariola remarked. "Oh, the face Mrs. Metterschmidt made when you implied that she was drunk! I shall never forget it!"

"Neither shall I," Mother said standing from her chair. "I need to retire, Girls. Chester will most likely wake me up in an hour."

"Mother," I said as I followed her to the stairs, "why don't you just tell the Friendly Society you no longer need their charity?"

Mother arched her back in a sigh.

"If I did that Natalie, it would only lead to more invasive intrusions than what occurred tonight."

"I don't understand."

Mother sighed and continued up the stairs.

We retired to bed. The porch light shone from the Kaiser for another hour. Knowing Mrs. Metterschmidt, she and Mrs. Kaiser were talking about places my mother could hide her fictional admirer. I became more inspired to get out of Englewood. I never wanted to be as bored as Mrs. Metterschmidt and Mrs. Kaiser, always intruding on my neighbors because housewifery was unfulfilling.

ALEXANDRA

I enter the office of the Englewood Herald to a round of applause and wolf whistles. Shauna Cousins gives a standing ovation.

"Damn, Girl! Who'd a guess you still got it!"

John Yeldman sheepishly crouches over the computer. I walk over to his desk and grab his copy of the police blotter:

Ohio State Police reported a suspicious vehicle parked at the Englewood Reserve on Friday Night.
Officer on scene reported Anthony Wilson, 37 and Alexandra Wilson 34 both of Englewood were in the vehicle.
No arrests were made given the Wilsons' marital status.

"Seriously, Yeldman, you are going to print that?"

"I have one job here, Wilson. I review the police reports every night and determine which reports make this week's blotter. Unfortunately for you, the police are having a slow week. I could barely fill half of the quarter page I am allotted."

I roll the paper as Yeldman takes his glasses off. As I lift my arm to jovially swing the paper across his face, Chip flies down the stairs from his office.

"Alexandria! Alexandria! I found him! I found him!"

Chip approaches me red faced from running. He handed me a piece of damp paper crumpled by his fist. The ink is smeared into nearly illegible letters. Chip's face reddens at my instinctive response of aversion to sweat.

"I found Heinrich Adolphson. He's still alive, residing in Limestone Manor Retirement Center. I called the staff. They are willing to let you see him. He never gets visitors."

I am not prepared to interview the man who was potentially the phantom. When I called Chip last Saturday, I hoped he'd discovered Heinrich Adolphson was dead with no local relatives. I could quickly write the feature fluffed with suspenseful garnish to give the readers a potential identity while maintaining a local mystery. Then I could move on to the next feature. So much for my best-laid plans, yet with everyone at the office privy to my marital life, I could use an excuse to leave.

"Call the staff and let them know I'm on my way," I say shifting my bag on my shoulder.

I pass Cousins' desk. She makes kissing noises as I leave.

Limestone Manor is nothing like Irma Hoople's home at Brookhaven. The outside is constructed of Limestone bricks. I enter inside to see the interior is built of the same Limestone bricks, resembling an unfinished basement. Many elderly residences are parked in wheelchairs in the hallway staring at me with glassy eyes.

A heavyset African American nurse wheels another patient into the lobby. Her name tag reads Bianca.

"May I help you?"

"I am here to see Heinrich Adolphson."

"If you are trying to get money from him, forget it. He has none. That is why he is here and not Brookhaven."

"I'm with the Herald. He has agreed to be interviewed for next month's feature."

Bianca parks the wheelchair and motions me to follow her. We walk down a narrow hallway.

"The windows in the room are small," Bianca explains without a solicitation. "They have to be ever since a patient with dementia climbed out a window in the middle of the night. Found dead by the side of the road hit by a car. The only window that provides ample light is the entryway you came in. We can't bring them outside. A careless employee left a patient out overnight a year ago. Patient caught hypothermia. He had a family, and they sued. That is why you received the grand reception."

"I am not here to write a piece about local retirement centers," I assure.

"I wish you would. Then the Powers that Be would take notice their policies are limiting our patients from having the quality of life. This place is a graveyard for the living. Mr. Adolphson is right here. I don't know why you want to do a story about him. If he makes you uncomfortable, do not hesitate to push the nurse button."

The nurse continues down the hall. It seems surprising that she didn't make a move towards introducing me to Heinrich Adolphson. I knock on the door.

"Just come in will you! I'm as decent as I'll ever be!"

A fetid odor greets me as I enter. I don't think I want to allow my brain to inquire what it is. An old man with sporadic white tufts of hair crowning his head lay in bed. His white t-shirt and the white sheets covering him from the waist down bring out the jaundice in his leather skin. His lips curl up in a sneer as I come in.

"Tell me where the baby is!"

I feared the possibility of the Phantom being mentally unstable. What did I expect of a man who was suspect of running off people of the road dressed as a skeleton? If Adolphson continues to rant for ten minutes, I could have enough crazy talk recorded for Chip to abandon the idea of the Phantom altogether. Or better yet, Heinrich Adolphson could kick me out which means less time I have to spend on this story.

Quickly putting on a professional demeanor, I begin the interview,

"I think you have me confused with someone else, Mr. Adolphson. I am Alexandra Wilson of the Englewood Herald."

Mr. Adolphson shook his head and grumbles, "No, you can't be who I think you are. Damn, I forget what year it is. Lately, my thoughts just wonder..."

I sat in a vinyl upholstery chair next to Mr. Adolphson's bed.

"You said you were with the Herald. What does the Herald want with me?"

I pull my phone out of my purse.

"Do you mind if I record the conversation?"

"Do what you want," Adolphson grumbles.

I place my phone on the end table by his bed.

"Mr. Adolphson, I am doing a piece on Englewood Mysteries. One of the mysteries was the Route 40 Phantom that was reported scaring truckers in the early 1950s. I have come to see you because your name has been mentioned as the Phantom's possible identity."

"Who has named me?"

"Mrs. McKinley Hubbard," I answer.

"McKinley Hubbard," Adolphson scoffs. "I remember him. That good-for-nothing cop was always poking his nose where he shouldn't be poking. So his old Battle Ax is still alive?"

Battle Ax? Mother Hubbard's strength can't be denied. She was a cop's wife who braved through the loss of her daughter. Yet she is the sweetest person I know. Clearly, Heinrich Adolphson is a disgruntle ex-parole her husband arrested back in the day.

"She is my neighbor."

"Has she ever mentioned Natalie Studebaker?"

"Nope. Is she another person her husband arrested?"

"She's someone Mrs. Hubbard let die."

My phone glows Shona's face. I hit ignore. As Shona's face disappears, Adolphson's face contorts.

"Who's she?"

"I'm sorry. That was my sister. She forgets I have a job."

"That's sister of yours. She doesn't look like you."

"We're different mixtures of our parents. Now, let's talk about your life in nineteen fifty-two."

Adolphson dramatically eyes the digital clock on the dresser across the room.

"It's getting to be two thirty. I need to be taking my nap. Why don't you come back tomorrow? Bring your sister."

"My sister lives in New York."

I go to grab my phone when Shona's face pops up again.
"You better answer that. It sounds like she needs to get a hold of you."

I pull my business card out of my purse.

"Thank you for your time, Mr. Adolphson. We will be in touch."

I awkwardly pass the Limestone Manor residents soaking up the limited sun they could absorb from the glass door. Mentally, I note that Anthony and I need to start a retirement account so we can spend our final years living instead of rotting in a limestone block tomb.

I drive straight home. The only thing this day brought me is the promise of Heinrich Adolphson giving me the run around until the deadline. Come Tomorrow. Bring your sister. Adolphson is a lonely old creep.

Finally, I am at my driveway. I just need to decompress. Anthony and Natalia are at soccer practice. I can just lie down and watch some dumb reality show about spoiled housewives. Better yet, if Nona is home I can have a glass of wine and whine to her as she makes dinner.

"Alexandra?" I hear an all too familiar voice greet me from behind.

A yellow taxi is driving away leaving my little sister at the foot of my driveway clutching a black duffel bag at her hip.

Anybody strolling down the street would think Shona was a solicitor harassing me instead of my sister. Adolphson was true about one thing; we honestly don't look alike. I inherited our mother's red hair and our father statuesque bone structure. Shona inherited our father's Black Irish coloring and our mother's crescent moon profile of a protruding nose and sloping chin. Not only am I staring at Shona's features because I am fearful to ask what she is doing here, but I am also trying to make sense of her outfit. She has a sage colored sweater over a cobalt colored floral print shirt with a red plaid skirt and brown argyle socks. On her feet are cross trainer sneakers.

"Hi, Alex!" Shona shouts.

I snap out of my thoughts. "Shona, what's going on?"

"I have been researching Mom's adoption. I have gotten to the point where I need to complete my research in Dayton, so here I am!"

I'd ask where she is staying, but I know the answer is my house.

"Well, come inside," I say reluctantly.

We come in through the garage. The lights are off, and the smell of sautéed garlic is absent from the kitchen. Nona isn't home. Shona takes off her shoes and plops down on the bench of the kitchen table. She unzips her backpack and pulls out documents.

"So, I called Good Samaritan hospital, and they said that they are in the process of scanning all the documents into an electronic system; however, they told me not to hold my breath in regards to finding something from the 1950s. The facilities have moved locations tons of times, and there have been a couple of floods in the past sixty years...."

"Shona, Does Mom know you are here?"

"Yeah, I called her as I was leaving."

"So she knows what you are doing?"

"What do you mean?"

"You are researching her adoption. Don't you think that should be her journey?"

Shona shrugs, "She has no interest in it."

"Then maybe she wouldn't want you poking around in her business."

"Alexandra, we have a right to know who our grandparents are. We would be medically negligent if we didn't research our ancestry. Many diseases, such as cancer, are genetic. Plus, for family planning..."

"Family planning?" Anthony asks.

Anthony is entering from the garage with Natalia close behind.

"Shona, what are you doing here?"

"I am explaining to Alex about the importance of doing our ancestry for our health..."

"Not the answer he was going for!" My smart mouth daughter chimes in.

"Natalia! To the shower with you!" I order.

"Where's dinner?" she asks as she walks through the kitchen.

"Nona is bringing it home," Anthony answers.

****

Nona comes home a half an hour later with fried chicken from Meijers' deli with garlic mash potatoes from the dairy section of the store. I pour her a glass of wine while Anthony leads her to the kitchen table to put her feet up. Natalia is reading a book from "The Magic Treehouse" Series.

Anthony and I are fixing the family's dinner plates when Shona emerges from our office, which we hastily cleaned to turn into her bedroom while she stays here. She is wearing billowing sateen pants and a University of Rochester sweatshirt.

"Oh, we shouldn't be eating fried chicken," she says, "the human body has no tolerance for Transfat and...."

"Then don't eat it!" Nona snaps.

Not once in the ten years Nona has been snappish to anyone. Natalia drops her book into her lap in astonishment.

"Sorry," Nona murmurs.

"Don't be," I answer as I put her plate in front of her, "you worked."

"Shona ought to be grateful," Anthony adds. "She is really testing the limits of her sister's hospitality."

Thus begins our chilly dinner. If Mother Hubbard isn't here, it isn't unusual for Natalia, Nona, Anthony, and I to eat in silent. Our decade living together condition us to be comfortable in quiet, a stark difference from my childhood. Shona and I grew up in a household where constant talking at the dinner table was a sign of family bliss. If our mother was ever quiet during dinner, we sat in agony waiting for the other shoe to drop.

"So, Natalia, have you been reading the book I gave you?"

"Mom says it is not age appropriate."

"But reading 'A Room of One's Own' is vital for all women."

"Natalia is only in the third grade, Shona," Anthony replied.

"When I was Natalia's age, my mother and I discussed the works of Virginia Wolfe. She had me reading Sylvia Platt when I was eight because she believed the mind should not be limited to chronological age…"

I have to interject, "Shona, I lived with you when you were Natalia's age. All your discussion points about Sylvia Platt you borrowed from my Cliff notes."

Then the meal became silent.

"So exactly how long is Shona staying?"

Anthony and I are in our bedroom. He is undressing while I attempt my nightly skin care regiment in front of my bedroom vanity. The task is impossible due to my stress induced headache.

"Seriously, she just comes here unannounced expecting to stay here indefinitely."

"It's only until she finds out who our grandparents are. Besides, I though Italians practiced hospitality."

"Do not throw my culture in my face. It's a low blow, and I am only half Italian. I am Anglo enough to kick her out as you should have. In fact, my father had no problem turning my Aunt Fina away when she came around looking for a hand out."

With Anthony riled up, I bite my tongue to stop uttering a comment that his Aunt Fina might have been a pot smoker like her niece. It is not the time to bring up his sister, Angie.

"Anthony! I have a killer migrate! Unless your next words are 'Let's have sex', shut up!"

Anthony crawls into bed muttering, "Not in the mood."

This is a first in our decade-long marriage. My headache is so bad that I don't care to analyze my husband's lack of libido. I slap moisturizer on my face and crawl into bed myself. Anthony keeps the light on his nightstand.

"When Mom decided to take a job, she did it with the intention of supporting an extra mouth-a baby's, not your sisters."

"John Lennon always said that 'Life is what happens when you're busy making other plans," I groaned.

"Lennon didn't have a freeloading sister-in-law. She is going to crash here while Mom is not only working but trying to keep house for us…"

My neck cracks as I position it on the pillow. That subsides enough pain to get me to think a bit clearly.

"You are right, Anthony. That is an excellent idea."

"What?"

"Shona, should do the chores and run the errands in exchange for room and board."

Anthony rolls away from me muttering, "Whatever."

NATALIE

I rode my bike to school that Monday with the intent of quickly getting home to drop off my books, change into my Dungarees, and quickly make it to Adolphson's auto part shop to make in time for my shift. I misjudged the timing. I came home with enough time to drop off my books and at least grab my Dungarees.

I rode onto Adolphson's lot right as my shift was supposed to start. Adolphson was smoking a cigarette in the lot. He gave me a glance over.

"I thought I told you to change into pants."

"I didn't have time to change, but I brought my pants with me. May I use your restroom?"

"Restroom?"

"You do permit your employees to void?"

"Girls don't pee and poop! Do they?"

Heinrich Adolphson made a quizzical face that indicated he was ignorant to the fact that women relieved themselves like men.

Rooney popped his head from underneath a car.

"We have a restroom!"

"Rooney!" Adolphson shouted, "Don't you even think…."

Rooney placed his hand on my upper back. "Right this way…"

Rooney led me to a small outhouse on the outskirts of the lot. He pushed open the door for me. I was greeted by pictures of women winning elections, being lifted on an industrial beam, and chased by polar bears in their underwear. A sickly sour odor rose to my nostrils.

Rooney laughed, "See! All you need in life, Doll Face, is the right bra!"

I heard a slapped. I turned to find Adolphson behind Rooney.

"Ahh, man! Why did you have to do that for?

"I told you to clean this up! We have a lady working here!"

Rooney kept rubbing his head. Adolphson motioned me over to the shack. Once near the shack of the business, he pointed to a door.

"You can change there. Just be quick about it."

Inside the room laid an uncovered mattress and a lamp. Books strewed across the floor. I wanted to pick one up, but Adolphson banged on the door.

"I don't pay you to dilly dally! I need you to work."

I came out in my Dungarees. Adolphson motioned me over to an office.

"I apologize about Rooney," Adolphson said as we were walking. "The boy ain't civilized. A drunken Irish man raised him. Old Man Rooney is a brute. Chased his old lady out years ago leaving his son not knowing how to act towards a woman."

"It's okay," I lied, knowing I better not be criticizing my fellow employee.

"No, it ain't," Adolphson said, as he opened the office. "I run a respectable business. You are a lady who must be treated accordingly. We just haven't a lady working since my ma died. My pa died two years ago, leaving me with this mess. It needs to be organized, but I can't make heads or tails out of it. Hell, neither could he. The office was Ma's place."

I walked into the room. It didn't seem daunting when I glanced inside

100

three days ago. Something crunched under my saddle shoe. Thinking about what was underneath made me wince. I began questioning if I should be here.

"Is there anything you need for the job?"

I wanted to say a lighted match, be rid of this and go up the road for a new position. I knew that would be disrespectful to the only person who gave me a chance at employment.

"If you please, sir, may I have some empty crates or boxes?"

"I have a bunch of empty soda crates in the back. I'll go get you some."

Adolphson left me alone with the papers and the bugs wanting revenge for their dead comrade under my shoe.

For the first couple of weeks, I was the only one not dilly dallying at Adolphson's auto parts. While I sort past receipts into crates, Adolphson and Rooney shot the breeze. They'd be smoking, or Adolphson would be reading the paper while Rooney was off doing whatever Rooney did. The Cadillac they been working on since Adolphson hired me saw little progress.

One day, Adolphson peered in the door.

"I have a Pepsi crate. Just two more Pepsis to go and it is yours. Why don't you come out and take a break?"

I followed Adolphson to the open area. The crisp early October air smelt delightful after breathing the stale office air. The cool breeze scattered the dust away from my skin. Adolphson opened two bottles of soda and handed me one of them. I sat on the newly empty crate as Adolphson stood and looked out onto the road.

"It's getting cooler out. We have been making more money this summer selling bottles of soda than on car repairs. Now that summer is over, we lost income."

"But you're a mechanic, not a grocer."

"If you haven't noticed the name 'Adolph' is in the shop's name," Adolphson gruffed. "People haven't trusted us with their cars since Adolph Hitler became a household name."

"Why don't you change it?"

"My family wasn't a bunch of dictators!" Adolphson barked. "Why should we change our name when we didn't do anything wrong?"

Adolphson steel colored eyes pointed directly at me. His boldness excited me as well as made me frighten. I never saw a man emote.

"You're right," I murmured, taking a sip of soda.

The sip became a gulp. As the fizzy bubbles ease my composure, I found myself able to engage in chit-chat.

"Your family came from Germany?"

"According to Ellis Island, they came from Poland," Adolphson said lighting a cigarette. "My grandparents left for the United States after World War I."

"I don't understand why it matters whether you are German. Almost everyone in Englewood has German ancestry. Nobody here cared two cents about the war in Europe in until the Japanese bombed Pearl Harbor."

Adolphson crotched down on a crate and asked: "What are your thoughts?"

"About a World War II?"

Heinrich nodded.

"I don't think I am allowed to think about war. I'm a girl!"

Heinrich rolled his eyes, "Everyone has an opinion about everything. So, out with it! What are your thoughts?"

"I feel the same about any war. War gets created when men feel they have something to prove."

I shook my head stun at my words. Heinrich pointed his cigarette at me.

"You lost someone during World War II."

"My father," I answered. "He wasn't a soldier. He was a doctor."

Heinrich's eyes dart to the front of the lot and froze. From a distance, a small figure dressed in navy walked towards us.

"Hell's fire," Adolphson groaned. "What does he want?"

A young police officer with a round face approached the front of the shack.

"Why, Why, ain't it McKinley Hubbard," Adolphson snapped.

"Officer Hubbard to you, Heinrich Adolphson!"

"Deputy Hubbard," Adolphson retorted.

"I have not come here to exchange remarks with you, Adolphson. I have come to investigate a matter that was reported to the precinct. Paul and Brian Stanley stated that you stole their Cadillac."

"Did they now? I'll tell you what Hubbard, you can take a look around all you want. I have nothing to hide."

Deputy Hubbard went straight towards the blue Cadillac parked in the front. Adolphson ducked into his room. Hubbard crouched down at the license plate. He peered at his notebook and ran to back to the front of the shack.

"Heinrich Adolphson, I am placing you under...Why hello, Miss."

Deputy Hubbard stopped directly in front of me. Adolphson emerged from his room and handed Hubbard a piece of carbon paper.

"Here is the agreement between the Stanley brothers. They pay me three hundred dollars; I fix their car. So far I have only received one hundred and twenty-five dollars; therefore, I have only put in one hundred and twenty-five dollars worth of work. When they pay me the money, I'll continue to fix the car."

Hubbard nodded but his eyes fixated on me, "Paul and Brian Stanley are sixteen years old. As minors, they cannot be bided to such a contract."

"Then they can bring their old man here and we can work this out like men. Now, be on your way."

Hubbard stood stalwartly in front of me.

"Excuse me, Miss, I need to ask your purpose for being at Mr. Adolphson's business."

"It's none of your business," Adolphson sneered.

"I am his clerk," I answered.

"Do your parents know you have sought employment, Miss?"

"Yes."

Adolphson hooked his arm around Hubbard's shoulders and moved him towards the path to the road.

"Hubbard, Hubbard, please allowed me to ask you one question: Are you a virgin?"

Hubbard straightened his hat indignantly. "I am still a Christian, although I don't see how my beliefs concern you!"

"You're leering at my employee in a matter that is nearly indecent. Now, if you are a man who is still ignorant to the mysteries of a woman, then your actions are understandable. You just need to get yourself some pootang. Whether you are wise to the ways of the woman or not, you need to get out of here before I make a call to your supervisor."

Deputy Hubbard proceeded down the path to the road.

"You haven't seen the last of me, Heinrich Adolphson! I see to it that the city of Englewood claims your junkyard and turns it into a respectable business of progress!"

"He's right about the contract," I said. "My mom works for a lawyer. I can ask about how...."

"I'm not worried about the Stanley punks," Adolphson said. "They may have the gull to report their car stolen but they won't have the nerve to tell Daddy that they busted the car drag racing."

"Drag racing? Isn't that illegal."

"It's my bread and butter," Adolphson muttered. "You better be going."

"I still have an hour left of my shift."

"I'll still pay you for it," he said whiling reaching into his pocket, "Is Whitman's General on your way home?"

"Yes," I answered.

Heinrich pulled out a nickel. "It's best that you don't go straight home. Hubbard may try to follow you. Buy yourself another soda or an ice cream and stay put for an hour."

"Thank you, Mr. Adolphson," I said, taking the nickel.

"It's Heinrich to you, Miss Natalie," Adolphson said touching my cheek.

I hopped on my bike hoping that Heinrich didn't see me blush. I peddled so fast to left the wind chilled the heat from my cheeks.

I laid on my bed that night replaying my conversation with Heinrich in my mind. NO one ever asked me what I thought about war. As a child, we were spoonfed what we thought about World War II: We were patriotic and supported our soldiers no matter what. As a girl, I was taught that the only thing I should be worried about was keeping my house tidy so my father would have a welcoming place to return to.

What struck me most of our conversation was Heinrich didn't chastise me when I claimed the war was a man's game. He immediately knew I had lost someone! Had my own mother heard me say what I said to Heinrich, she would have slapped me across the face. She would never admit to having the same thoughts a decade earlier. I remember that conversation all too well.

I was laying in my bed ten years ago while my mother screamed at my dad in the kitchen.

"We're having a baby, Charles! How can you stand there and tell me you are willing to risk never knowing this child?"

I still clearly remember the strain in my father's voice to remain calm even though he was irate with my mother for not seeing his opinion. "Winifred, our country is at war. They need doctors."

"Then let the army recruits doctors from cities that have an abundance of physicians. You are the only doctor in Montgomery County. Your country needs you here. Your children need you here. The only reason you are going to war is to prove something to your long decease father! He should not matter anymore! Our children should matter!"

"I have enough, Winifred!" My father had yelled before he stormed out into the night.

He returned two days later with a fancy maternity dress for Mother, a doll for me, and a christening outfit for the baby who he only saw in pictures. Mother and I pretended all was well until he shipped out. I learned that night that men never actually cared to be partners with their women. I never wanted to be a wife because my opinion was never to be respected. The more I thought about Heinrich Adolphson, I felt my paradigm starting to shift. I always thought of crazy ideas when I was tired.

I pulled open a book in hopes to stop thinking about him.

ALEXANDRA

Shona didn't get off the right foot with Anthony when we were first married. Her reaction to our union was little to be desired. I remember there were pay phones outside of the Las Vegas chapel. Even though we had cell phones, we thought it would be cute to call our family from the booths.

Nona was overjoyed despite burying her husband the week before. I got my father's answering machine. He showed his elatedness by sending us a fat check once he got back from Cabo. When I called Mother's house, my news was met with silences. Shona took the phone.

"How can you be married, Alexandra, when our parents can't?"

I hung up as Shona remarked, "To a soldier even!"

Anthony and Shona didn't meet until Shona graduated high school. During the party, my step mother lit a bonfire. Shona and her friends found old furniture from storage and threw it in fire pit shouting, "Viva the avant-garde!"

"What are they doing?" Anthony asked with a roll of his eyes.

"Denouncing the value of old objects that tie us to the old order," I guessed.

"What are they, Hippies?"

"Hipsters."

"What's the difference?"

"I don't know."

Contrary to what Anthony believed, my sister was far from flighty. She may no longer want to grow up to be a Unicorn trainer like she professed when she was a kid, Shona still maps out her life. For the last four years, she had her path to her doctorates degree planned out. This is the fall where she was going to start grad school. What is she doing at my house?

There is only one way to get to the bottom of this. Natalia is at school. Anthony and Nona are at work. I think Shona is sleeping downstairs. With the assurance of privacy, I dial my mother's office from my bedroom.

"Susan Richards."

"Hey, Mom. It's Alex."

"Why hello…."

"Is this a bad time?"

"I have class in an hour."

"I'll let you go."

"No, it's all right," Mother snorts, "I am giving the same tired lecture on Kate Chopin I give to my Freshman Comp students every semester. I can recite it better than I can recite Mother Goose to babies. What is going on? Are you and Natalia okay?"

"Yeah, we're fine," I begin, "I am calling about Shona."

"Shona? What happened?" Mother panics.

"She showed up out of the blue at my house last night."

"Was she drunk on Pabst? She and her friends drank it like water this summer."

"No," I drawl, trying not to be insulted at my mother implying the reason my sister was visiting me because she drank herself stupid.

"I thought she was following her friend, Gwen, to Williamsburg and moving into a crack den apartment. It's good to hear she is with you. She has had a rough go of it since she broke up with God."

"Shona was religious?

"No, Shona was dating boy name Godfrey. His parents were pragmatic atheists. They named him Godfrey to proclaim he was 'free from God' as his mother put it."

"Shona is straight?"

"You sound surprised."

After I had transferred to Ohio State, Mother went out of her way to raise Shona in her image. Of course, I am surprised that there is a deviation in Shona's personality from hers. If I speak my thought aloud, I would sound snotty. It's time to get to the matter at hand.

"Mom, the only person Shona has been calling about for the past couple of weeks is you! She found an adoption certificate when she was cleaning out Jo-Jo's room."

"Oh," Mother says trying to calm. "She found that."

"You knew you were adopted?"

"Alex, my mother looked like Snow White, and I looked like Pippi Longstocking. It was obvious we weren't genetically linked."

"You never told us."

Mother sighed, "Honestly, Alexandra, I didn't think it mattered. My parents are still my parent whether it is birth or adoption listed on the parental certificate. Heck, you were such disrespectful snot growing up who would have unfairly disclaimed Jo-Jo whenever you were mad at her. My nondisclosure only prevented conflicts."

"You were born in Ohio," I state, " the same hospital as Natalia even."

"That's lovely to know," My mother murmurs. "Now, be patients to your sister as she goes on this journey. Allow her to have this diversion from her broken heart."

"Shouldn't this be your journey?"

"Alexandra, you are so near sighted," My mother says. "Shona lost the entire love of her life. You only had to deal with the loss of his leg."

"You are seriously not comparing my husband's amputation to a college break up."

"Some amputations are ones of the soul, Alex. I have to run. Take care."

I stare at my phone. I will never understand my mother's rationale. Souls cannot be amputated unless you're dead. Here my mother, the one who chides me for running away to Ohio, allows Shona to hide from her broken heart by running away to my house. I got to accept that nothing in my family makes sense.

Nona had Anthony drop her off at work so Shona could use her car to run errands. I go downstairs and quickly jot a grocery list for Shona and leave her our grocery money before I go to work along with a note to pick up Nona after her shift.

I didn't make it to the Herald today. Some teen queen died from an overdose last night. As the entertainment editor of the Dayton Flyer, I spent my day reading tweets from her fellow celebrities for the next morning's print. I left the office teary-eyed yet able to put my life in perspective. The underlying theme from what I read was that fame and fortune don't matter if you don't have the love a family. Yet, the moment my sister enters the kitchen with different bags of vegetables and fresh herbs all perspective becomes lost.

"Man, that was a long day. You think with the amount of farms Ohio has per capita that the state could host a bevy of Farmers Markets. I had to drive around all day to find only one. I'll have to get creative, but I think I could pull off in making my Tomato Tofu soup...."

My concentration from helping Natalia with her homework turns to Anthony simmering as he sorts Shona's vegetables.

"How much change did you get back, Shona?"

"None," Shona answers Anthony. "I had to go out of my way to stretch the limited money Alex gave me. But don't worry, I was able to afford the stone ground wheat bread..."

"For how much!"

"It was only five dollar which is a bargain...."

"A bargain? Alex gave you a shopping list, right?"

"Oh, that silly thing," Shona naively laughed, "That list was loaded with cancer causing preservatives. Alex's idea of bread was a genetic sponge version of Wonder Bread!"

"That list was two weeks of complete meals! Is all you bought were ingredients for one batch of soup?"

"I can make an abundance of it, and we can freeze it so it can last for throughout the week," Shona replies gaily.

Anthony puts his hands over his face, breathing heavily. Natalia, who now runs from my attempts to cuddle, inches towards me and ducks herself into my arms. Anthony rarely exposes his temper. He never loses composure in front of Natalia.

Anthony forms his hands into a steeple resting them on his forehead. Opening his eyes, he looks at me.

"Isn't Shona supposed to be the genius of your family?"

Suddenly Shona's quiet voice rose, "I never said I was a genius, but I do know that we need to get our food from sustainable organic resources in order to preserve..."

Anthony mockingly bent his arms in confusion. "Wow, who knew? Certainly not me. I only have an Associate's Degree in Applied Medical Science. My job as a Physical Therapist Assistant hasn't resulted in giving any knowledge about the human body compare to your B.S degree in what was it again?"

"Modern Literature and Women's Studies," Shona squeaks.

"What kind of job can you get with that degree again?"

"Anthony!" I interject. "You are going too far!"

"Well, she better start contributing to the household budget soon, or she is out!"

Anthony leaves the kitchen.

"Can I watch TV?" Natalia asks.

"Sure," I whisper giving her a hug. Once Natalia is out of the kitchen, I swallow a sigh.

"Shona, contrary to liberal opinion, veterans don't receive enough in benefits. Between Anthony's medical bills and tuition, we have spent many years financially in the red. We are staying in the black this year because we stick to a strict budget. Organic food is a luxury we can't afford."

"This is how I survived in college. I would make vats of soup and eat it for a month my senior year because I was so sick of Beef-a-Roni. I just wanted to feed your family healthy food."

What could be a beautiful moment of two sisters understanding their differences turned into chaos as Anthony storms into the kitchen, "Shona! Weren't you supposed to pick up my mom! Where is she?"

Miraculously, Nona appears with boxes of Marion's pizza.

"Dinner is here!" she shouts.

"Mom! How'd you get home?"

Mother Hubbard enters. Nona kisses her.

"This kindhearted woman waited with me for an hour for me to be picked up. When she realized no one was coming for me, she offered to buy me dinner. I was going to have the rest of you starve, but she insisted I bring pizza for you all."

"I feared that something terrible happened," Mother Hubbard adds "None of you would be so negligent and leave Nona stranded."

"Shona happened," Anthony seethed taking a pizza box from his mother. "Thank you, Mother Hubbard. For the next week, all we will be eating is Tofu and Tomato soup. This pizza will be a real treat."

Nona looks around at the vegetables and herbs strewed about the kitchen.

"Why didn't you shop at Meijer's before my shift was up? You would have gotten a discount, and I would have a ride home."

Nona leaves the kitchen. Mother Hubbard stands to stare at Shona. Shona puts her arms across her chest to hide within herself.

"Mother Hubbard, this is Shona, my sister," I introduce trying to make my voice lighthearted as possible.

Mother Hubbard walks up to Shona and touches her cheek. "You look like Natalie."

Shona places her hand over Mother Hubbard's which remains on her cheek. I shake my head in confusion.

"I always thought Natalia took after Anthony's family."

"I am not talking about Natalia," Mother Hubbard answers. "It 's nice to meet you finally, Shona. I'd best be going. Jenelle will be home soon. I have to pretend I ate the quinoa she left me. She is a health nut as well."

Mother Hubbard leaves. I can't help but notice that she is as pale as a ghost. In fact, she looks like having seen one.

I turn to Shona. "Come on, let's put these away before they spoil."

"It's what kids in Rochester do, Anthony," I say while I sit at my vanity mirror as he paces the floor. "They spent a dollar on a thrift store shirt so they can spend a hundred dollars on an Artisan meal."

"They spend their parent's money," Anthony remarks. "So we certainly can't forego eating during the next two weeks, what bill do we not pay?"

I sigh. "Maybe we should wait and see how much Nona gets paid on her first check before we know what we need to cut? We are a three income household now."

"No! Mom's money is for building the family, not to make up for Shona's recklessness!"

"Okay, let's put this in perspective, Anthony. Your mother got a job so we can have another child without me in on the discussion. Now you shot down my input on how to deal with a financial crisis. I should be the one having the most input. Unlike the two of you, I have two jobs!"

"And Mom is working so you can quit one! You need to start prioritizing on what is important. Your biological clock is ticking."

I stare boldly at his reflection. "That is not what you say to a woman you want to impregnate. It kills the libido."

Anthony pulls his free weights from underneath the chaise lounge.

"Mine was massacred tonight."

I climb in into bed with a pillow over my head. Sleep is futile as Anthony grunts with each lift of the weight.

NATALIE

On Saturdays, Chester rode bikes with Jimmy Gordon while Mariola and I helped Mother clean the house. We took turns dusting, scrubbing the kitchen, and scouring the bathroom. Afterward, the four of us went to Rob's Diner for dinner.

The Saturday after my first week working at Adolphson, I found myself scrubbing the toilet. I grumbled to myself that this was no way to spend a weekend after spending a week with sorting papers among the dust and bugs.

Mariola had the pleasant job of dusting and sweeping the living room. She was near when there came a knock at the door.

"I don't know anything about where they are," I heard Mariola say.

"Good Afternoon, Miss Chinnici, I wish to see Mrs. Studebaker."

I stopped mid-scrub at the male voice. I tiptoed over to the top of the stairs. Deputy Hubbard was standing at the door. Mother walked out of the kitchen.

"Officer Hubbard, is everything okay?" she gasped.

"There is no emergency, Mrs. Studebaker," Hubbard said taking off his hat, "but I do wish to inform you about your daughter's employment. Are you aware that your daughter, Natalie, is working for Heinrich Adolphson."

"She told me that she was a clerk for a mechanic. I naturally assumed it was Dale and Sons on Main Street."

"Ma'am, I don't mean to alarm you, but are you aware that Mr. Adolphson is suspected of criminal activity of theft and vehicular

115

endangerment?"

"I haven't seen his name appear on the criminal docket when I am in court. I am just aware that the city wants the land his auto body shop is on," Mother explained.

"As I said, I do not wish to cause alarm and I am pleased to hear that no criminal activity has taken place. I simply was under the prerogative that you of good standing within the legal system needed to know there are concerns about your daughter's employment."

"I appreciate that," Mother replied. "Please stop here again if you hear of anything in regards Mr. Adolphson."

Hubbard put on his hat. "I will, Ma'am.

Mariola opened the door. Hubbard tipped his hat to her.

"Nice to see you again, Miss Chinnici; however, I wish our meetings would be under better circumstances."

"Thank you, Sir," Mariola said as she closed the door.

That night, Mother got a call from the Gordons inviting Chester to stay for dinner. Still in her Dungarees and her hair wrapped in a kerchief, she looked in the living room mirror and groan. "I don't feel like primping to go to Rob's diner. Maybe we should stay in tonight? Mariola, how are you coming along on your civics report?"

"Not too well, I'm afraid."

"Why don't you go to your room and work on it? Natalie will bring a sandwich up to you."

"Very well," Mariola said as she went the room we shared.

I was about to follow Mariola to our room when Mother called out, "Natalie, I could use your help! Why don't you fetch the glasses and pour some milk while I make sandwiches?"

Mother pulled some leftover chicken and a jar of mayo from the refrigerator as I went to the cupboard for the glasses. Mother shuffled about as she retrieved bread from the pantry. From the other side of the cabinet door, I heard, "Officer McKinley Hubbard stopped by today."

I felt my face redden with anger. I kept the cupboard door open so Mother couldn't see my ire.

"He seemed to be concerned about your employer," Mother continued, "as am I."

I slammed the cupboard. "McKinley Hubbard is a liar!"

"Why, Natalie!" Mother gasped, "This is unlike you."

"Well, it is unlike you not to seek the truth! McKinley Hubbard came to the shop Friday with his unfounded accusation. The truth was that the two spoiled Stanley boys stacked up their car and wimped out telling their father it was stolen when they refused to pay Mr. Adolphson the money!"

Mother dipped a knife in mayo and sighed. "Heinrich Adolphson may be in the right this time; however I am every aware of times he was not. He was in a heap of trouble when he was your age. When you told me you have found employment, I trusted you enough to make a sound choice. I blame myself. I should have inquired further."

"Who are you to judge?" I cried as I turned my back to my mother at the refrigerator. "You are not one, nor are you God."

Mother stabbed the mayo in the jar. "I am your Mother and it is my responsibility to ensure your well-being! That is enough of your insolence. Take this sandwich to Mariola."

I passed my Mother as she held out Mariola's plate with the bottle of milk in my hand. I reached for a glass.

"You confirmed of some thievery I heard when Deputy Hubbard was here," I said as I poured the milk.

"What was that?"

"Heinrich said that the town wants to steal his land," I replied, "and you admitted it that the court has had hearings about it."

"Englewood wants to expand its business district," Mother replied thrusting the plate in my hand. "We could have a strip mall full of shops like they do in the cities if Adolphson would let the city buy his shanty shack. It's amazing how he stays in business when no one in town trusts him."

"That's because the town unfairly thinks he's a Nazi because 'Adolph' is in his name!"

"Ohh, Natalie," Mother groaned. "Englewood is a town built on German Heritage! There is no merit to your words! Now march upstairs to give Mariola her dinner. Don't even think of coming down for yours until you sweeten your disposition!"

Luckily, I wasn't hungry. Once in our room, I placed the sandwich next to Mariola at the desk and plopped on my bed to read. Feeling the blood boiling in my veins, I couldn't concentrate on my book.

"Mariola, how did you become acquainted with Deputy Hubbard?"

"He was training under the officer that arrested my mother," she remarked.

I couldn't help but smile. It was Mariola's mother's arrest that was the unfortunate circumstances. I knew I shouldn't revel in Mariola's painful past, but at least in that, I had an ally against McKinley Hubbard.

"He did what?" Heinrich growled as he wiped his hand on an oiled rag.

"McKinley Hubbard came to my house snitching on me like a rat!"

Heinrich leaned against the side of an old jalopy that took the place of the Stanley boys' Cadillac. Rooney was looking under the hood.

Heinrich rubbed the stubble on his chin for moments. He turned to me with steel eyes. "He didn't make any claim that I violated you in any way, did he?"

118

"I wouldn't be standing in front of you if he had! My mother wouldn't allow it! Although he did leave her feeling suspicious about something..."

"What!"

"McKinley Hubbard mentioned that you are under suspicion for theft and endangerment," I stammered. "But I told my mother that those suspicions weren't fact."

"If only...." Heinrich muttered staring out onto the road.

Rooney popped his head from the jalopy's hood. "The engine's shot!"

Heinrich turned to the car. "Well, we have to do what we have to do!"

"There ain't a dang thing we can do!" Rooney shouted. "We've been patching that hunk of junk with random parts for years! The engine is a molten metal mess!"

Heinrich sighed, "That is old man Wilkins' car. He's been the one loyal customer to the family since the shop open. I can't tell him there is nothing I can do."

Rooney growls a whisper, "Then we ride tonight! Dale and Sons are expecting a delivery. Maybe..."

Heinrich hit Rooney on the arm and motioned his head to my direction. Rooney shirked back underneath the hood. I walked around the jalopy, taking in the detail of its familiar structure. "It looks like a Model T."

Heinrich arched his brow. "You know your cars?"

"My father had one in the twenties. He framed a picture of him standing next to it in his study."

Heinrich touched the car lovingly.

"Old Man Wilkins couldn't afford his own Model T. He scrounged up pieces from the junkyard near a Ford plant in Cincinnati and built this car by hand. It has lasted him the last thirty years. I just got to dig it. This car's seen its last day..."

"What if I told you I know how we can get a Model T engine?" I

119

chimed.

"I'd say you're crazy," Heinrich chuckle. "They don't make them anymore."

"I happen to know a family who has a Model T they only bring out once a year for the town's Fourth of July parade! I could distract them while you and Rooney extract the engine. They live on the outskirts of town. No one will see you and they won't notice it is gone until ten months later!"

Heinrich pulled out a cigarette from his pocket. "I already have the heat on me from Hubbard!"

"Who has already labeled you as a thief!"

Heinrich lowered the cigarette from his lip. I stood before him with my hands on my hips.

"I have lived in this town all my life," I continued. "Once they put a label on you, you can never dispel it! Even if you have Jesus Christ defending your character! Instead of running a fool's errand to prove them all wrong, revel in the freedom of proving them right!"

Heinrich snapped his fingers. "Rooney, get your kit!"

The Metterschmidts lived on the outskirts of town. Fields lay behind their house. To the side was the shed that housed Mr. Metterschmidt's Model T. Monday nights the men met at their respective club, Elk, Lions, and Kiwanis. Having the men away from their homes mitigated the danger of Heinrich and Rooney getting caught.

I knew Mrs. Metterschmidt spent Monday nights cleaning without Mr. Metterschmidt underfoot. Being alone, she would be quick to call the police if she saw Heinrich and Rooney lurking in the shadows of the setting sun. I stood in her doorway as Heinrich and Rooney were parked in the fields, hidden in the tall grass.

I knocked on the door shivering in the crisp fall wind, yet sweating due to nervousness. The box in my hand bounced a little from my palms as my spine quivered.

The door opened to the unusual sight of Mrs. Metterschmidt wearing curlers in her hand and a ratty robe. "Why, Natalie Studebaker? What on earth are you doing here?"

I held out the small box in my hand. "Good Evening, Mrs. Metterschmidt. My family wishes to gift you these caramels to show our appreciation for all the kindness you have bestowed upon us."

Mrs. Metterschmidt grabbed me by the arm and pulled me inside. "Get inside!"

Mrs. Metterschmidt firm grip caused me to trip over my own two feet. I clutched the box to avoid the caramels from spilling from the box. Once I regained my footing, my palmed opened revealing a crumpled candy box.

"What were you thinking to come around at this hour without a coat!" Mrs. Metterschmidt exclaimed.

"As I said, ma'am, my family wishes to ….."

"I heard you the first time," Mrs. Metterschmidt remarked. "Does your mother know you are here? Of course, she doesn't. She and I had a conversation of the contrary this afternoon. In her opinion, The Friendly Society and I can just mind our own business as she put it."

I wished I had known that before I formulated the plan with Heinrich and Rooney. I thought the caramels from Whittman's could follow enough sweet talk to keep her busy as they extracted the engine. If what Mrs. Metterschmidt said about my mother's encounter with her was true my flattery was raising suspicion.

"Come now," Mrs. Metterschmidt motions to her living room, "I was sorting through donations from my church's congregation for the homeless. I can see if there is a coat you can have."

"Thank ma'am," I said.

I stood in the living room as Mrs. Metterschmidt shifted through piles of clothes. "Are you going to the football game on Friday?"

"No, ma'am, I am not that keen on sports."

"A woman doesn't attend ball games because she is into sports, Natalie Studebaker. She attends to make connections by showing support for her school. This is the game the representative from OSU is coming to."

If there was one thing Meredith Metterschmidt loved more than receiving flattery, it was handing out criticism. As much as I hated to engage, it was a sure-fire plan in keeping Mrs. Metterschmidt distracted.

"I know the college recruiter doesn't want to see me."

"True, but he will want to determine the popularity of the players," she said holding an ugly tweed coat. "You could benefit as well. Some boys do sit on the sidelines. Maybe you can make connections there."

"I do my homework on Friday nights so I can devote Saturday helping my mother with the chores."

"The issue I discussed with your mama this afternoon, Natalie, is that her priorities are not right," she replies folding the tweed coat. "Whereas she has made peace with not sending you to Ohio State University in the fall, she still allows you to keep your nose in your books. You can't expect the boys to notice you if you hide behind books."

"The only boy who looks at me is Daniel Arthur," I said, naming the boy in my class who leered every girl with his creepy gaze.

"Daniel Arthur! Why I know his mother! He is from good stock. I can introduce the two of you if you would like."

I shivered at the thought of being in the same room with Daniel Arthur. I tried not to judge outcasts like me, but Daniel Arthur's penetrating gaze skived me.

"I wouldn't want to put you to any trouble, ma'am."

"Why it wouldn't be any trouble," replied Mrs. Metterschmidt, "in fact, your arrival here today persuades me that setting up an introduction with Daniel Arthur is the right thing for you."

Suddenly a voice from outside pierced the night with an "Alley Op!" saving me from further discussion. Mrs. Metterschmidt ran to the front window.

"What is it, Mrs. Metterschmidt?"

"I am certain it is one of those Greasers. I don't need to make them out in the dark to know that it is them. I wonder what ruckus they are causing tonight!"

"I best be getting home," I said.

"Why yes, you must. Take this coat so you don't catch your death of cold. We'll be in touch. It is good that you are thinking about turning your focus on what matters."

Trying to make my smile appear genuine I said, "Thank you for everything, Mrs. Metterschmidt."

"Thank you for the caramels. I will see you around, Natalie."

I sprinted off the Metterschmidt's porch the moment the door closed behind me. In my saddle shoes, I jogged a block until I caught up Heinrich's truck. Heinrich opened the door. I climbed in with my entire body charged with an unknown energy.

"I can't believe we pulled it off!" I exclaimed, "After years of putting up with the smug, uppity bitch, I pulled one over her!"

Heinrich chucked, "Natalie Studebaker, I thought you were a lady when I hired you."

He squeezed my knee and we drove off back to the shop.

ALEXANDRA

I wake up with Anthony's side of the bed empty. That is not unusual since he likes to run before work. What is unusual is the yellow Post-It note stuck to my vanity mirror. I crawl to the foot of the bed and reach for the mirror. After a good yank I get to read the following:

I remember, one of us has a rich daddy. That person is not me.

"I don't have a rich daddy!" I shout.

Ugh, what possesses my war veteran husband to behave like a bitchy, waspy girl? We have been in dire financial straits without name calling and dragging our parents into this situation. Why is my husband acting like a child now?

Still, Shona spending our entire food budget on soup ingredients has us in a bind this month. I need to ensure my daughter is fed by any means necessary. I need to make the call. I just wish 'Vincent Price' was still alive. He would help me no questions asked even though calling him was my last resort. My dad's current significant is the opposite. Daddy Warbucks-whom I dubbed due to how he resembles Albert Finney-is very vocal how everyone can prosper if they just work hard enough. I never dare to call my dad and ask him for a penny. Desperate times require desperate measures.

I scoot to my nightstand and grabbed my phone. "Call Dad."

"Calling Dad."

The phone rings before the most masculine voice I know answers, "Hello?"

"Jolene?"

"Hello, Alex."

"Are you at my dad's?"

"I'm answering the phone at his house, aren't I?"

"What are you doing in the city?"

"My construction firm is renovating the building your father lives in. I saw Patrick and Al one day. Al told me he thought it was silly for my crew to stay in a motel in Brooklyn, so he arranged for them to remain in an empty penthouse while I stay here. He's a good man, that Al."

"Sounds like he is," I reply, hoping that he bestows his kindness to me.

"So you're calling your dad about Shona?"

Jolene always got to the point. Clearly, my mother spoke to her about my call yesterday.

"Yes, I am."

"It's good that you have taken her in. It was a blow to her when God broke up with her. Then he got into the Masters Program, and she didn't, Man, that did her in."

"Shona was denied from the U of R MFA program?"

"Yup, she didn't get in."

"How? Shona's brilliant."

"The staff unknowingly judged her harshly during the application review because she was Susan Richard's daughter. They expect Shona to be Susan, but she can't be."

"Didn't she apply elsewhere?"

"Your mother convinced her that she was a shoo-in for the program. This all has hit Susan hard too."

Suddenly, I am brought back to my freshman year in high school when I tried out for the one flute spot in the Jazz band. I didn't get it even though I practiced two hours a day. Not making the band wouldn't have been as bad as my mother's prolonged glances of pity which were worst that her stares of disapproval.

"Hey, Patrick!" Jolene calls from the phone, "It's Alex."

I hear the click of a phone lifted from the receiver. " I got it, Jolene. Hi, Pumpkin."

"Hey, Dad, how are you?"

"Great. Very Great. I am so glad to hear that you are taking Shona under your wing. She is a little lost right now. It's great that you and Anthony are allowing her respite."

"Yeah," I sigh.

"What's the matter, Hon?"

"Well, it just costs us," I reply.

"How so?"

I recount last night's soup debacle. He asks me how much my food budget is and then questions if it is really that low. A Decade of being a millionaire boy toy blinded him to the struggles of Middle-Class America.

"I'll see what I can pull together for you, Kiddo. I just need to talk to Al."

"Thanks."

"You hang in there, Peanut. I'll talk to you soon."

I hang up and get ready for my day. As I shower, I think about what got me through hard times. When my parents divorced, I went through five journals in a month. I won five short story competitions after Anthony came back from Iraq with half his leg blown off. Getting lost in a story kept my sanity during hard times, which now makes me realize what I need to do for Shona.

In the kitchen, Nona fried egg. Shona is sitting at the bench in her pajamas eating yogurt and granola while reading this week's issue on the Herald. Nona hands me a plate of eggs and toast and an empty glass. Apple juice and orange Juice are out on the table. I put my plate down and pour myself some juice.

"This town is really small," Shona comments, "The front page is about a how the community refuses to acknowledge the death of a child molester."

I grab the paper immediately as Shona places it on the table.

"Daniel Arthur died in prison," I say.

"I remember Mother Hubbard telling me about the case," Nona replies, "That man ruined a lot of lives."

"Isn't writing that the town refuses to acknowledge his death contradictory?" Shona remarks.

"Did you read the article?" I ask, "I reviewed it for the author. Nora Neuman has a knack for writing stories about survivors that puts them in an empowering light. It's an honor that she contributes to my paper when she is in Ohio."

"What's so great about her?" Shona inquires.

"She's retired from the Associated Press. Her husband grew up here, and his mother isn't well. They moved to Englewood after she retired. She might be in the office today, why don't you come to work with me?"

"Really?"

"Yeah, there is a lot one can learn from Nora Neuman. She's a brilliant writer. I wish I can capture the human experience half as well as she can."

"I'll get dress!"

Shona runs now to her room. Nona gives me a look.

"Nora's mother-in-law died in August. She left for Europe shortly after."

"I know, this article on Daniel Arthur is comprised of bits of an article we wrote together last year."

"Why are you telling Shona she'll meet Nora when she isn't there?"

"Don't worry, Nona, there is a method to my madness."

"Madness," Nona snorts as she places the frying pan to the sink.

Madness is more of a Hail Mary I am throwing towards Chip. We both stare at Shona sitting at my desk below.

"I don't know, Wilson, how can I be assured your sister isn't one of those East Coast types that will want to try to convert our readers into their worldview without attempting to understand the Midwest way of life?"

He won't. Shona possesses the typical twenty-something arrogance. Still, she is a person who is need of a chance…and a distraction.

"Look, Shona is brilliant," I explained, "She just needs experience. If you think I'm a good feature writer, wait until you see what she writes under our guidance. You don't have to pay her. Kids her age love working for free if they get job experience."

Chip sighs.

"She has to have some interest in Midwest to allow her search for our mother's past to bring her here. Think of this as a feature: Two local sisters raised in New York discover the past of their mother who was born in the town they ran away to. In fact, my mom was born in the same hospital as Natalia. Isn't that interesting?"

"It is, but can you prolong your interest into the story?"

"Why are you asking that?"

"Well, I gave you an assignment two weeks ago. You have hardly made headway with it."

"This feature Shona and I could work on will make a bigger splash than the Phantom, Chip. Face it; you assigned me to a story that only two people care about: Yourself and Heinrich Adolphson."

"You are about to give the public a name to the faceless phantom, Alex! This will be huge!"

"Half the people who care about him are dead! It was sixty years ago!"

Chip put a brotherly hand on my shoulder.

"Alex, one of the things I feared when I read your piece about Lisa Hubbard's bout with cancer is that you will only finish pieces that interest you. If you are going to be successful in your new role here, you are going to have to find a way to put your heart into every story. If any story lacks heart, our subscriptions are on the line, as well as your job."

"You want my heart into this story; I'll give to you."

"That's the…"

"…in the form of my sister. Give Shona an internship here and I will give you your Phantom story."

"You run a hard bargain, Wilson," Chip sighs as he holds out his hand. "It's a deal."

I run down the stairs and grab Shona off my desk chair.

"Congratulations, you are now interning at the Englewood Herald. Off to your first assignment."

"Really? I wasn't interviewed or asked to show my portfolio," Shona replies I as drag her car.

"This is one time where nepotism is working in your favor."

Shona stands back in horror as the lifeless living residents of Limestone Manor greet her. Ten of them are parked against the receptionist desk. Bianca rolls another resident to the door.

"You again?"

"Hello," I greet, "Is Mr. Adolphson available?"

"I'll go see if he is receiving visitors."

Bianca turns down the hall.

Shona leans over to my ear. "Why do they slump them here?"

"So the residents can get sun without them being sued," I whisper.

"That is no way to live," Shona whispers back.

Bianca comes back into view.

"Ladies, Mr. Adolphson will see you."

We follow Bianca to Mr. Adolphdon's open door. The open window makes today's stench subtle. Still, Shona wrinkles her nose. Mr. Adolphson turns his head in our direction.

"They only bathe us twice a week," he says without a hello. "I asked for one the day after your sister came. She was supposed to come the next day. But, if it was to fetch you, I'll forgive her."

Come Tomorrow. Bring your sister. Damn, Shona's sudden appearance that day made me forget Adolphson's creepy parting.

Shona sits down on the chair. I stand close. Mr. Adolphson reaches out to take one of Shona's curls. Instinctively, I poke him with my pen. He chuckles.

"You two are a blast from the past."

"I am afraid I don't understand," Shona replies.

"How much do you know?" Mr. Adolphson asks.

"Alex briefed me in the car. She told me you were a phantom who scared trucks."

"I may," he laughs, "What's your name again?"

"Shona," she says with an outreached hand, "Shona McNally."

My phone rings. My father's picture pops up. I excuse myself and go into the hall. As much as I don't want to leave Shona alone with the old creep, I can't have her know I went to Daddy for money.

"Alex," a firm voice says on the other end of the phone, "Alvin Warber, calling. You called your father earlier today. It seems that Shona has caused you a setback."

"I wasn't prepared for her visit, but I'll work her into next month's budget," I stammer.

"Alex, I have always liked you. You are not like the other children that have crossed my life. You have never asked a dime from me. For you to ask your father for such a little amount means you are in dire straits."

"Only momentarily…"

Daddy Warbucks voice booms, "I am transferring ten thousand dollars to your account."

"That's too much! I can never repay you!"

"It's a gift! Not a loan! Now don't be spending it in one place! You have a good day, now!

I attempt to squeak a thank you but immediately hear the beep signaling that Mr. Warber terminated the call.

I walk back into Mr. Adolphson's room. Shona sat next to his bed transfixed to their conversation.

"How long were you together?"

"I only knew her for a year," Mr. Adolphson explained, "but that year impacted my life. It changed when she enter and never became the same after she left."

Mr. Adolphson closes his eyes. I watch as Shona places her hand on his.

"You're tired. I should let you be."

Adolphson puts his other hand on Shona's.

"Don't be like your sister. You come back tomorrow."

"I will."

I can't get Shona to move out of here fast enough. I am pulling her to the door when I heard a familiar voice calling, "Hey, Alex Wilson!"

Janelle Hubbard walks towards me with her arms out. I envelop her bones in a hug.

"I was wondering when I was going to see you! Your brother told Anthony and me that you were coming in this week! I thought Mother Hubbard would be bringing you to our place for dinner about now."

"I have been working the moment I arrived here in Englewood. I haven't unpacked my suitcase. I'll probably do it this Saturday when Nana watches the game. Will you guys drive her to the Keegans house?"

"Ah, don't you want to drive her yourself, Wolverine?" I mock

"Fool, you know I won't be there."

"Well, we don't want you in Buckeye Country anyways."

"Why can't she come?"

Janelle and I stare at Shona. She was oblivious to our confusion.

"This is the twenty-first century. Certainly, even Alex's friends can accept differences amongst people…"

The silence clings to the three of us like a dense fog. Shona can't be implying that Janelle is being excluded because of her race.

Janelle isn't having it. "You must be Shona."

"Yes, I am."

"Let me tell you this, Shona; I don't go to the Buckeye watching parties because my blood runs maze and blue, not scarlet and gray. You were right, Alex. Your family doesn't think highly of you."

"I didn't mean to offend," Shona whines, "It's just that Midwestern people aren't as…"

"I got to get back to the hospital. I'll call you later, Alex."

I wave to Janelle as she leaves.

We drive home in silence. I am livid that she'd think that insinuated that my friends were closed minded. As she sits next to me in the passenger oblivious to how she behaves, my ire boils my blood. The she starts spouting nonsense.

"I like being in your house," Shona says.

"That's good."

"I feel that there is a calm, loving spirit that protects the house."

"Could be," I mutter.

"The last two nights, I have just slept so comfortably."

"The Midwestern aren't as what!"

That ends Shona's zen. She squeaks an inaudible answer.

"Louder!"

"As open minded as people from the Liberal states."

"That is so closed minded! Where do you get off coming to Ohio and criticizing us every chance you get?"

"I didn't mean to!"

"Well, you got to stop it; otherwise, your internship will end sooner than it begins."

The remaining part of the car trip is silent. Shona and I exit the car slamming the door shut. We enter the house with a big slam of the back door. The vibration causes Anthony to spill the orange juice he was drinking from the carton by the fridge. Shona goes to the cupboard to get a mug.

"Why did you call that doctor 'Wolverine'?"

"Because she graduated from the University of Michigan," I answer with my back turn, "OSU's biggest rivals. It doesn't matter. She is Mother Hubbard's granddaughter and my friend. Quit being quick to judge people as narrow-minded!"

Anthony starts to yell, "What is going…"

I continue to the bedroom. I just need to go to bed.

NATALIE

I couldn't sleep the night we swiped the engine from the Metterschmidts. Every molecule wanted to burst. Never in a million years did I believe I could best smug Mrs. Metterschmidt. Finally, I felt what victory was like!

The rush from the heist was a severe high to come down. I couldn't concentrate in class. Joretta Barr would walk in with a new broach or scarf pin and I felt my fingers getting twitchy. I sat on them to calm them down. At times, my legs bounce because the twitch was so strong.

"Natalie Studebaker," Mrs. Harkness, my Civic teacher yelled. "Is something the matter?"

Everyone looked at me. I pressed my buttock harder against my fingers as Jorretta Barr's shot me a smug look. I wanted to slap her face so badly.

"No ma'am," I whispered

Mrs. Harkness stepped over to my desk with a sharp look. "Well then, remember that you are a lady and ladies sit still!"

Mrs. Harkness breezed back to the chalkboard as the other girls giggled. I made mental notes to refer her to Heinrich for car parts.

Chester came down with the mumps a week after the heist. Mother forbade me to go work after school. Mr. Kristoff had only allotted her time off while Mariola and I were at school. I intended to walk to school with her until I noticed she had an unfavorable companion.

Deputy Hubbard tipped his hat to Mariola and me as we exited the school. Mariola started to glide over to him. I grabbed her arm.

"What does he want?"

"Officer Hubbard always walks me home."

"Why?"

"Because he does," Mariola says irately.

Mariola continued over to Hubbard. I quickly followed, immediately linking her arm in mine.

"Miss Chinnici is not in need of your services, today, Deputy Hubbard."

"Hello, Miss Studebaker. If you are walking with Miss Chinnici, it is best that I escort you as well."

"Whatever for?"

"You don't need to explain," Mariola whispered.

Mariola turned silently. Officer Hubbard gesture for me to follow. I dismissed him with a shake of my hand.

Jorretta Barr passed me with a gaggle of her pals. A handkerchief floated from her books. Instinctively, I picked it up the ivory cloth embroidered with pale blue lilies. My handkerchief had an embroidered "V" for my Aunt Victoria. I never brought them out in public because I hated the questions of why I had a hand-me-down snot rag.

I walked up to Joretta's group. I was about to tap her shoulder when I hear, "Miss Bossley told me of a scholarship hopeful."

"Who is it?" asked a girl.

"Natalie Studebaker," Joretta giggled. "Imagine her as a football player! I never even seen her at a prep rally. What's with her sudden interest in football?"

I turned and stuff the handkerchief in the pocket of my sweater. Walking away with the handkerchief wasn't as thrilling as stealing one of Joretta's broaches, but it was still nice to pull something over that smug nose snot.

I entered the house to find Deputy Hubbard talking to my mother with Mariola standing close to his side. He held his hat in front of him.

"…When Miss Chinnici told me of the vile things Mr. Whittaker was saying on her way home from school, I knew there needed to be some action. Unfortunately, unless Mr. Whittaker acts on his threats, I can't make an arrest."

"Thankfully your presence has deterred him," Mother replied. "Thank you, Deputy Hubbard, for telling me about Mr. Whittaker. I hope you escorting Mariola hasn't gotten you in trouble with Captain Vincent."

"It has not ma'am. With your permission, I would like to continue escorting Ms. Chinnici from school."

"It would be quite all right," Mother replied.

"Thank you, ma'am," Deputy Hubbard said putting on his hat. "Good day to the both of you. I'll see you tomorrow, Mariola."

I opened the door as he approached paying no head as he tipped his hand in farewell. Mother's eyebrows arched as I quickly shut the door.

"Mariola, you should have told me about Mr. Whittaker," Mother said.

Mariola stared at the ground, "His words were not things you say to polite company, ma'am."

"I agree, that is why I needed to know that you were exposed to such vile threats."

"What threats?" I chimed in.

Mariola's face redden. Mother shot me a look.

Turning back to Mariola, Mother said, "You should not feel shame in this, only Mr. Whittaker."

"I don't think he does," Mariola muttered.

"Then he is not a good Christian and God will judge him accordingly," Mother replied.

Mariola went upstairs to our room. Mother ordered me to start dinner while she tended to Chester.

Mariola and I cleaned the kitchen after dinner. Mother walked in still wearing her house dress carrying her change purse.

"You girls have helped me a lot this week while Chester's sick. Why don't the two of you go to Whittman's General Store and buy yourselves some treats?

"What about Chester?" Mariola asked.

"Don't you have to be at work?' I inquired.

"Not tonight," Mother answered, "Chester is on the mend and Mr. Kristoff has allowed me to work from home. It is time to give you girls a break."

Mother pulled to nickels from her change purse. "Both of you should deserve a little extra to your allowance this week," she said as she pressed a nickel into our palms, "Enjoy."

Mariola forgot to untie her apron as she tore out of the kitchen. I ran to follow her out of the house.

"Golly, I don't know what I want," Mariola squealed as she ran, "A chocolate bar or a bottle of soda."

By the time we got to Whittman's store, we were sweating. Mariola ran to the soda machine. My hand went into my blouse pocket to pull my newly acquired handkerchief. It went back to my side when I saw Joretta Barr at the soda counter.

Jorretta sat with her mother and Mr. Butterfeld sipping a strawberry phosphate. She stared off into a distance as her mother's fiancé talked.

"You see Joretta, Communism means no freedom. As Americans, we have to ensure freedom for the world. That is why we send our boys to Korea."

I wiped my brow on my sleeve and walked around. I didn't feel like having a treat. Running to Whittman's with extra pocket money was something I did when I was a kid. Now that I worked towards college, I wanted to become a woman. I never saw a woman running to the store for a soda.

I perused the woman's toiletry aisle. There were so many creams, lotions, powders, and cosmetics. I didn't know their purpose. Although my mother had an array of products on her vanity table, she never allowed me near them. Her cosmetics were for professional purposes only. She believed that young girls needed to be concerned about being modest.

I stopped at a shelf of lipstick tubes. I opened one and twisted up the red pigment. When they didn't think I could hear them, Rooney and Heinrich talked of red lipped hussies on the drag. I often felt a twinge of jealousy I didn't understand. Mother would never let me my own tube of lipstick. I tucked it into the waistband of my skirt.

I turned around to find myself face to face with Mariola. Disappointment froze her face.

"What are you doing Natalie?"

"Nothing."

"I saw you tuck lipstick in your skirt."

"What are you implying, Mariola?"

"I know what happens when a person stashes an item in their clothes."

"Of course," I replied, tucking my blouse into my skirt. "Your family stole for things they couldn't obtain by lawful means."

"You're not starving," Mariola harshly whispered.

"What's it to you?" I shot back. "Hey, I thought you were going to get a bottle of soda?"

139

"I couldn't decide which one to get," Mariola replied meekly.

"You've dallied long enough. We have to get out of here."

I walked over to the counter and grabbed a stick of Black Jack gum off of the display. Mr. Whittman walked over from the soda counter.

"Will that be all for you ma'am?"

"Yes, sir," I replied handing my nickel.

I walked pass the patrons at the soda counter. Mariola lingered at the front counter. Everyone stared at her. Mariola put her nickel on the counter and walked out of the store.

Mariola was a surprisingly fast walker. I chased her a block screaming her name. She never broke her stride. I finally caught up to her as she stepped into our yard. I extend the package of gum towards her.

"Here, have this."

"I don't like Black Jack," she said as she walked inside quietly.

Mariola didn't talk to me the next morning. She had to understand what I felt being Italian and all. Like me, she was on the fringe. I needed to talk to her but couldn't around Mother. Unfortunately, Mariola practically ran to school with her long strides. When Mariola turned to go to the bathroom once we arrived at school, I breathed a sigh of relief. Now was my chance to talk to her.

Joretta and Mary Iris were at the sinks when we entered. Joretta swiped a mauve hue across her lips.

"This color doesn't work," Joretta pouted.

"I told you, it is for an olive complexion," Mary Iris commented. "Your skin is too creamy for that color."

Mariola walked over to the stall. Joretta grabbed her arm. Gently, Joretta clutched Mariola's chin and wiped the lipstick upon her lips. She turned

Mariola's face examining her work.

"You're right, Mary Iris. That color is for the darker complexed."

Mary Iris muttered in agreement as she pulled a bottle of fizzy cola out of her knapsack. She opened the bottle by tilting it against the sink.

"Mary Iris, you shouldn't be drinking soda, Joretta commented, "It rots your teeth."

"But I just opened it," Mary Iris said in mock horror. "I can't let this go to waste."

Jorretta grabbed the bottle from Mary Iris' hand. She pointed it towards Mariola.

"Do you like Fizzy Cola?"

"Sure?" Mariola replied.

"Here you go," Jorretta giggled as she handed Mariola the bottle.

Jorretta and Mary Iris left the bathroom in giggles. I walked over to snatch the bottle from Mariola's hand; however, she quickly turned her back to me.

"You are not going to drink that!" I shouted as Mariola put the bottle to her lip. "They gave that to you to mock us!"

"Only you," Mariola answered. "I didn't steal anything."

"So you are just going to let them embarrass me like that? What kind of friend are you?"

"The friend who spent her own money so you wouldn't be a criminal," Mariola shot back. "If you are embarrassed that Jorretta Barr saw you trying to swipe that lipstick then you should have thought about that before you tucked it in your skirt!"

The homeroom bell started ringing.

"Dump that in the sink! You can't take that into class."

"I am going to stay in here and finish my soda," Mariola said as she headed for the stall.

" If you are not accounted for in homeroom, you'll be truant. Truancy is against the law!"

"I'm sorry, Ms. Natalie, I don't believe you are a reliable source of what is lawful and what's not!"

With that, Mariola shut the stall door in my face.

ALEXANDRA

I spend the night at my computer spending Daddy Warbucks's money. Anthony comes into the bedroom to find me at my vanity slumping over the computer.

"You better be writing the next Pulitzer prize winner," he grumbles.

"I am paying off car loans."

"Car loans?"

I shift my eyes towards Anthony.

"I got your little Post-IT this morning. I called my dad. Daddy Warbucks called me and transferred a sizable amount of money that has allowed me to replace the grocery money, pay our car loans and my student loan. If we take the money we budget for the cars to pay off our credit cards every month, by year's end the only debt we'll have is our mortgage."

Anthony sighed. "I'm glad you paid off our debt, but don't you think you should have talked to me before you made payments?"

I lift the Post-IT from the table.

"I know you didn't graduate with a Communications degree like I did, but any idiot knows you don't open a productive conversation with ridicule."

"Hey, I had a right to be angry! Your sister spent all of our grocery money."

I shake my head, "If this were your sister, we wouldn't have even had that disgusting soup Shona made for us. Angie would have used all our money to buy pot."

Anthony's shoulder muscles began to rise. "You have no right to speak of my sister."

"If you are not ready to have an honest discussion about Angie, then consider the topic of my sister off limits."

Anthony grabs his running shoes and leaves with a slam of the door.

Everyone is quiet when I go to the kitchen for breakfast. Nona sits at the kitchen table with the Englewood Herald in her hand. Anthony is at the coffee pot pouring himself a cup.

"Your article came out," he muttered. "You did a good job."

Accepting the cup of coffee he's handing me, I whisper, "Thanks."

Nona puts down the paper, wipes her eyes with a napkin then blows her nose. Anthony leaves giving me a peck on my cheek and giving Nona a kiss on the head.

I spend my day at the Herald answering emails from people who connected with Lisa Hubbard's story. I send Shona out to visit Heinrich Adolphson. I am not in the habit of answering emails about my pieces, but Lisa's story…well, it's magical. Mother Hubbard told me in life Lisa had a way of bringing people together. In the form of the article, Lisa's spirit is doing the same thing.

Nona spends the day processing the Tomato Tofu soup into pesto. It is surprisingly delicious. After dinner, I scoop some in a Mason jar for Mother

Hubbard.

Janelle waves at me when she sees me cross the streets. She must have just come home from work. Once I reach the garage she envelopes me in a big hug.

"Alex, that was a beautiful story you wrote of my aunt!" She points to her name tag, "Everyone always asks me what the 'L' in 'L. Janelle Hubbard stands for. Today I had a great story to show them in the paper. Not only that, you made my daddy cry! My mom Skyped with me today and told me Daddy didn't cry once when Aunt Lisa died yet cried for five minutes after he read your article online. You're good, girl."

I started blushing. I like praise, but don't always know how to handle it. Thankfully, Janelle is savvy in any situation and can mitigate my awkwardness.

"What do you have there?" she asks pointing to my jar.

"Tomato Tofu Pesto."

"How'd one come up with a concept such as that?"

"It's a long story."

Janelle leads me into the house. Mother Hubbard sits at her screen in porch. She holds a sewing frame in her hands. The fabric in the frames has the letter O half sewn in."

"Hi, Nana," Janelle says as she kisses her grandmother. "Alex is here. She brought us pesto. Would you like me to make you a turkey sandwich? I bought ciabatta bread from Kroger's this morning. It will go well with this pesto."

"I'm not hungry, Honey."

Janelle points to the empty bottles of protein shakes, "Did you have anything solid today?"

"You're the one nagging me about the benefits of protein shakes, so I'm drinking them!"

"How you been sitting here all day?"

145

"I am trying to finish this quilt for baby Obama, but I keep getting interrupted by the phone. All of Lisa's friends that I barely saw these past thirty years been calling all day. I reckon that is the hazard of never changing my phone number."

"Who's Baby Obama?" I asked.

"Lincoln's baby" Mother Hubbard answered. "Mostly, the Hubbard men are named after Ohio-born presidents. When I had Janelle's father, it took a lot compromising on my husband's part to have Marcus's middle name be Taft instead of his first. Then again, I wanted Marcus to be Marco. That was another compromise. Anyways, Lincoln's name ended up being Lincoln because Marcus loved Abraham Lincoln. He talked about him nonstop when he was in second grade. When Barrack Obama ran for president, it ignited the same passion in Lincoln as his namesake did for his father.

"Anyways, Girls, I am getting tired. I am going to head to bed."

"Do you need help, Nana?" Janelle asks.

"I'm old! Not invalid! I'll be just fine."

Mother Hubbard left merely whispering goodnight to us.

I follow Janelle to the kitchen. She offers me a bottle of Yuengling beer before she makes herself a sandwich.

"I didn't know Lincoln was going to be a father."

"He's nowhere close," Janelle replies, "He broke up with his girlfriend a few months ago. When he is not working, he's sleeping. He's got no time for a girlfriend."

"Your nana's personality has seemed a little...off the last couple of times I've seen her." I comment, "Is she alright?"

Janelle spreads pesto on ciabatta. "I've seen this in many of the patients. She's preparing."

"For what?"

"For the Lord."

"She's can't be preparing for the Lord," I dismiss, "She's too young."

Janelle looks up at me in disbelief. "How old do you think my Nana is?"

"Well, not old enough to meet the Lord."

"She's in her eighties. I lost a patient yesterday twenty years her junior. When Papa Hubbard was dying, we thought she would join him soon after. We were all relieved to hear her tell him on his death bed that surviving Aunt Lisa's death taught her she could survive anything and that she still had to be here for Lincoln and me."

I lean against the entry and sigh. "Mother Hubbard is the one constant ever since Anthony and I moved to Englewood. I just don't want to fathom a day she isn't here."

"How do you think I feel? She's my Nana."

"My grandmother died a couple of months ago. I wasn't heartbroken as I will be when your Nana goes to the Lord."

Janelle puts her table knife in the sink. She turns towards me grabbing the sink from behind.

"My mom once confided to me that she was surprised how Nana related to Lincoln and I better than her mother. Probably a racial assumption on her part. The thing is that my Granny was raised in the same community of Black North Carolina Baptists she raised mom in. Lincoln and I were the only biracial children in whatever suburb wherever Daddy was stationed. Nana being the only Italian Canadian here in Englewood knew what it was like to be different from everyone else and struggling for that sense of community. She taught us how to turn those feelings around to reach our goals. She inspired me to strive to be the best runner in high school and to complete my medical degree. Through those endeavors, I found my community. When she dies, I'll be lost for inspiration."

"You said she was Italian Canadian," I reply, "I didn't know she was born in Canada."

"Yeah, she was. Come, I'll show you a picture."

Janelle leads me into the living room. Mother Hubbard's entire adult life lines the fireplace in photographs. Janelle goes to the far left end and pulls what appears to be a smartphone photo of a picture. A line of prisoners with big circles on their back was walking away from the camera.

"Canada imprisoned people of Italian heritage in internments camps during World War II. Nana's father was detained for that time. Vandals burnt down her childhood home. I guess they received word that Nana's father was killed in camp and decided to leave for the States, although Nana never talks about how they got here or how her mother died during that time.

"Long story short, Daddy flew all of us to Toronto when he heard of the exhibit at the Columbus Centre. Nana saw this photo and swore the man in the center of the line to be her father. Daddy snapped this with his phone. He printed this for her when we returned home."

Janelle pulls her grandparent's wedding photo from the mantel.

"Ever wonder why the majority of this pictures have light spots?"

I have a brain that perfects imperfect details in pictures. Now that Janelle points them out, I see two glares circling Mother Hubbard's head as sits in her bridal gown.

"Nana always believe that these light spots in photos were her parents' spirits. And here," Janelle says as she pulls down a picture of Mother Hubbard hugging Lincoln and Janelle when they were toddlers, "Nana insists that the light above our heads is Aunt Lisa."

Janelle's phone rings. She excuses herself. I stand in underneath the middle part of the banister. In an eight by ten frame is the one complete family photo the Hubbards have taken. Lisa is in her hospital bed surrounded by her parents, her brother and his then fiancé. Cheryl Hubbard was pregnant with the twins at the time.

Janelle runs to the kitchen calling out, "I have to go. A Patient is in crisis."

"I'll lock up," I call out as Janelle runs out the door with her turkey sandwich in her mouth. I admire her. I could never be a doctor and maintain a happy disposition like she does. I wonder how she does it.

I walk to Mother Hubbard's room to see if she is awake. I find her sleeping on her bed still fully clothed. I wrap her quilt around like a burrito. I am about to her off the light when I hear her call out, "It's just time to come clean!"

"Mother Hubbard? Are you awake?"

"There is no shame in it anymore, McKinley. I am just going to tell those girls the truth! There is no point in hiding it now."

I flip off the light. She's just talking to her late husband in her dreams.

I go to the living room and sit in a chair to finish my beer. I just need to be alone to process what Janelle told me about Mother Hubbard preparing for the Lord. It can't be happening. Mother Hubbard isn't sick. If it's true, I can't handle it. I have too many cases of Life happening right now. I can't deal with something as monumental as Mother Hubbard's death.

I stare at the final family photo. I see a light spot next to Lisa. The more I stare at it the light spot becomes a female face. Suddenly I see a full rounded face of a woman with sandy curls and tortoise shell glasses. I blink. The face is gone.

I pour the remaining beer in the kitchen sink then head home. I am going to quit drinking. Clearly, beer messes with my brain.

NATALIE

The day I returned to work finally came! I pedaled excitedly to Heinrich's shop. I'd missed seeing Heinrich to the point where I deluded myself that he missed me. I didn't arrive at the reception I was expecting.

Heinrich stood outside of the shack. When he saw me, he merely gruffed, "Welcome back."

"Thanks," I squeaked.

I slunk to the receptionist desk. The appointment book was empty. There were no receipts from the past week scattered on my desk. I grabbed my knapsack and pulled out my homework pretending to read a chapter.

The tube of lipstick rolled out of my knapsack. I forgot I put it in there they day after Mariola and I went to Whittman's shop. While Heinrich looked out into the distance, I applied the red hue to my lips. Suddenly his eyes pierced me. I froze holding the lipstick to my bottom lip.

Heinrich walked to me pulling a rag out of his pocket. "Wipe that off! I don't run that kind of establishment!"

"Golly!" I exclaimed, "it's just lipstick!"

"I don't hire hussies!"

Off from a distance, we heard whistling. Coming up on the dirt road was McKinley Hubbard. Heinrich walked over to the stoop. Hubbard continued to whistle until he met with Heinrich. He stopped with his arms akimbo.

"Adolphson, I demand to know the whereabouts of Seamus Rooney!"

"Go elsewhere. He called in sick today."

"As he should be! I am here on account for the ruckus he caused last night at the Evangelical Free Church! He disrupted a social while intoxicated, attempting to take liberties of the young ladies in attendance."

"Rooney's not right in the head," Heinrich seethed. "Old Man Rooney is always beating on him. If you are fixing on making an arrest, find him. If Old Man didn't beat his boy, the boy wouldn't be drinking to kill the pain. Rooney was only at the church trying to find salvation afterward like his mama told him to before Old Man Rooney did her in."

"While Rooney was trying to find salvation, the Phantom struck again! This time, he made off with crates of apples from a grocer's truck."

"Well, I'll be....."

Hubbard walked up to Heinrich shaking his finger. With his short stature, he resembled a toddler imitating a parent.

"I bet if I had a warrant, I'd find a bushel of apples in your garage. I know you don't have cars in there. Nobody in Englewood trusts you!"

"That's because everyone in Englewood is an idiot!" I chimed.

Heinrich and Hubbard looked at me in disbelief. Embolden, I left my counter and strutted to them.

"I don't appreciate you spreading rumors about my place of employment, Mr. Hubbard," I continued. "What right do you have to abuse your authority around here? Your limited authority, I may say?"

"You may not, Miss Studebaker," Hubbard objected, "In fact, I have the right mind to escort you home..."

"You won't be walking fifty feet near me! Make any attempt to or say any word that will sabotage Mr. Adolphson's business, and I'll see that you are exposed as the fraud you are! Especially," I continued, "to Mariola Chinecci. She doesn't like cops that much. She only tolerates you because she fears you'll hang her like your buddies hung her mother!"

Hubbard glared at me, "I bid you good day, Miss Studebaker."

As Hubbard left, I fluffed my skirt and went back to my counter.

Heinrich's eyes rest on me. I pretended to concrete on my homework. He walked up to the counter.

"You didn't have to say anything to him."

"If I didn't, the little ant would still be here," I muttered into my textbook. "As a member of the elite society, I know how to put boys too big for their britches in their place."

"Elite society?" Heinrich scoffed, "Since when?"

"Since birth. I'm a doctor's daughter."

"A late doctor's daughter."

"What's it to you if my father's deceased?"

Heinrich walked over to my counter. He slammed my textbook shut.

"Listen, Little Miss! I don't appreciate my employees waltzing in, made-up, and back talking me! You can take your highbrow attitude and beat it!"

"I just lied for you and got Hubbard off your back! A little appreciation would be nice!"

Heinrich stared at me red faced.

"I don't think Rooney would display that much loyalty," I muttered. "I'm hungry. I am going to get myself an apple."

I walked over to the shed. Inside was a dark sedan loaded with apples. Sitting in the middle of the front seat was a plastic skeleton. I walked over to the car and plucked an apple from its pile from the open window. My wrist bumped into a hard material I couldn't see. I turned to the door at the sound of Heinrich clearing his throat.

"What made you believe Hubbard?"

"It wasn't a matter of believing Hubbard," I answered, "it was a matter of knowing that you are the only person in town smart enough to pull this scam off." Taking a bite of the apple, I finished, "Also, you're poor enough to have relatives who worked carnivals at some point in time."

Heinrich sneered, "Why you better watch your mouth, Missy."

"It's Pepper's Ghost," I replied. "You have the glass at an angle towards the skeleton. I bet you a weeks' wage that if I'd find a blue light on the interior roof."

Heinrich walked over to the sedan. My heart pounded in my chest as he reached inside. A green light illuminated the room. I walked back to my counter dejectedly. Five minutes later, Heinrich walked over carrying something behind his back. He leaned his elbow on the counter.

"How'd you figure out the illusion was -what did you call it-Pepper's ghost?"

"Simple science."

Heinrich tapped his fingers on the counter. "Girls don't take science class. They take home economics."

"My father was a Kiwanis. They use to run the spook house at the Randolph Township Fair. I would help him set up the ghost room. I learned all the tricks. Angling glass bends light while creating illusions."

Heinrich nodded. "You like to think yourself as observant, intelligent, and one not easily fooled by what she sees and is told to believe."

"I know myself," I said annoyingly.

"Yet, you are working to go to college where you are paying professors to brainwash you…"

"To become someone better than a housewife."

Heinrich snorted. "Everyone knows a girl goes to college if she isn't lucky to find a husband in high school."

I twisted my faces as well as the back of my skirt. Heinrich was purposely trying to get my goat. If I punched him like I wanted to it would only satisfy him knowing he could get to me.

Heinrich looked at me bemused. "Or it could be that such a high brow girl such as yourself couldn't dream of being a farmer's wife or a shopkeeper's spouse. Therefore, you must go to college and proclaim to have a desire to be a doctor or lawyer. Now, there are no such things as female physicians and lawyers. You will be going to class to pick one to be your husband and be their housewife! Do you see the irony in this?"

I did, but I wasn't going to give Heinrich the satisfaction that he got me. I painted the cute smile on my face.

"If I am too good for red lipstick then I am too good to waste my life here with the likes of you."

I packed my bag as Heinrich replied, "You are too smart for your own good. Most girls wouldn't have guessed a blue light was a ghost. Since you were half right, I should honor the bet." He dropped a book on my backpack, "This is worth more than a week's worth of wages. This will expand your mind."

I picked up the book. "'The Town and the City' by John Kerouac."

"I like Jack's style," Heinrich commented. "It's similar to Thomas Wolfe. You familiar with him?"

I shook my head. My mother warned me not to say that I only preferred British Classics because it made me sound snobby. Standing in front of Heinrich, I felt uncultured. I never heard of Wolfe or Kerouac. I felt my literary paradigm pop in my brain.

"Go home. Start reading," Heinrich said. "There is nothing for you to do here."

I clutch my book and run to my bike. If I said goodbye, I only squeaked it. I needed to get away from Heinrich before my desire to embrace and kiss him overcame me. Books meant more to me than roses and diamond rings. Still, Heinrich giving me a book didn't mean he desired me. It could be another attempt to get under my skin. He succeeded.

I opened "The Town and the City" that night at bedtime. I couldn't put it down. The next morning I awoke to find it book laying across my face. I continued to read it at the breakfast table when Mother wasn't looking and in class whenever I was able to hide it behind a textbook. Heinrich let me be every day as I sat with the book in my hand the entire shift. This book became a part of me. I applauded Mary Dennison views of society as "insane disorganized stupidity". Kerouac's prose of rain made me yearn for a downpour. Even when I was heartbroken when Waldo Meister died, I couldn't drop the book. At last, I got to the last page, then went immediately to the first page.

A week into my continual loop of "The Town and the City" Mother received another friendly visit from Meredith Metterschmidt. Mrs. Metterschmidt had a stack of magazines and booklets in her arms. I briefly looked from the living room couch then diverted my eyes back to the book. Mother gave a cordial greeting, yet I could hear the annoyance in her voice.

"Winifred, the Friendly Society has collected these guides for Natalie this week. It has been noticed by the daughters of the society that Natalie has her nose stuck in her book all week, and we at the Friendly Society decided to collect suitable reading material for her."

Mother took the booklets from Mrs. Metterschmidt.

"Household Hints? Good Housewives Guide? Why would you collect this for Natalie? She is only a student."

"For less than a year," Mrs. Metterschmidt retorted. "Are you aware of what Natalie is reading?"

"A book," Mother answered, "as she has been doing since she learned to read. That is not unusual."

I lowered my book. Mrs. Metterschmidt motioned mother outside. Once they closed the door, I ran upstairs to Chester's bedroom. Chester sat at his desk as Mariola stood over him. I flew open the window.

"Gall, Natalie!" Chester whined, "It's breezy outside! Shut the...."

"Hush!"

I pressed my ear to the screen. It took a second before I could make anything out.

"Well just be lucky Joretta Barr is making friends with your house girl."

"What housegirl? I have no one in my employ."

"Your charge or whatever you call her."

"Mariola because that is her name."

"Well this Mariola walks with Joretta Barr and told her the book Natalie is reading. It's a good thing they are friends. If Joretta didn't tell her mother who told me what your daughter was reading, we would never have caught this."

"I am still confused about your purpose here, Meredith," Mother said.

"Winifred, are you aware of the Beat generation?"

"I am afraid I don't."

"Mr. Metterschmidt has a sister who lives in New York City. The Beats are a group of college dropouts who wear black and take opium in the bars of Time Square."

"What does that have to do with Natalie? I can assure you she doesn't do drugs."

"One of these Beats have been peddling a book about the city and somehow it has fallen into your daughter's hands. How did she get the book?"

"I think she borrowed it from a friend."

"Your daughter doesn't have friends. She doesn't 'fit in' as they say. Raised under your influences, I amaze at the limited ability she possesses to do so."

"I beg your pardon!"

"Well, with a mother who wears black and is barely at home, what can one expect?"

"I'm a widow! I do what I do to honor my husband!"

"You're husband's been dead for a decade. You need to move on."

"That is not the respect you give to a man who dies in war!"

"Your husband was a doctor, not a soldier."

From the window I saw Mrs. Kaiser peer from her window. She gave a quizzical expression then appeared at her door. Suddenly she walked across the street to our yard. Mother led Mrs. Metterschmidt by the shoulders.

"Hellen, please assist Mrs. Metterschmidt home. I am afraid that she is not on her right mind."

"Excuse me!" Mrs. Metterschmidt shouted.

Mother continued to speak to Mrs. Kaiser. "I am very worried about her. I mean you remember a decade ago when she worked in the tank factory in Dayton while Mr. Metterschmidt sat in the house continuing his End of Prohibition celebration. Well, Meredith here has forgotten that, amongst other things."

"Why I never!" Mrs. Metterschmidt exclaims Mother gently push her into Mrs. Kaiser's hands.

"I would help her myself, but I have to prepare for bed. Not all of us have a father who can provide us our bounty. I am one of the few who has to work. Not that I mind, Hellen. I do so to honor my husband, who died while healing the wounded in the war. Tootles, now."

I dashed away from the window bumping into Mariola and Chester.

"Golly!" Chester exclaimed, "Did you hear what Mother said?"

Mother's heels clicked through the hall. Chester and Mariola scrambled to resume their position at Chester's desk. I sat on his bed pretending to read a comic book. Mother appeared in the doorway.

"The three of you to bed!"

Mariola and I settled in for the night. As Mariola was about to turn off her bed lamp, I asked, "Are you really friends with Joretta Barr?"

"McKinley asked her to walk me home since he can't do so anymore."

"Why not?"

"He wouldn't say."

"Well, it is probably for your protection Mariola," Mother said from the doorway.

She walked over to my nightstand and swapped Heinrich's book with another.

"What are you doing?" I whined.

"Giving you my copy of Charles Dicken's 'Bleak House.' It will occupy you for a month and mitigate talk."

"But…"

Mother waved her hand dismissively. "I don't care for visits from the Friendly Society. Unless you want to face them yourselves, you read what I approve. Be lucky I am giving you an actual book to read than those silly housewife magazines."

With that, she turned off my light and walked away with my book.

ALEXANDRA

"Did you ever read Jack Kerouac?"

Shona and I sit in Heinrich Adolphson's room at Limestone Manor for the fourth time this week. Sitting with him has been unproductive. He spends our visits asking questions about our family, our history, yet never divulge about what possessed him to drive around like a phantom in the fifties. If he was demented to scare truckers off the road, he must be getting off on stringing us along these past weeks. With my story due in two, I was getting annoyed that he wants to talk books.

"I watched that movie that stared those vampire chicks," I retort.

"I watched 'On the Road' as well," Shona answers, "but I enjoyed the book more."

"I had known of him before anyone else here did," Mr. Adolphson grumbles, "don't know how I came across my copy of 'The Town and The City.' I didn't read much then. I don't know what possessed me to open that book. He didn't go by Jack, then, he went by John. Anyways, Kerouac hooked me on books. Read all of Kerouac's and those who influenced him. Then as the years went by I read other things. But Kerouac … he had it down. Do you girls read?"

"Our mother had us reciting Sylvia Platt at birth," I remark.

"Little good it did you," Shona snorts as she playfully elbowed my side fat. "You filled your brain with that R.L. Stine's and Christopher Pike's nonsense growing up."

Mr. Adolphson shoots a disapproving sneer towards Shona.

"There is nothing wrong with R.L. Stine and Christopher Pike. It is judgments from academic snobs that prevent the common man from reading. Or limits what words get out to the masses. Not everyone is an overly educated WASP. Why should all the books be written for them?"

"I disagree," Shona say, "there is no such thing as being overly educated."

"Education itself is subjective," Heinrich remark before turning his head my way. "Who did you like better, Stine or Pike?"

"Stine," I answer. "He kept the story relatable. Pike at times came off as perverted, and I never understood why he was obsessed with a starlight crystal. Yet his book 'Remember Me' is still one of my favorites."

"Stine is from Ohio. We Ohioans know how to tell stories. It's what we do."

"That is how I make my living here."

Shona scowls. Lately, I've sense that Shona reveres Mr. Adolphson as some respected elder. His approval my teenage reading material irks her. After hearing her come off as condescending about what I read, I can't help but take small pleasure at her being miffed.

"I got a feeling you're the Mama's girl," Mr. Adolphson says pointing to Shona, "and you're the daddy's girl," he says pointing to me.

"Alex can call Daddy and get whatever she asks for," Shona replies, "I never ask him for anything."

"That's because Mommy gives you everything you want so you don't need to call Daddy."

"A house divided," Heinrich snort. "It's common. I had a sister myself. She was Daddy's girl; I was Momma's boy. She was older than me. Broke Daddy's heart when she ran off with that boy whose name I don't recall. I don't care. I don't even know if Greta, my sister, is alive. Don't think about it much. She doesn't care I am rotting here. It is a miracle the two of you get along."

Shona and I met each other with arched eyebrows.

Mr. Adolphson continued, "Natalie and I had a child. We didn't get to find out which parent she would gravitate towards."

With that, Mr. Adolphson stared ahead. Shona and I sat waiting for him to finish a story. Minutes later he dismissed us with the wave of his hand.

"I'm tired, Girls. Go and come back tomorrow."

"Tomorrow's Saturday, Mr. Adolphson," I say, "We can schedule to reconvene on Monday."

"Just come whenever," Mr. Adolphson grumbles as he closes his eyes.

Shona and I walk to the car. Shona maintains a calm façade until we enter the car. Quickly she turns into our uppity mother.

"I don't see why I can't come over tomorrow?"

"We need you to help clean the house while Nona makes food for the Buckeye game. It is our week to host."

"I'm not going to watch the game."

"You don't have to. You could talk to the women in the kitchen, play with the Natalia and the neighbor kids, or lock yourself downstairs. I don't care. You're not getting out of cleaning the house because as one of its inhabitants, you equally created the dirt."

"I should go back and visit Heinrich tomorrow, but maybe I shouldn't. I can't believe what he says about education being subjective. I don't get why this town settles for mediocracy..."

"Mediocracy?"

"Well, it seems that this town doesn't strive to do more in life than family making...."

"If you had things going your way you'd be Mrs. Free-from-God about now. You shouldn't be poo-pooing anyone's fortune in love just because you haven't received your own."

Shona clamps her mouth. So that is it, she is at the phase in her break up where the bitterness she feels is leaking from her cracked porcelain vase. She stews for a moment. I watch her mouth open as she figures out another statement of protest against Ohio's need to be bourgeois. Thankfully, my phone beeps.

"Check my phone. I can't be reading text messages while driving."

Shona sighs and takes my phone from the cup holder.

"It's Natalia. She says she and Julia are at the UDF and need to be picked up."

"What are she and Julia doing there?"

Shona shrugs and places the phone back in my cup holder.

Thankfully, the United Dairy Farmers gas station and ice cream shop was only two blocks from Limestone Manor. Natalia and Julia were sitting on the curb drinking milkshakes. They see my car pulling up and stand up talking at once.

"Mom, Julia wanted to visit her Maw-Maw…."

"Yeah, but I had forgotten that she went to Florida…."

"And we didn't know if you knew where she lived…."

"I would have called my Mom but she is at work, and she doesn't let me have people over when she and my dad aren't home and I thought if we went to my Maw-Maw's Natalia could hang out with me…"

Like a conductor, I wave my hands to shush them.

"You girls aren't supposed to be going any place but your own houses unless you notify a parent. Did any of you think to do that?"

"Well," Natalia starts, "we were going to call after…"

"Because we were going to be with a relative…." Julia continues.

"Enough," I clip. "Let's go to my house. I'll text your mom, Julia, to let her know that you're with us."

The girls let out a girly squeal and head for the car. Walking towards it, I notice it's empty. Where is Shona?

Natalia waves, "Hi, Aunt Shona."

I turn around to find Shona at a vegetable stand at the corner. The fall pumpkins are out. I walk over to her as she examines a bin full of pie pumpkins. The girls follow.

"Are these pumpkins magnificent?" Shona gushes. "They are perfect for roasting and making into soup!"

"Pumpkin soup? Gross!" Julia exclaimes.

"No, it's delicious," Shona explains with a gleam in her eyes. "In fact, I should buy some to make it for tomorrow so everyone can try it."

"My Nonna is making meatballs," Natalia replies snidely, "we don't need your soup."

"Watch it!" I snap.

Too late, the gleam in Shona's eyes is gone. As petty as it seems, that soup was the first thing that made Shona happy that day. Her life isn't going as she thought. The last thing she needs is her bratty niece's remarks.

"Hey," I say, "Nona would be insulted if we don't let her make her Meatball Capolavoro sandwiches for the game. It's an Italian matriarch thing. But, Chip, our editor, usually hosts a fall festival party next month. You can make the soup then."

Shona gives me a small smile yet walks dejectedly to the car.

The next night all the neighbors gather at our house. The men congregate to the living room television, the women to the kitchen, and the kids are running around outside before it gets too dark. Shona comes up from her room in the basement and walks into the kitchen. The women are placing the plates, Tupperware, and crock pots in the kitchen. Women view my sister from the corner of their eye then turn to greet her with a tepid hello. Nona places her meatball subs on the kitchen table, catching a glimpse of Shona.

"Look, she emerges!"

Shona gives a shy smile. The other women grabbed a bottle of beer or pour themselves some wine. I handed Shona a bottle of hard cider.

"I thought you were planning to hide out for the evening."

"I was checking my Facebook and saw that last night was the Feast of the Goddess," Shona mopes, "Mom posted pictures…"

"Ohhhh," I realize when I saw the hurt in Shona's eyes.

For most of her adolescences, Shona helped Mother press the Grecian robes and prepared the food longing for her day to frolic and read poetry with the other women scholars in the university's garden. Since she wasn't accepted into the master's program, Shona wasn't invited. All I can think to do in response is hug her.

"Feast of the Goddess?" Mother Hubbard chimes from behind our embrace. "Is that a lesbian gathering?"

"
No," Shona replies curtly.

"It's an academic gathering," I quickly say. "Our mother assists the women's studies professors in the annual gathering to welcome the graduate students entering in the program."

"I see," Mother Hubbard says as she turns to the plate of meatball subs.

I turn my lips to Shona's ear.

"Mother Hubbard is the most accepting person in this room. She asks to understand. You'll just have to forgive her for being eighty and losing her tack." Then giving her a slight push between her shoulders I say, "Now get yourself some food."

Shona joins the women at the table. She fills her plate with only the raw veggies and fresh fruit. Mother Hubbard moves to the center of the bench to make room for Shona. Mother Hubbard smiles wide as Shona sits down.

"It is so nice to meet a member of Alex's family, Shona. I met Anthony's family but just never yours."

"It's only Anthony and me," Nona replies.

"I met many of your sisters when Anthony came back from Iraq."

"Everyone except my sister, Fina," Nona remarks. "The moment Alex sent the Red Cross telegram, all of the sisters I can rely on arranged a caravan to Ohio without a thought about their own lives. That is how we do it."

The women murmur in appreciation.

"So what brings you to Englewood, Shona?" Lynn Keegan asks.

"I am researching the particulars to our mother's adoption. She was born in Dayton."

"Wow!" Shelley Hughes exclaims, "Did you know that your mother was born here, Alex?"

"Nobody was more surprised than me."

"How is your researching coming along?" Mother Hubbard asks.

"Not as far as I would like," Shona says. "I am interning at the Herald. It's been occupying my time."

The women keep spouting off questions to Shona: What did she study at school? What were her hobbies? Does she like sports or crafts? Shona answers all of them politely. Suddenly the dreaded question is uttered: "Are you seeing anyone?"

Shona clamps her mouth and looks down. For whatever reason, Nona finds it fitting to answer the question for her, "She's been moping about some guy."

"Oh, Dearie, what happened?" Shelley asks.

Shona sits up a bit taller to make herself look composed.

"It was a silly matter, really. We went to see the community theater production of 'Who's Afraid of Virginia Wolfe?' Godfrey made a snide comment that anyone who wants to keep their sanity was afraid of Virginia Wolfe. I reminded him that the play was about an old couple's jealousy of a young couple's ability to conceive. As he continually made snide remarks about Wolfe's mental instability, I tried to educate him about the deaths of her parents and the sexual abuse she endured. God just replied that some people are just genetically positioned to be crazy. I tried to get him to see the error in his judgment…"

Mother Hubbards takes Shona hand and strokes it. "Aww, Honey, it didn't matter that the two of you have different ideas. You just weren't the one."

"That's the worst," Shelley replies, "I was in love with Bobby Hinton. I wasn't the one for him. Rebecca Shaker was. It broke my heart when he dumped me and started dating her. In the end, it worked for the best. I have my husband and kids."

"Joseph." Nona remarks. "I was so in love with him. His dad was from Sicily like my parents, but his mother was a WASP. For whatever reason, she didn't like me much. She wanted Joey to marry a girl like her. He was such a Mama's boy that he obeyed her every wish. After college, he married a Korean girl who was nothing like his mother. They have beautiful kids…"

"Touchdown!"

The women run to the living room screaming, "Rewind, Rewind."

Shona sneaks out of the kitchen.

During halftime, I seek out Shona. She is sitting outside on the brick porch ledge.

"What are you doing out here?"

"Natalia is telling the other kids that there is a ghost of a prom queen that haunts my bedroom. She's pretending to lead a séance."

Shona stares out onto the street. She is down in the dumps and just needs some time to stew to complete the grieving process of her break up with Mr. Free-from-God. I start to retreat to the house until I hear, "You really ought to have a room of one's own."

I walk over to the ledge. "I did. You are sleeping it."

"Why is Natalia in there?"

"That's where the kids go when it gets dark whenever we host the Buckeye game. I'm upstairs with our guests, so usually it doesn't matter if the kids play in my office. I can kick the kids out if you want me to."

"No. It's fine."

"Well, I'll let you be."

No sooner than I turn I hear, "It just can't be that simple: Not being the one."

I turn back and climb onto the ledge next to her.

"I'm afraid it is, Shona. Honestly, Virginia Woolfe has never determined an outcome on a relationship."

Shona shoots me a disbelieving look. Suddenly my relationship with my mother is brought into light.

"Well, not romantic relationships," I state. "Look at the relationship between our mother and step mother. In the rare times I visit, the most intellectual reading I've seen from Jolene is when she sits down with a copy of 'Popular Mechanics.' Otherwise, Mother turns her head the other whenever Jolene's issues of 'Bikes and Babes' arrives in the mail."

"I'm not following."

"What Mother wouldn't excuse in her daughters she excuses in Jolene. In their relationship, there is an overabundance of acceptance between them. As long as each fulfills the other's core need of love and trust, they overlook the trivial aspects of the other's personality. They both strive to accommodate the other because the love is strong."

"You speak as you know them, Alex. You rarely came to visit after you transferred to Ohio State."

"I know this; Jolene likes her solitude in her woodworking room. Yet, she gave that room up so you and I could have a room to sleep in when neither Mom nor Dad could keep the house in the divorce. Even though, Mother walks as the upstanding academic lesbian now, she spent nearly thirty years keeping face with Jo-Jo. She strived to have a better heterosexual marriage than her mother or at least the appearance of one. She rode us hard to prove she could prove she could parade us as the better, successful daughters. She gave up the entire façade when Jolene came around. I know I didn't live with them for long, but it was long enough to see the truth."

Shona hang her head staring at her plaid high-tops as she swings her feet from side to side.

"What about Dad?"

"What about him?"

"What was his excuse for not being around?"

"Well, he and mom divorced so they could be their true selves."

"Yet, he couldn't stay in Rochester?"

"Grandma Anna disowned him," I answer. "It had to be painful to be in Rochester. He didn't have anyone there like Mother did."

"He had me."

I feel lame. Not once did I think that Shona could have the same feelings of unworthiness about Dad that I did about our mother. I don't even know what to say. Shona does. She breathes in a sigh.

"God said that he no longer had patience for my daddy issues and my pursuit to live in my mother's shadow. He told me that he couldn't be with a reflection of pompous intellectual who thinks she is superior because of her sexuality."

"He said that?!" I spat with disgust. "He is certainly not the one for you.

168

The One would never say that to you."

"What would "the One" say?"

"Wouldn't have to say a thing," I reply. "The person who is the one for you would let you know that you are special and worthy of his or her love through actions and deeds."

I hug Shona. For moments, we watch the wind scatter leaves across the street in our embrace. Then a thought pops into my end causing me to ruin the moment and open my mouth.

"Have you ever thought about talking to Dad about how you feel?"

"Have you ever talked to Mom about how you feel?"

Point taken.

"Well, you can always talk to me about anything, and you can stay here as long as it takes for you to figure things out."

Shona squeezes me tighter. "Thanks."

The front door opens, people start filing out. Due to their jubilant nature, I take it OSU won the game. Everyone waves to Shona and I as they leave. From behind I heard Anthony's voice.

"Are you girls going to stay out here all night?"

We giggle and look out at the stars for as long as we want.

NATALIE

"Those Stanley punks want war!" Rooney screamed.

I stood amidst white toilet paper streamers trying not to look at the crudely painted swastikas on the shack. Heinrich paced the yard with his nostrils flared out.

"When did this happen?" I asked.

"Last night," Heinrich said. "The Stanley boys are sore that we got them in trouble with their old man. Now they want revenge."

"I thought they were never going to face their dad."

"He faced them," Heinrich said. "He came over here with the money yesterday morning. Must have whooped the boys a good one."

I scanned the entire area. The Stanley boys didn't leave a surface untouched.

"I'd say call the police, but with our luck, they'd send McKinley Hubbard over," I muttered, "He would think this mess as justice."

"You're no fool," Heinrich replied.

"I say we drive!" Rooney exclaimed. "Just drive into Dayton in the middle of the night and give those crumbs a lesson. We can mess their place up good."

"Sure, if you want to spend a night in the can," Heinrich replied. "Cut the wumgush, Rooney. Their daddy's loaded. If we retaliate, we will be the first place he sends the cops. He'll pay them enough to lock us up for a decade."

"We can't let those ankle biters defeat us!"

"Don't blow your top," Heinrich replied as he walked towards the shack, "If you go in all hot headed, you'll only in up back in the clink."

"Then what are you going to do?" I asked.

Heinrich placed his hand on the small of my back. Walking me towards the car, he said, "Let's go to the movies."

I stopped.

"The movies? Crumbs just defaced your business and you just abandon it to see a picture show?"

"See man!" Rooney shouted. "The Dame agrees with me!"

I hated to admit to myself that it was true. Knowing the Stanley boys' kind, they would be driving by any time now to admire the damage. As a child, I was exposed to high society kids and their hijinks. Not once did I see any one of them get what they deserved. The thought of the Stanley boys' smug faces as figured they wouldn't get punished for their crime made my blood boil.

Heinrich pushed me to his car. "I'm not abandoning anything! I just need to clear my head. Come on, 'Captive Women' is playing at the cinema."

Heinrich parked a block behind the Dayton theater. He led me through the alley. Standing between a door and a dumpster was a redhead resembling Marilyn Monroe in a uniform. For a moment, I stood mesmerized as she perfected the smoke ring. Heinrich nudged me ahead. I nearly tripped. "Oh!"

The redhead turned her head towards us. At the sight of Heinrich, she sneered, "I know nothing!"

"Which means you do know something, Velma," Heinrich growled.

"I know nothing that is going to keep you out of trouble!" Velma shot back.

"You're not my keeper, Velma! If you know of anything about the Stanley crumbs defacing my property, you tell me!"

"You know more than me," Velma said in a soft voice, "I only heard they sought revenge. I didn't know what they did. What did they do?"

Heinrich's face twisted into a sneer. A vein pop on his neck. Velma stuck the cigarette in her mouth. Clearly she wasn't a fool to say anything about the matter. Instead, she pointed her head towards me.

"Who's the little girl?"

If I weren't raised to act like a refine doctor's daughter, I would have popped the smug tart. I rolled my eyes in response. She turned up her nose at me.

"This lady is Natalie Studebaker. She is my clerk."

"A lady," Velma scoffed, "You can't be more than sixteen. Seriously, Heinrich, what do you have yourself messed up in?"

"I am here to bring no trouble," Heinrich said, "We just want to see 'Captive Women.'"

"You got a quarter?"

"You have the twenty-five dollars you own me?"

Velma opened the side door. "Enjoy the show."

Heinrich leads me to a dark theater. Shivers went up and down my spine as the light shut off and the screen illuminated us. We sat down in the middle of the empty theater.

The only time I had been to the movies before was when my parents took me to see "The Wizard of Oz." I was four at the time. My mother loved the book growing up and begged my father to see it. The story went that I cried loudly when the Tin Man came on screen. Father removed us from the theater indignant of how I embarrassed him. He declared I was banned from the movies, which he maintained until he died. My mother didn't have the financial means to lift the ban afterward.

As far as I cared, I didn't need to see a movie right then. "Captive Women" was a nuclear war propaganda movie where the scantily clad actresses fought for the city of Manhattan. I felt myself drifting to sleep. Suddenly I felt a hand stroking my check.

Suddenly, Heinrich's hand was on my shoulder. It felt natural. I dug him and he dug me. Suddenly his hand started to lower itself. I brushed it away. His hand stayed on my shoulder for ten minutes. Then it began to drop to my chest. I slapped it away. He turned his head and lowered his mouth onto mine.

"Did you really wanted to see this movie," he chuckled.

I shook my head and went in for another kiss. I allowed his tongue to explore my mouth the entire movie. I never dreamt kissing would feel so good.

Suddenly, the lights in the theater turned on. Heinrich shrugged. "What now?"

"Well…the movie's over."

"So it is," Heinrich replies. "So what now?"

I didn't know how women expressed their needs. I didn't think they were allowed to. I rummaged through my brain to make a witty sentence of my desire. Like the girl I was, I blurted "Well, it doesn't mean we have to quit what we were doing!"

Heinrich laughed. "It will be getting dark. Won't your mama start to worry?"

"She works late."

Heinrich wrapped his arm around my shoulder. We were starting walking to his car.

"Heinrich!"

Velma stood in the doorway. Heinrich walked over to her, leading me by the shoulder. With a sly grin, he said, "This better be good, Velma, cause

I got big plans tonight."

"I got wind of the Stanley boys' plans for tonight!" Velma said. "They're drag racing with some other rich crumbs near the Cemetery in Brookville."

"How would you know about this, Velma?"

"I was at the drug store because I was out of cigarettes! The Stanley boys were announcing their plans to the entire store from the soda counter."

Velma pulled out a cigarette. Placing it between her lips, she continued, "I didn't go past the front counter. They didn't see me."

"Well then," Heinrich replied, "My plans for the night have changed. Thank you, Velma. You're a real doll."

Heinrich turned us towards his car. Velma shouted behind us, "Don't get yourself into trouble!"

Heinrich didn't say a word as he drove. I didn't realize we were heading back to the shop until we passed the cemetery my father was buried in on National Road in Englewood. Heinrich pulled into the shop, jumping out of the car before it completely turned off the ignition. I followed him to the garage. There we found Rooney passed out against the sedan with a half full bottle of beer in his hand. Heinrich grabbed the beer and splashed its contents on Rooney's face. Rooney's eyes open, but he turned the other direction.

"Get up you drunk!" Heinrich barked, "We're going to ride!"

"Ride?"

"Yeah," Heinrich said, "We are going to teach the Stanley crumbs a lesson they'll never forget."

"What lesson would that be?" I asked.

Heinrich turned to me and sneered, "That I am their worst nightmare!"

Squished in the back seat with Rooney, Heinrich drove us down National Road to Brookville. We were instructed to keep down. The twenty-minute ride into Brookville wasn't pleasant. Rooney had a horrid case of beer farts. I bunched my skirt to my nose as I sat with my head bent to my knees.

There was a mile stretch of National Road dividing the Catholic and Protestant cemeteries. Heinrich pulled into the Catholic cemetery. The Catholic side provided dense tree coverage. Heinrich open the driver side window. I lifted my head to suck in the fresh air.

"Not a sound," hushed Heinrich.

I attempted to peer over Heinrich's shoulder, but Plexiglas separated us. The setting sun directly beamed upon the windshield. All I could see were the distorted colors of dusk.

As the orange and pink twilight started to fade, muffled hollering began. I pressed my ear on the Plexiglas. Heinrich's shadow turned towards me. "The Stanleys are betting some other crumbs a hundred bucks to drag."

Heinrich pulled a black ski mask over his head. "Be prepare to flick the light when I give the signal."

Engines revved from a distance. Heinrich turned over the ignition. Suddenly the car sped from the gates.

"Now!"

I flick the overhead light. All the Stanley boys could see was a skeleton glowing from the passenger sheet. Pretty little rich kids screamed. Suddenly, the car vibrated, pushing me into Rooney. I heard metal crunching. I closed my eyes as the car rotated several times. Finally, it moved in a straight line.

As the car drove away, I heard, "That better not be you, Adolphson! If you summon Satan again, I'll do more than decorate your shop!"

Heinrich dropped Rooney off at his father's house before driving to mine. Once we arrived, Heinrich opened my door and guided me out of the car by the hand. Linking our arms, he walked me to the front door. The porch light was off.

"You're not going to be in trouble with your momma because your home after dark."

"She's probably still at the office," I said. "She is never home on time."

Heinrich leaned against the doorway, smiling his crooked smile. "You should have seen the faces of those Stanley boys. We sure taught them a lesson."

"I wished I could have," I said. "I couldn't see much when the light was turned on. Gosh, to be able to see the horror on those boys' smug faces...man, I would trade my right foot...."

Heinrich interrupted me my placing his mouth against mine. With his arms, he pulled me in close to him. For five seconds I floated in blissful eternity.

"Now we can continue what we were doing," he laughed.

The porch light flicked on. Heinrich broke our embrace.

"See you tomorrow, Kid."

Heinrich walked back to his car. I opened the door livid, prepared to yell at Mariola or Chester for turning on the porch light. My face met my mother's bosom.

"Chester, help Mariola with the dishes!" she called out to the kitchen as she grabbed my arm, leading me to my bedroom.

"You, Little Missy, have found yourself going to bed without supper."

"Luckily, I'm not hungry," I replied.

Mother nudge me into my room. She closed the door behind her.

"Where might have you have been?"

"At work."

"Don't lie to me," Mother remarked. "Officer Hubbard drove by the shop and found it vacant and covered in Nazi marks. You weren't there."

"The shop was vandalized!" I cried, "Yet, Hubbard didn't do a thing to catch the crumbs who did it!"

Mother leaned against the door with her arms across her chest. "Was that your employer walking you to the porch?"

"Yes."

"Let's only hope that Mrs. Kaiser didn't see the two of you. If I receive a visit from Meredith Metterschmidt, you'll be in more trouble than you are now. You were supposed to be home for supper. Instead, you were carrying on while Mariola took care of your brother and the house."

"Good for her," I said. "I was working."

"Mariola is NOT our house girl, Natalie Lauren. She may be under my charge, but that doesn't mean she should act as a servant to our house! Since I have a capable daughter to assist in the household duties, Mariola shouldn't be burden with running the entire house! Effective immediately, you are no longer employed! You'll resign tomorrow. From this day forward, you come home with Mariola and assist your brother with his homework as Mariola makes dinner! Do I make myself perfectly clear?"

I nodded so she would leave.

"Think about your actions and where they are taking you," Mother said, as she closed the door.

I got ready for bed thinking of that there is no way she would know where I was if she was working all afternoon.

ALEXANDRA

"Come, and let me show you my secret world," read Chip, "the world I keep under lock and key. Together we'll walk the secret gardens, once belonged to only me."

Chip lowers the paper and stares at me across his desk. I smile in response. Chip shakes his head and sighs.

"Alex, I...I just don't know what to do with this. This wasn't your assignment."

The "this" Chip is talking about is a poem my mother wrote. Shona and I found it years ago. We were searching for Christmas presents in her study. Instead of gifts, we found a notebook of poems. Shona and I thought it was beautiful, so we copied it with the fax machine. We never could approach her with our positive review in fear of being punished for snooping. Every year on October 11th, I contemplate sneaking the story into print. This year I found myself without my completed assignment. Now I sit anxiously waiting for Chip's reaction wondering if I have a job or not after this.

Chip puts down the paper. "Alex, any other editor would terminate you right now. This is downright insubordination. Plus, how you titled it is going to cause controversy: 'Poem of the town's estranged lesbian.'"

"It's my mother's," I explain, "As I told you, she was born in Dayton."

Chip gets up from his chair and stares through the foreperson window.

"Alex, Englewood isn't ready for this. You and I can read this poem and know it is about a woman allowing someone to see her true self. There is a childlike whimsy to the poem of your mother inviting another into her imagination. Yet, if Englewood reads the word lesbian phrases like 'secret garden' are viewed as vulgar. We'll lose subscribers. In this day in age where many fine newspapers have gone under, we can't have that!"

"I never had to hide the fact that my parents are gay, Chip. I fail to see the big deal."

Chip turned to face me.

"Here's the mindset of Englewood, Wilson. People can hold discriminatory views of subcultures, but in turn love anyone in the same culture they discriminate because that person is vetted through their deeds. Yes, people accept Alexandra Wilson, daughter of gay parents because Alex Wilson is a great friend, neighbor, and employee. They accept your parents because they know you."

"Then print the poem and let the town know my mother."

"Your mother who refuses to come and visit you because she has generalized our community as being full of undereducated rednecks," Chip remarks.

I see Chip's point. In years past, I lock the poem in my desk remembering that my own mother never found me worthy enough to share her secret world with me.

Chip flings his arms out. "'Found Poem of Englewood's Lost Child.' That is how we'll title it. You and Shona will follow up with an article on your mother's adoption. The paper will fund your research."

"Why, Thank you, Chip!"

Chip turns around with his arms akimbo.

"You will finish the Phantom story, Wilson! I expect you to complete in it time for next week's issue."

I sigh, "Chip, I don't mean to be ungrateful, but I have to say you have me on a fool's errand with this story. If Heinrich Adolphson was the Route 40 Phantom, he does not confess to it."

"Wilson, you're a reporter. Think of a way to get him to tell!"

"I hate being in the same room with him and hate having Shona with him. He has this weird fascination with our lives. He is constantly answering our questions with personal questions. The only other thing he talks about is a person named Natalie Studebaker..."

"Natalie Studebaker! Start with her!"

"You know her?"

Chip's face fell.

"I know of her. She's next to my father and grandmother."

Chip's relatives are buried in the cemetery next to the Marion's pizza.

"Is there anyone alive that knew her?"

"Your neighbor, Mrs. Hubbard."

She's someone Mrs. Hubbard let die.

Adolphson's words echo in my head. This isn't something I need to rope Mother Hubbard into. If I ask her one question about this Natalie Studebaker, it will only give credence to Adolphson's absurd accusation. I will have to try my hand at creative writing to make my deadline.

"You'll have the story by next week," I promise as I leave Chip's office.

Later, I am sitting in the kitchen typing the introduction to the Phantom feature. Nona is at the stove cooking. Natalia comes running into the kitchen from the back door.

"Mom! Mother Hubbard told me that Italians were put in concentration camps!"

"In Canada," I reply as if it could soften the blow.

"What does this have to do with the garlic you were supposed to fetch?" Nona calls out.

"It's here," Shona says as she walks in behind Natalia. "Mother Hubbard had extra. Gosh, people sure like to tell stories around here. I made one comment about her mantel full of pictures, and she had to tell me the story of each of them. I have to go back sometime. We had only gotten through a fourth of them before her granddaughter told her it was time for Wednesday mass. I am so curious, how did she make it to America when the Canadian government seized her family's resources?"

"I don't know," I say, "I don't think she's ever told us a story from before she was married. I only knew about her father's incarceration because Janelle told me. I don't think she ever told us she was from Canada. Has she ever talked to you about her childhood, Nona?"

"Nope," Nona replies with an outstretched hand."

Shona hands Nona a clove of garlic. "I told Janelle to enjoy church with her nona, and she replied 'My nine of what'? I thought it "nona" was an Italian matriarchal title because that is what the family calls you."

Nona chuckles. "If you empty the cotton from your ears you'll hear that Natalia calls me Nonna. That is Italian for Grandmother. I am called "Nona" because I am ninth in a long maternal lineage of Angelina Sophia's. My daughter, Angie was tenth. I didn't want her called Dieci."

"Wow! That name is old!" exclaims Natalia.

"You were supposed to be the eleventh," Anthony comments as he enters the family room. "Mom, why are you cooking? You worked today."

"I like my granddaughter being Natalia Lorraine," Nona comments as she stirs her pot. "I also like to cook for her. That is how I show her I love her. You can join me in family love by chopping the garlic for me."

Anthony sulks over to the counter next to the stove. I get back to my computer. Natalia starts playing on her smartphone. The silence was comfortable to all but Shona.

"Why Natalia is named Natalia Lorraine?" she asks.

"Your sister was delusional when she was pregnant," Anthony remarks. "She insisted that the house was telling her to name the baby Natalie Lauren."

"The house?"

True, I heard what sounded like a mother lecturing a daughter when I went to bed at night when I was pregnant. Not pleased at my husband's smug look, I simply say, "I thought Natalie Lauren was a beautiful name. Anthony wanted an Italian name, so we compromised with Natalia Lorraine."

"Compromised?" Anthony snorts.

My phone beeps. I glance at the screen. It's a text from Donna Clayborne.

Wilson, can you cover for me at the Historical Society meeting for me tonight? My husband's out of town and my babysitter canceled.

Sure. What time?

In twenty minutes.

Good thing the Randolph Township Historical Society is only a five-minute drive from my house.

"Clayborne needs me to cover a historical society meeting. I have to leave now."

"When are you going to eat?" asks Nona.

"When I get home," I said.

"Can I go?" Shona chimes, "maybe I can do research there?"

"You can," I say as I gather my notebooks, "but you aren't going to find any court records if you are researching about Mom. They house high school artifacts from the fifties and sixties."

"It still could be interesting," Shona said.

"Go," Anthony barks.

I leave shooting Anthony a look. Whatever mood he is in, he better lose it before I get back.

"I didn't know Anthony has a sister," Shona says as we pulled into the Historical Society's parking lot.

"Had a sister," I reply whiling parking the car, "she died right after we got married. She was driving under the influence of marijuana."

"Hmm. Hey, how do you think Mom is going to react when she finds out you printed her poem in the Herald?"

"Mother doesn't read the Herald," I say, getting out of the car.

"She subscribes to it," Shona replies as she shuts the car door.

"And uses it to pack boxes."

We enter the renovated church that house the Historical Society. Upstairs houses the exhibits of the old villages of Englewood, Clayton, and Union. Shona gravitates towards the handouts given to student visitors. I follow the voices coming from the downstairs. I walk down to find the society's officers engaged in a lively discussion.

"If Richard Weimer wants us to sponsor his granddaughter, then he can fly himself from Florida to vet her," an elderly bearded man.

"It would be a nice event," says an kind looking woman, "it would attract the local book clubs."

Susie Mae, the President of the Historical Society, gets up from the table to greet me at the stairs.

"I told Donna Clayborne that there wasn't nothing to cover. As you can see, whether to host the next event is quite debatable."

"Sounds interesting," I say, "What's going on?"

"A granddaughter to two of our founders, Richard Weimer and his late wife Joretta, wrote a book set in 1950s Englewood. She's a creative writer."

"And we are the Randolph Township Historical Society!" bellows the man, "not the Historical Fiction Society!"

"How about I do this," I suggest, "I write up a brief section on what this author is proposing. I'll end it with the society's email address. If the public thinks this is an excellent idea to host this author, they'll let you do."

"We are more than capable…." The man began.

"That is an excellent idea," says Susie Mae. "I always like to reach out to the public and get their thoughts. It's the public's interest that keeps us going."

So I sit and listen to the Historical Society discuss the pros and cons of hosting a founder's granddaughter for an author talk while taking notes. From the corner, we can hear the sound of drawers being pulled.

Susie Mae leans over, "Your assistant must be doing the scavenger hunt we made for junior high kids."

I lean my chair back so I can see around the corner. Shona is pulling out the drawers that house the high school graduation composites of the old Randolph Township high school. Shona sees me looking at her. She motions me over the drawer she opened. The conversation is wrapping up. I get up and walk over to her.

Shona points to the paper she is holding.

"On here it says to look for the girl who is not in the yearbook, but is in the graduating photo of the class of 1953. Look!"

Shona points to a girl with ringlets, chubby cheeks, and chunky glasses. I peer closer to notice that her nose slopes into a sharp point like Shona's.

"Hey, you found your fat doppelganger."

"Look at the name!"

"Natalie Studebaker," I read.

"That's the girl Heinrich Adolphson talks about all the time."

"Oh yeah…."

"I see you found the mystery girl of 1953," Susie Mae says from behind.

"Why is she in composite but not the yearbook? Shona asked.

"No one knows much beyond that Natalie Studebaker dropped out," Susie Mae answered. "It was late in the year. The composite was already developed, but the yearbook wasn't published yet."

Susie Mae points to a girl with perfectly coiffed hair. "That is Jorretta Weimer, or Jorretta Barr as she was known back then. She knew Natalie Studebaker. She said she kept to herself. She told me that Natalie told everyone she was going to OSU then suddenly stopped coming to school after the prom. No one knew the reason."

"It's an Englewood mystery," I reply.

"It was the fifties," Susie Mae says, "she found herself in some trouble..."

Susie May is interrupted by another committee member. My eye founds a tan girl in the corner of the composite. As I try to read the name, Shona closes the drawer and turns to walk upstairs.

"Hey, I think Mother Hubbard was in that class!" I say.

I follow Shona as she stomps out of the church to my car. I quickly wave and shout out "thank you" to the officers leaving behind us. I enter the car with Shona sulking in the back seat.

"I can't believe how girls were treated in the fifties!" Shona declares as I enter the car.

I turn towards the backseat. "What got you all riled up?"

"It was the fifties, Alex. Natalie Studebakers is being made to look like she's a loser drop out, but I bet she it was because she found herself in 'trouble.'" Shona finishes with air quotes.

"Trouble that has nothing to do with you," as I put the car in reverse.

"She must have been pregnant!" Shona exclaims.

NATALIE

I was able to maintain my employee at Heinrich's shop for one more week. I don't know who snitched to Mother, Mariola or Chester. Most likely Chester was the snitch. Either way, Mother came marching over to the shop one day and dragged me home. She monitored me from work through the telephone. I was required to answer at 3:05 pm every day. Mrs. Kaiser, who shared our party line, seemed to have an urgent call at that time every day. We always heard the phone click.

To pass the time, I took up knitting. After school, I went to the couch as Mariola helped Chester with his homework and cooked dinner. As long as Mother witness me cleaning the kitchen after supper, she left me alone.

I didn't stop seeing Heinrich. Every Saturday night, Mariola and I went to Whittman's store. There Heinrich would wait to pick me up and take me to the movies. I couldn't tell you which ones we saw. We only paid attention to each other.

The weather started getting colder. Mother ordered wool coats for us from Montgomery Wards. The leaves fell from the trees. December had come before we knew it. Suddenly it was Christmas.

I woke up to a trumpet in my ear on Christmas Day. There was my brother playing "Happy Birthday" at my bedside. I threw my pillow at him.

"Aww, Natalie, why'd you do that for? I am only wishing you a happy birthday! Look what Santa brought me! I can join the school band!"

"I thought you stop believing in Santa!"

"I can believe in Santa again now that Mom makes more money."

Chester leaves my room tooting his horn. I groan as I got up. Looking at Mariola's bed, I see that it's empty. I put on my dressing gown and slippers then head downstairs. The television is blaring with the music of Bing Crosby's 'Fireside Theater'. The odors of yeast and vanilla danced from the kitchen to mingle in my nose.

I found Mother and Mariola in the kitchen twisting dough. Mother looked up at me with a sigh.

"Oh, Natalie, I hoped Chester didn't wake you up. I told him to let you sleep on your birthday."

"He did."

"He woke up at the crack of dawn," Mother chuckled, "He was so excited to see what was under the tree. He had all of his gifts opened before I awoke. Of course, his favorite had to be that trumpet of his."

I shrugged.

"Well, I am sorry he woke you."

Mother led me out of the kitchen by the shoulders to the dining room table. A gift wrapped in pink paper sat upon it. Mother kissed my forehead.

"Happy Birthday, Darling."

Mother nudge me to the gift. With a sigh, I opened it. Inside the box was a black suit with white polka dots. It was similar to the dress suit Mother wore to work.

"Isn't it lovely?" Mother sighed. "It is perfect for your graduation."

"I suppose," I said.

"I thought that you could wear it tonight," Mother said, "when Uncle Walter and Aunt Flora come for Christmas Dinner."

I gave a small smile. Mother bustled to the kitchen.

The morning the four of us sat to a breakfast of eggs, sausage, bacon, and a dessert bread Mariola called Pandoro. The mother insisted Mariola

187

and I opened our presents as Bing Crosby crooned Christmas Carols. The theme of our presents were sets: be them sweaters, stationaries, or pens. Mariola received a cookbook and I received another novel by a Bronte sister.

From the television Bing sings "I'll be Home for Christmas."

"Can't we turn this off?" I quietly asked.

Instead, Mother turned the volume knob. Bing's voice surrounded the living room.

"Oh, this song first played the Christmas after Dr. Studebaker was killed. It makes me think of him whenever I heard. It's as he makes it home for Christmas."

Mother started to weep a little. Chester hugged her. Mariola knelt beside her. I couldn't take it. Every year, we heard that song and I became forced to mourn a father used the war as an excuse to abandon us. Today was Christmas and my birthday. I didn't want to grieve anymore.

"Excuse me," I whispered.

I walked upstairs with the box that contained my new suit. I twisted my hair, put on silk stockings, and pilfer some of Mother's cosmetics and perfume. I put on my new suit and replaced it in the box with a blanket I knitted.

Quietly as I could, I tiptoed down the stairs. Everyone was attentive to the television. The creaking of the closet door hinge gave me away.

"Why, Natalie, where are you going?" Mother asked.

"I have an errand to run."

"Where to? It's Christmas Day. Everything is closed."

"I have to deliver a present," I send as I put on my wool pea coat. "I'll be back soon."

Mother started to rise from the living room floor. I quick zipped my boots and dashed out the door.

It was a temperate winter day. Even so, it was cold enough to chap my cheeks and cause my nose to drip as I walked to Heinrich's shop. Right when the shack becomes visible, I wipe my nose and throw my handkerchief in the snow. I lightly swiped the purloined lipstick across my lips with hopes it left a subtle stain.

I proceeded to the shop. From a distance, I saw Heinrich perched on top of a car smoking a cigarette. If the box I carried didn't make my gait awkward, I would have run to him. Instead, I attempt to glide to the top of the hill. Given the ice that glossed over the hill, an elegant stride was an impossible feat.

"Why I'll be," Heinrich greeted. "You were the last lovely thing I expected to see today."

"Merry Christmas, Heinrich!"

I held the box out to him. Heinrich stomped out his cigarette and motioned me to the shack. I followed.

"Where's Rooney?"

"Christmas time makes him and Old Man Rooney sentimental," Heinrich said, opening the bedroom door for me, "Or at least the drinking they do does. He'll be back tomorrow when Old Man Rooney sobers into his usual loving self."

"Golly," I replied.

"Sorry that it is chilly in here as it is out there," Heinrich said. "I don't exactly have the means to keep a fire in here. I was going to start a bonfire in the back to get warm."

The walk had me sweating me my coat.

"I'm quite all right. If fact, I hope it's alright by you if I can take it off."

"Do whatever you want," Heinrich mumbled as he grabbed a mug containing stale coffee.

As the pea coat slipped off, Heinrich choked.

"Damn, child," he swore, "when did you become a fine woman?"

"Since this morning when I woke up and became eighteen," I said turning around in my suit.

"Happy Birthday," Heinrich replied, "the extra year looks good on you."

"Why thank you," I blushed. "Now, aren't you going to open your present?"

Heinrich opened the box to find the knitted patchwork blanket I started since Mother forced me out of my employment. A smiled formed on his lips.

"This is nice," he said. The natural growl in his voice almost came out in a purr.

"Not working left me with a lot of time on my hands. I had to take up some hobby or else I'd gone crazy."

"Did you now."

Heinrich didn't need to know that I intended on knitting him a hat, mittens, and scarf but I only had the patience to knit small squares. My rudimentary sewing skills allowed me to attach the squares to form a blanket.

Heinrich lay the blanket on over the one sheet that covered his mattress.

"Nobody ever cared enough to make me a blanket. I had hussies who would coo that they couldn't bare that I was so cold during the winter. They didn't care enough to do something about it."

"Well," I huffed, "there is a reason why they are cheap hussies. You know, I can never understand why you deny yourself the finer things in life," With a pivot to my hip, "You work hard enough."

Heinrich sat on his mattress and chuckled. "The finer things in life, huh? I never had a need for fancy stuff. I am not of the materialistic sort."

"Well, I…didnot mean material possessions…"

Heinrich leaped from the bed and wrapped his arms around my waist.

"I do like fine women. You're an excellent breed, Natalie. In fact, you're the only woman worthy of christening this beautiful blanket with me."

We spent hours naked underneath that blanket. Physically, making love the first time hurt, but Heinrich's tenderness eased the pain. By the third time, I fell into a natural rhythm. In between our love making, we talked and laughed. He told me about pranks he played on his sister. I told him of the decade's worth of antics of the Englewood Friendly Society. There were moments of silence. For once, I now realize what the verse, "heavenly peace" meant. We fell asleep as evening fell.

We woke up to a knock that nearly shook shack.

"What the hell?" Heinrich cussed.

"Heinrich Adolphson! Open this door now!"

"That damn, McKinley Hubbard!" Heinrich growled.

Heinrich threw his side of the blanket upon me. He scrambled into his clothes. I turned on the shadeless lamp next to the mattress. Standing up, Heinrich awkwardly got his boots on his feet. As he put on his coat, he mouthed, "Stay here."

Heinrich shut the door behind him. I quickly gather my clothes before starting the arduous task of dressing with my ear pressed against the door.

"Rooney is at his Pa," Heinrich remarked.

"I am not here to see about Seamus Rooney!"

"You have no business with me. Leave now!"

"I am here about Natalie Studebaker! Is she here?"

"You have no business with her," Heinrich growled.
I quickly buttoned my suit and jacket.

"I have a formal complaint that she is here. I am entitled to search the premise…"

191

"You will do no such thing!" I yelled as I stepped out the door. "I'm here on my own accord. Without complaints too might I add?"

Heinrich lowered his head. Hubbard's eyes stood fixated on me.

"Ms. Studebaker, I need you to come with me."

"I'll do no such thing!" I remarked. "Now do what Mr. Adolphson said and leave! If you don't, I'll have my mother press a complaint against you to the courts!"

"It was your mother who called the station looking for you," Hubbard replied.

My heart sank. Mother just had to get into my womanly business. But I wasn't a girl no more. I could stay if I wanted. When Heinrich walked to me and gave me a parting kiss, I knew otherwise.

"Just go with him," he whispered, "we don't need any trouble."

I walked over to Hubbard's car without meeting him in the eye. Hubbard opened the back door. I kicked the passenger door. He opened it for me. Getting into the car he sniffed the air.

"What's that sour smell?"

"Nothing you're man enough to handle."

Mariola peeked from the curtain as Hubbard pulled up in our driveway. Getting out of the car, I could feel eyeballs darting at the back of my head from the Kaiser's window. Mariola opened the door as we headed for the stoop. Hubbard tilted his hat at her. Mariola put her finger to her lip. I went inside. Mariola waved to Hubbard and shut the door. She motioned me upstairs.

Mother emerged from the kitchen in her Christmas dress and heels.

"Mariola! Please see that Chester gets to bed."

"Yes, Aunt Winifred."

Mariola tiptoed up the steps.

Mother grabbed my wrist and dragged me into the kitchen. Holding me by the shoulders, she started to sniff the air. Suddenly she released me and walked to the sink, snatching the bottle of Joy and a piece of steel wool.

"Go to the washroom and remove the filth off of you!"

"I'm not dirty!"

Mother swung her arm and smacked me across the face. I stood in front of her in shock.

"Don't lie to me, Natalie! It may have been a decade since I had a whiff of that aroma but I remember it well. On me, it was love. On you, it's sin!"

With that, she fell onto the kitchen table and bawled. Five minutes to eternity, she lifted her head.

"Ever since your father died, it killed me that I couldn't afford both a Christmas and a birthday present for you. It killed me that for nine years, I couldn't afford to buy more than socks and undergarments this time of year. I hated that we ate only sandwiches for our Christmas banquet!"

I covered my ears at Mother's shrill screams.

"Finally, when I can afford a decent Christmas, you abandoned the family and humiliated me! Every Christmas caller inquired of your whereabouts. I had no answer! Your Uncle Walter even stopped by. He could have written you a check for Ohio State! Instead, he gave your present to Mariola."

"He has never given us money," I remarked, "Uncle Walter is of the mind that you should stop thinking of Father and find yourself a new husband to take care of you."

Mother looked at me with a steel face.

"Not that I agree with Uncle Walter's prerogative that you need a man, but I wish you quit thinking about Father."

"Why, Natalie!"

I found myself becoming indignant.

"I remember the arguments the two of you had before he went to war. He abandon us in the noblest way possible, but it was abandonment never the less. And I hate hearing that Damn Bing Crosby song played every year on my birthday. I hate hearing you weep over a man who didn't care to be home for Christmas."

"That's your excuse to give your most sacred possession to the first guy who winked at you!" Mother hissed.

Even in her anger, Mother could glide gracefully as Ginger Rogers. She slid to me and grasped my chin. Her manicured fingernails dug into my skin.

"Young Lady, did it ever occur to you that people in this house have endured worst circumstances than you have. You lost your father. Your brother never met him. Mariola lost both her parents, not just one. I lost the love of my life! To make matters worse, the way my daughter carries herself in town prevents me from obtaining another man."

"What have I done?"

Mother released my chin. She turned her back and headed for the sink. She grabbed a pan vigorously scrubbed it.

"It's my fault, really," she began, "I allowed you to walk through town with a superior air. Instead of balancing your focus to minding your etiquette as well as your study, I raised your unfit for any young man in this town. I supposed it is only natural for a dumpy awkward girl turns to a greaser. Of course, I thought I did raise you with a better sense of judgment, but clearly that isn't the case. Well, I suppose it is too late to save your reputation once word gets about tonight, but it isn't too late to save mine.

She turned to me. Her eyes were slits. I backed away until I hit the kitchen table.

"I raised you as a woman of a worldly mind only to understand you don't have one. You act like a brainless girl; you will be treated as one. Next week, I'll enroll you into finishing school. You will only read what you are assigned. By God, Natalie, you will learn to sew for I am never ordering you a dress again!"

The moment she fell to the sink to weep, I ran out of the kitchen to my room. As I opened the door, Mariola quick turned off her bedside lamp. I turned the overhead light switch on to find Mariola wearing an ivory quilted bathrobe belted around her waist twice.

"That's mine."

Mariola shook her head. "I rather it was; however, your uncle said it's mine because you were not here."

"You must be pleased with yourself."

"I wouldn't say that, Natalie. Today was the saddest Christmas I ever witnessed."

I arched my eyebrow at her.

"When I traveled with the gypsy camp, all I would be lucky to receive was a string of leather with a glass bead from my gypsy godfather. The celebrations were fun. We roasted potatoes over the fire and sang. I thought the Anglos were having better Christmases because they gave each other so many presents. I would trade all my presents if it meant not seeing Aunt Winifred cry today. I guess I didn't know how good I had it."

Mariola laid her head down on her pillow.

"It's not my fault..."

Mariola placed her pillow over her head. Her muffled voice floated, "You didn't know how good you had it."

ALEXANDRA

"So how is Anthony handling Shona living with you guys?" Heather asks over the phone.

"Indifferently," I answer as I type a few lines on my computer at the Dayton Flyer's office.

"Really? That's interesting. I didn't think Anthony could handle your family's... uh... culture?"

The truth of the matter is that I haven't truly talked to my husband in some time. If he'd sweeten his disposition, I would make an effort. Sure, getting used to Shona's presence took time; however, Anthony's pouting about the situation didn't inspire sympathy from me.

"Are you doing a piece of Midwestern family dynamics?" I ask.

"Nope, I am busying reporting the tween Hollywood feuds and how dance offs are settling disputes in the Hollywood juice bars."

"Tell me the latest."

Heather met one of Anthony's Air Force buddies after graduation. She moved out to Sacramento with him. The relationship didn't last. Heather joined the Hollywood paparazzi as a means to make money to get back to Ohio. She'll never admit to how much she loves her work. Now she feeds me stories from Hollywood for my entertainment articles in the Dayton Flyer.

"You know, my boyfriend is a screenplay writer," Heather says after she wraps up her dance off report. "Shona moving in with your family might make for an interesting script."

"It's not that interesting."

"Aww, come on, Alex, Middle American family sitcoms are making a comeback."

"I am glad you find my family amusing. Talk to you next week."

Anthony isn't finding Shona's addition to our family dynamic amusing. Every night he retreats to our room after dinner and lifts weights. Shona, Nona, and I alternate in helping Natalia with her homework. Tonight is my night. Natalia is learning long division, a subject I flunked in third grade. By the time Natalia is finished, my nerves are fried.

Shona agrees to read a story to Natalia once she is ready for bed. I go to my room where Anthony is lifting his weights. He stops when I enter.

"What are we going to do with Shona? She has no direction."

I arch my eyebrow at him as I head to the vanity. Gathering my pajamas I slung over the mirror that morning; I change for bed.

"I mean it, Alex, she just bounces around from one idea to the next. This morning, she was streaming 'The Sessions' the proclaimed she was going to be a sexual surrogate. Now isn't she supposed to be a research assistant or a genealogist?"

I grumble as I pull my pajama top over my head.

"She is no help whatsoever around the house. I mean, she's supposed to be smart because she went to a private college, but Natalia got a B-minus last week because of her. Shona turned Natalia's paper on pioneer days into a feminist rant. She finds a way to spout feminist and lesbian issues when assisting Natalia in math! That's just numbers!"

I mutter under my breath, "Too bad Angie isn't here to tutor Natalia in science. She'd be great a botany."

"What did you say about my sister?"

"Nothing. Nothing about the sainted Angie."

"You have no right to judge my sister."

I roll my eyes, "You're right. Neither should the guy whose wife and baby she killed while driving under the influence. We should call him to arrange a petition for Angie's sainthood."

"My sister lost her life in that accident too!"

With my arm akimbo I stare at Anthony as he points a finger at me.

"Did it ever occur to you that if Angie didn't smoke a bunch of pot at the rally that protested YOUR involvement in Iraq, maybe she would be alive without ever having killed anyone!"

"Alex, What the…"

"You have no right to disparage my family when the only shameful family member belongs to you! Imagine if Angie was alive! We would constantly have to talk to Natalia about drugs to explain her behavior! At least my sister models a healthy curiosity and studious nature for our child! Your sister only modeled family abandonment, drugs, and murder!"

"And you model how to be a bitch to our daughter!"

"If you aren't man enough to deal with strong females, then leave!"

I point to the door. Anthony takes off his flannel pants and puts on boxers and jeans. He leaves the room as he pulls a shirt over his head. I fell on the bed as I hear the car pull away from the driveway. Laying there, I hear Shona brushing her teeth in the bathroom. Nona's turns her radio off from downstairs. Once I'm assured that the rest of the house is asleep, I go downstairs with my laptop.

In the kitchen, I pour myself some chardonnay from the fridge. I sit staring at my laptop as it boots up. My mind starts wondering.

Throughout our marriage, Anthony and I witnessed couples who were passionately in love suddenly split. We always wonder why their marriage died. We never see the fight that caused those marriages to end. Now I sit alone after breaking a carnal sin of an Italian marriage, questioning a husband's manhood and talking ill about his family. Now I question, "Did I just kill my marriage?"

If I am going to enter the Herald's office tired from the insomnia I just cursed myself with, then I should have the completed pages of the phantom story to justify it. I grab my smartphone and click on the voice recorder app. Heinrich Adolphson's voice speaks.

"We Ohioans know how to tell stories. It's what we do."

Ah, that day. Unfortunately, Heinrich hasn't provided us with a suitable story since that visit. Since our visit to the historical society, Shona's made attempts to research Natalie Studebaker. She can't find a birth certificate listing her as a mother. In fact, Shona hasn't found anything tying Adolphson to a Natalie Studebaker. I'm lost for the story. I place my head in my hands and stare at them absently.

Suddenly a voice from the other side fills the space, "The only woman that can survive a marriage to a Wilson man is a strong willed woman. Now, my son always said he hated them, but he never did like the woman who couldn't make up her mind...."

It's Peter, my father-in-law. I never met him when he was alive. Anthony and I couldn't afford to travel to California as Peter's health declined. When Anthony and I started living together, I became involved with his Sunday phone calls to his parents. Peter always told the greatest stories about his childhood, his time in the Air Force during the Vietnam War, his marriage, and children.

Peter was moved to hospice care the time Anthony had to leave for Sacramento to train for his deployment. I called Peter daily with a recorder next to the speaker phone. I had a good twenty stories before he passed.

When Anthony called me with the news of Peter's passing, I begged my father for the money to fly me to California for the funeral. I can't remember what surprised Anthony the most when I entered the funeral parlor: that I made it to the funeral or that I cried, "I'll never get to sit with him and heard his stories in person."

Either way, Anthony proposed we eloped to Vegas after the funeral.

I lean back in my chair with my eyes close as Peter's voice flows through my ears.

"Now he would hate that I told you this, but I remember when he dated...well he's not here, so I'll just call her what she was, a skank. So this skank named Trista kept telling both Anthony and his friend Rusty that she wanted them to be her boyfriend, but she just couldn't decide which one because they were both so sweet. After a week of her BS, Anthony just told her to make up her mind. When she insisted that she couldn't, Anthony shouted, 'I'll make it up for you! I'm out!'"

I open my eyes as Nona enters the kitchen. She pours herself a chardonnay and sits down across from me. She chuckles as Peter finishes the story with how Rusty and Anthony remained friends and dated twins shortly after that.

"Those times seem like another lifetime ago," Nona sighs. "It's good to hear Peter's voice. Why did you transfer it to your phone?"

"I didn't."

"You had too. You didn't even have a smartphone eleven years ago when you made those recordings."

"I uh..."

Nona nods her head, "Peter swore he would never leave the kids and me. Even in death he keeps his promises."

"Maybe I backed them up in a cloud..."

"You have a stack of photos waiting to be scanned from fifteen years ago. You never have the time to back up your work as intended."

I began to search the files on my computer. Clearly, Nona is wrong. I have the files somewhere. They must be link to an application....

"I'm glad to know that Peter is here. When Natalia was born, I wept because I knew Peter would have loved her. Well, he does. For an Anglo, he had an Italian sensibility of family. We were everything to him. Anthony is just like his father. He will return."

"In death?"

"In an hour. Well, give him two given what you said."

"Seriously…"

"Seriously, he loved his sister. Now, how do you think he feels having to tolerate Shona while knowing that if Angie were alive, you wouldn't let her in the house?"

"What Angie did was intolerable and inexcusable."

"Alex, there isn't a person angrier at Angie than me. She caused me to lose my daughter less than a year after I buried my husband, not to mention my house and half of my family heirlooms. That man whose family she killed came after me with a vengeance as the beneficiary of her 'estate'. He didn't care that I lost my child too. So many precious things I sold off. Worse, I don't have my daughter. I love my son, you, and Natalia. I may have been here on my own free will if Angie hadn't died," Nona sighs, "I gave birth to two children, not one. I will always love Angie despite that her death caused me grief."

I twirl my wine. Anything I say will seem like I'm minimizing Nona's grief. I can't do that. I try to go back to my story.

"He holds a lot of guilt introducing Angie to the drug that kills her. Whenever you speak of her death, you might as well accuse him killing her himself."

I stop typing.

"Are you saying to me that Anthony did pot?"

"You didn't know?"

I shake my head.

"Anthony was the typical surfing, skating California punk. He had intelligence, but no ambitions. After school, he was at the beach with one of his boards, hanging and smoking with his friends. Sometimes, he took Angie with him. The summer after Anthony graduated, Peter was fed up with his behavior. He told Anthony if he couldn't make rent of two hundred dollars, he was going to drive Anthony to the nearest recruiter.

You can figure the rest of the story."

"That…it…ah, come on. You are telling me a story."

Nona shakes her head. "Anthony had the potential to be great as his father. He just needed a staff sergeant to drill the notion into him."

Nona stares off. Believing she isn't going to say anything, I go back to my computer. That when Nona decides she has more to say.

"Peter and I…we had enough. We gave the kids enough. We gave them all that matter. Anthony never wanted for anything. You and he raise Natalia with enough. But there is something he had that Natalia doesn't and that's a sibling. Seeing Shona around reminds him of what he and Angie had. He wants that for Natalia."

"Nona, really? Don't you start too."

"I understand your perception," Nona replies in a rather smug tone. "Your parents were gay when they married. They had you as the obligatory child to throw off everyone's scent. Yet, nine years later, they have Shona. For a time frame that large, one has to wonder what you lacked."

I roll my eyes.

"Now, I understand that you don't want Natalia to feel that way. I mean she is more like Anthony and Angie than she is like you."

"Enough throwing shade, Nona. If Anthony wants his baby, then he needs to make me want to jump him. Instead, he whines like a little girl."

"Ha, if Anthony was any less of a man, you would have been slapped across the face. Seriously, Alex I haven't seen you be such a bitch since after Anthony came back from Iraq…"

Nona grabs my wine glass. She is at the sink before I can reach for it. She starts pouring my wine into the basin.

"Nona! Are you crazy?"

"You're pregnant!"

"All you needed to say is 'yes, I'm crazy."

"The last time you were a bitch was after you repeatedly jumped Anthony's bones the moment he came home from Iraq. It was because you got pregnant with Natalia. Another thing I want to bring up! Anthony wasn't prepared to be a dad after he lost his leg…"

"Hate to burst your bubble, Nona, but you have to have sex to get pregnant. That has not been the case now."

"You did! It was in the papers! It was recent enough. We may still have it. I'll get it."

I can't take this craziness. As Nona searches for the Herald, I retreat to my room. Anthony comes home. I hear him and Nona chattering like crazy. Suddenly, the sound of Anthony's steps thunder to our room.

"Darling, I've heard."

"It's a real bad case of PMS, Anthony Carl Wilson. Wait, tomorrow, I'll be bleeding and rubbing my soil sheets across your face."

Anthony hugs me tightly.

"Saints be praised! You are pregnant!"

NATALIE

Thankfully, there weren't any finishing schools in Englewood. Unfortunately, the town had Mrs. Metterschmidt. During one of her "friendly" visit, Mother confided that she was looking for an etiquette coach. It was all too convenient that Mrs. Metterschmidt happened to give etiquette lessons for the local girls. With that, Mariola and I spent every Wednesday afternoon in Mrs. Metterschmidt's living room being lectured on manners.

Mrs. Metterschmidt's charm school became a blessing in disguise. After the lessons, Mariola, and the other girls would go to Whittman's store to practice the lessons at the soda counter. I would head over Heinrich's shop to spend time with him.

Spring delivered the curse to Mariola. Mother tried convincing her that having a monthly visitor meant Mariola was healthy. Whereas Mariola enjoyed regular nourishment, she didn't like the periodic visits of Aunt Flo. Mariola bled profusely. After school, she went straight to bed with a hot water bottle. Mariola's massive output overshadow that I wasn't bleeding at all.

"Have you told her, yet?" Heinrich asked, passing me a cigarette in bed one Wednesday night.

"Are you daft? She will have the courts send bulldozers and wrecking balls to tear your place now."

"I graduate in two months. After that, I'm out of her house. The baby isn't due until the fall."

"Where are you going to go?"

"Well, here, of course," I answered, "Where else would I go?"

Heinrich sighed, "This isn't a place fit for a baby."

"Well, you have two months to get this place spic and span."

"This is an auto body shop. A kid can't be running around here. He'll cut himself on the scrap metal."

"What makes you sure it's a boy?"

"It just better be a boy. It's a family business I got here. I can't teach a girl to fix an engine, now, can I?"

"Well, you got six months to figure it out."

No longer having the promise of attending college, school became pointless. I spent my days reading Heinrich's bookS hidden behind my textbooks. Teachers didn't solicit responses to my questions now that I was no longer raising my hand. By the lack of witnessing irked facial expressions, it seemed the teachers were relieved I raising my hand.

On the first of April, prom posters littered the school's hall. Girls were all a buzzed with the notion of being asked by their true love to attend to receive an engagement ring that night. At first, I found the idea of prom banal. I didn't need to flounce around in a poufy dress when I already got my man. I retreated to my book while walking down hallways and when I was waiting for Mariola in the bathroom.

"Mr. Butterfeld has already secured me a teller position at his bank," Joretta Barr said as she primped at the bathroom sink.

"That's unnecessary," Mary Iris said, "Robert is going to propose to you at prom."

"It will be a long engagement," Joretta sighed. "Ever since he received his acceptance letter, all he talks of is his studies at Loyola Unversity. He'll make me wait for the entire four years he is there. I might as well work and save up for a decent wedding."

"If he gets the sense knocked into him, let me know. I'll take the job when you're married. Maybe I'll meet a cute young business associate."

I rolled my eyes. Unfortunately, I was hidden much by my book as I thought. Joretta cleared her throat.

"You have something to say?"

"If I did, I would have, but there is nothing to say."

"Of course, she's got nothing to say," Mary Iris replied, "she's got no college acceptance letter, no job prospects, and no man."

"And you have no knowledge of me," I remarked, "I'm just one of those girls who doesn't need to brag about her man."

"What man?" Joretta asked, "I haven't seen a boy walking around with you here."

"I said man, not boy. He's out of school."

"Who?" Mary Iris inquired.

"My employer. I got a job and a man which is more than the two of you have!"

I storm out of the bathroom as I hear Mariola's stall flush. Joretta's voice floated out of the bathroom as the door shut behind me. "Now what is her problem?"

In the hall, I saw a flyer announcing the prom posted on a bulletin board. I tore it off and stuffed it into my notebook. I would show them!

"Absolutely not!"

Heinrich threw down his oil rag and stomped away from the Ford he and Rooney were fixing. I followed him waving the flyer in the air.

"Awww, come on!" I whined. "It could be fun!"

"If prom was fun I would have gone five years ago when I was in high school. All it is about are dippy girls fetching for a husband by dancing with them with their sweaty palms. The only beverage is fruit punch, and if you enhance it with your own 'sauce', you're kicked out of there. I already have a refrigerator full of beer and an occasional naked woman in my bed. Why do I need to go to prom?"

I resisted the urge to shout that the occasional naked woman better be only me. I never won an argument antagonizing Heinrich. Instead, I wrapped my arm around him.

"Every dippy girl in school doesn't believe I have a man. They are going to be parading around boyfriends. Imagine if I walked in with you. They would be green with envy."

I nuzzled his back. Heinrich pulled a cigarette from his pocket. Placing it in his mouth, he said, "Any day now the whole town won't be able to ignore that you been with a man. When that day comes, you'll sure wish they could."

Rooney slipped out from the Ford's undercarriage.

"Now why are you giving her a hard time, Heinrich? There has never been a dame proud to lay with you before."

Heinrich pushed Rooney back under the car with his foot. He grabbed his lighter and lit his cigarette looking out onto the road. I slithered into the crook of his arm. He stood looking at the road. I stood looking at the sunset waiting for him to speak.

"Who the hell is coming here?" he asked, releasing me.

I looked towards his line of vision. Mariola walked down the street and up the hill to the shack.

"What are you doing here? I thought you would be at Whittman's store with the other girls."

"I was. Your mother called the store and told Mr. Whittman to send us home. I pretended you stopped and admired someone's lilac bush and that I had to find you. That is what Mr. Whittman told your mother. We better be home."

"What did she want?"

"Mr. Whittman didn't say. Come on now."

"Don't go anywhere," Heinrich said, "I'll go get the station wagon and drive you girls home."

"I don't believe that is an excellent idea, Sir," Mariola remarked.

"Neither is you getting home long after dark," Heinrich snapped.

Mariola and I followed Heinrich to the shed. Rooney slid out from the car and ran after us. He caught up and wrapped a greasy arm around Mariola.

"What's your name, little girl?"

Mariola silently removed Rooney's arm from her waist with a look of disgust. She entered the backseat. Rooney practically pushed her to the other side. I walked to the passenger seat. Heinrich shook his head.

"Rooney is riding up front with me. It's for the best."

At Heinrich's whistle, Rooney leaped into the front seat. I joined Mariola in sulking in the back seats. No one spoke a word as Heinrich drove us to my street. He dropped us off at the street corner. I fumed the short walk home. Mariola and I entered the house to find Mother reading the paper in the kitchen.

"Good Evening, Mother, what is it that you need?"

"Nothing, in particular, Natalie, I just thought it was best that the two of you be home. We can't have you out admiring lilac bushes that aren't in bloom yet, now can we?"

"Very well," I said, heading for my room.

"Now, don't leave right away," Mother replied, "the both of you, come sit. Let me hear about tonight's lessons."

"I have studying to do," I remarked, leaving the kitchen before Mother could say another word.

During the spring semester, I had the last period free. Unfortunately, Mother forbade me to leave without Mariola. With the warm weather, I visited my tree and read. The day after Mariola interrupted my visit with Heinrich, I heard a whistle. There he was, leaning against the station wagon across the street. I ran over and embraced him. He immediately let me go.

"You're in enough trouble. We don't need to attract attention."

"You came to my school."

"Well, I can't call you at your house!"

"Why are you here?"

Heinrich crossed his arms and faced the street. "Rooney wants to go to prom with the Itty girl that came over last night."

"Mariola?" I guffawed, "She would never go with him."

"Well, you better find a way to make her go. I am not going to prom if Rooney ain't going. He actually wants to go. You can make it happen, can't you, Baby?"

I drew in a breath. "I'll try."

The school bell pierced through the air. Students paraded.

"That's my cue to leave," said Heinrich.

I ran to the front door to find Mariola as she exited the school. I couldn't wait to tell her the good news.

"Well, I don't even like him!" I heard Mariola say from the other side of the bathroom stall.

I peeked through the crack to see Mariola talking to Joretta and Mary Iris at the sink. Joretta was staring into the mirror, fluffing her hair.

"Now, Prom's not really about whether you like your date or not."

"Then what is it about?" Mariola asked.

"Well, I'm not quite sure," Joretta asked, "but you certainly don't want to be a girl alone at home on prom night."

"Ummm….."

"I am in the same boat as you," Mary Iris said with a hand on Mariola's shoulder. "Joretta is having me go with a friend of her boyfriend's. Still, it is the one night before my wedding that I will get to dress up and have fun with my friends. You should go. We could stand by the punch bowl and talk with the other girls. It will be fun."

Mariola gave a hesitant answer, "If you say so."

"You know what will be fun," Joretta squealed. "I am having the girls get dressed at my house. My mother's room has a floor length mirror and a vanity table with a lighted mirror. It will be like getting ready in a Hollywood dressing room. You will come, yes?"

"I could but what about Natalie Studebaker? She is the reason I am going. It wouldn't be nice to be dressing without her."

"Why of course she is invited," Jorretta answered in a falsetto.

"It would give us a chance to see the man she's been bragging about," Mary Iris remarked.

"Thank you," Mariola replied, "thank you both."

Joretta's voice floated as she exited the bathroom, "Our pleasure."

Mariola looked at my stern reflection as I exited the bathroom. "Do not look at me like that. I saved you from having to tell your mom about prom now."

Years of being the Friendly Society's charity I became attuned to their meeting scheduled. The next afternoon session I called Heinrich's shop without the risk that Mrs. Kaiser wouldn't be eavesdropping on the party line. After Mother's daily call in, I asked the switchboard operator to dial Heinrich's shop.

"Adolphson's shop."

"She's agreed to it."

"Ain't that nice," Heinrich replied.

"She also arranged to have us dress at a classmate's house, so I don't have to tell my mother. The only other matter to worry about is getting our dresses. I barely have enough saved up for one dress, let alone two."

"Now that is a quandary," Heinrich said.

"What should I do?"

"Why are you asking me?"

"Because you are the man…."

I heard a click on the other line. Quickly I finished, "Thank you, Sir, I will be sure to tell my mother when she comes home."

I hung up and ran to the window. Looking across the street, I found Mrs. Kaiser on her phone from the window. I went to my knitting. I had more important garments to worry about than prom dresses.

Three nights before prom I awoke to stone pelting my window pane. I dash to the window as Mariola began to stir. Outside on the curb was Heinrich's "haunted" station wagon. The glowing green skeleton pointed to my porch then drove away.

Pregnancy swelled my feet into pillows. With naturally cushioned steps, I walked down the stairs without a creek. I opened the door to find two delivery boxes in the familiar shapes of dress boxes. I picked them up and read the label by the glow of the streetlamps. Each was addressed to McKinley Hubbard. Quickly I brought them upstairs to my room. As I shoved the boxes underneath my bed, I heard a creak from the doorway. I scrambled to into my bed. Mother opened the door to my room.

"Natalie? Mariola?"

Pretending to be asleep, I laid perfectly still hoping my heartbeat couldn't be heard. I breathe a sigh of relief as Mother shut the door.

The first time in weeks, the air at school wasn't abuzz with prom chatter. Guys and gals alike were talking about the Route 40 Phantom's latest strike.

"This time, it was the mail truck the phantom spooked," Mary Iris said at the bathroom sink, "the paper said he stole a couple of parcels."

Joretta swiped a pinkish lipstick across her lips. "Does anybody know what he took now?"

I maintained my focus on washing my hands.

"The postmaster lives on my street," Mary Iris explained. "I saw McKinley Hubbard visiting him. The postmaster pointed out the names of the manifest and Hubbard marched off his lawn. My mother dropped by to return a cookbook. His wife said the manifest says that the stolen packages addressed to McKinley Hubbard; yet, Hubbard is insistent that he never ordered anything! The postmaster's wife stated that the stolen boxes contained dresses! Something kooky is going on?"

"Dresses?" Joretta scoffed with a shrug of her shoulder. "He probably ordered them for his mother."

"A seemly story," I remarked.

Jorretta looked at me with indignation that I would dare address her. Mary Iris twisted her mouth.

"A dress is a rather special gift for a boy to give his mother," I explained. "I think Hubbard is a poof. He probably ordered the dresses for himself.

A cloud of doubt washed Joretta's face.

"Well, I do find it funny that he's never been seen strolling around town with a girl…"

"He has with Mariola," Mary Iris remarked. "Are you two daft? The Phantom order these in Hubbard's name to taunt him! Everyone in town knows Hubbard has been trying to arrest the Route 40 Phantoms for years. He doesn't allow room in his life for anything else."

"But why would the phantom order dresses?" Joretta asked, "For once I think Little Miss Studebaker has presented a most logical statement. You are joining Mariola and the rest of the girls at my house tomorrow, right?"

"That is what I've been told," I answered.

"We are going to start getting ready at noon," Jorretta replied as she turned for the door, "See you then."

Prom was on the same day of Jimmy Gordan's birthday party. Mother accompanied Chester to the occasion. Before she left, she instructed Mariola and me which chores she would like to see completed before she returned. Five minutes after she left, I ran upstairs with the garments bags I stash the dresses in. Mariola had started dusting when I went upstairs. I grabbed her hand and ran out the door.

All the girls had curls in their hair and cream on their face. Without a word, Mary Iris sat Mariola on the vanity and curled her hair. Jorretta handed me a set of tweezers.

"You need to shape your brows."

The hours dragged with idle chitchat. I remained invisible in the corner as Mary Iris primped Mariola. Finally, it was four thirty, and we could get dress.

"Where did you even get these dresses?" Mariola whispered.

"They're just old things I use to have," I lied.

Mariola pulled a pale pink chiffon dress out of the garment bag.

"This doesn't look old at all."

213

Once dressed, Jorretta told all of us to line up. Striding in her emerald green ball gown, she went down the line cooing at all the girls.

"Mary Iris, the plum rose dress you are wearing is divine. Shirley, your golden cream lace is exquisite. Geraldine, blue is your color, but the low halter neckline is certainly scandalous. There better not be rumors about you floating around the halls come Monday. Why? Mariola...."

Standing in her pink dress accented with a nosegay of roses, Mariola was a sight to behold. Her soft black curls cascaded over her bare shoulders. A deep blushing pink lightly stained her lips.

"What that dress needs is a string of pearls rather than the gold cross," Joretta suggested, "I'll go fetch you some from my mother's jewelry box."

"That's kind of you," Mariola replied, "but I need to wear this. It was my mother's. It is important to me."

"Yes, of course," Joretta said. "Why, Natalie, that is such a high waist!"

Heinrich bought me a periwinkle scoop neck dress that cinched just below my bosoms with a full-length skirt. I thought I was beautiful and glowing. Joretta just laughed.

"If I didn't know any better, Natalie Studebaker, I would have guessed you were in trouble."

"Now why would you say that?"

"Because the only reason most girls of your short stature would wear a dress like that is because they are hiding something. You must be hiding a little weight. A girl ought to know that one should not eat sweets for a month before prom."

All of Joretta's cronies giggled. Mariola wrapped her arm around me as we filed out of Joretta's room.

The high school boys were in the foyer as we descended the Butterfeld's staircase. I scanned the crowd for Heinrich and Rooney, but they were absence. Mrs. Barr asked each date to meet their girl the staircase for a picture. Mariola reached the bottom of the stairs to no one waiting. My heart sank.

A loud knock shook the front door. Mr. Butterfeld opened it. Outside stood Heinrich dashing in a tan three-piece suit. Rooney stood in a maroon striped jacket over white pants.

"Why!" exclaimed Ms. Barr, "I didn't know your prom's theme is 'The Great Gatsby'!"

Everyone laughed.

"It's not, Mother. The committee picked 'Heavenly Night' for the theme."

The laughter increased. Heinrich grabbed me by the hand and pulled me to through the door. Mariola declined Rooney's offer of his arm. The crowd's laughter grew into a roar. Mary Iris held Mariola by the shoulders.

"Mariola, come on!" I ordered.

Mariola followed us to a red Corvette parked in front of the Mr. Butterfeld's driveway. The boys silenced their laughter once they saw the car. Heinrich and Rooney opened the doors for us. Heinrich clutch the wheel tightly, turning his knuckles white.

"I only could get the dresses without calling attention to who the phantom was," Heinrich said. "Rooney and I had to pull our fathers' old suits from the closets."

"I think you look classic," I said, bending over to give him a kiss on the cheek.

"You have a nice car, Sir," Mariola remarked.

"Why thank you," Rooney said, "it's on loan from the Stanley punks!"

"Excuse me?"

"Old man Stanley bought his boys a new car to crash," Heinrich muttered.

"Should you be driving a car that isn't your?" Mariola asked.

"It's not a doll's place to mind," Rooney retorted, reaching for Mariola.

Mariola slid to the door. Heinrich pulled up to the high school. The four of us exited silently. Heinrich and I linked arms. Mariola walked with her hands folded in front of her as Rooney wrapped his arm around her shoulder.

White balloons and crepe paper covered the school gym's interior. The basketball hoops were cover in garlands of white tissue paper flowers. With the only lighting being from the drama department's spotlights, the gym almost resembled Heaven.

The younger students of the school band started playing a Glenn Miller arrangement. I walked Heinrich to the dance floor. We dance. I smiled at him. He looked around.

"I suppose they won't be playing Elvis or Chuck Berry, would they?" Heinrich commented.

"I like Glenn Miller."

I pulled Heinrich closer, resting my head on his chest. I close my eyes as we sway to the music.

Five songs later, Heinrich muttered under his breath, "The nerve of her."

"The nerve of who?" I asked.

"Her."

I pulled my head up to see Heinrich pointing at Mariola standing near the punch bowl with Mary Iris.

"She's been talking to her friend the entire time while we're here. Rooney has been sitting near the bleachers with the other losers. She acts like she is better than him!"

"Mariola is just shy," I lied. "She lived in gypsy camps before my mother took her in. She's no more civilized that Rooney. She might be keeping her distance because she fears he'll discover her lack of upbringing."

"Then let's head over to a juke joint," Heinrich said.

Heinrich led me to the door whistling for Rooney. At the command of Heinrich's head tilt, Rooney bolted from the bleachers. He ran and grabbed Mariola by the hand, dragging her from her conversation with Mary Iris.

"I don't want to leave now!" Mariola exclaimed. At the sight of Heinrich's silted eye, she breathed, "It's too early to go. We just got here."

"If your date is leaving, you're going!" Heinrich gruffed.

Rooney and Heinrich led Mariola and me out of the school and to the Corvette.

"Ya know, Heinrich," Rooney asked, "I'm not hungry. How about we skip the juke joint?"

"Ask your date what she wants."

"Do you want to eat, Doll?"

"I'm all right," Mariola answered timidly.

"How about you, Natalie?" Heinrich asked, "Don't you need to eat?"

"Maybe."

"There's a Mr. Freeze down yonder. I'll get you something there."

Heinrich pulled into the deserted parking lot of Mr. Freeze ice cream stand. He got out of the car and opened my door. He took my hand and steadied me out of the car. He popped his head and said, "Have fun, you two."

Heinrich took me to the stand and ordered me a chocolate malt. He walked me to the side of the building closest to the moon. We leaned against the building with his arm wrapped around my waist. Occasionally, he sipped from my malt as we looked at the moon.

"Heavenly Nights," he sighed mockingly.

I giggled.

"You don't need walls covered in white crepe paper to feel in heaven. All you need is the moon and the stars. Those who want more, well, there the truly poor. A real rich man knows what he has and wants no more."

"You were right to have us leave those fools back at prom."

Heinrich put his hand on my stomach.

"I never had much. I never thought I was living without. As I think what I have to pass on to our son..."

"Or daughter," I interrupted.

Suddenly a clamor of sirens snapped us back into reality. We turned to our right to see blue and red lights.

Heinrich walked over to the parking lot. I followed behind to find Officer Hubbard handcuffing Rooney over the front hood of the car. Mariola was crying in Mary Iris's arms. Another vehicle arrived on scene. Joretta ran out of it to Mariola and Mary Iris.

"Oh I knew it!" screamed Mary Iris. "I knew he had ill intention!"

"What the fresh hell!" yelled Heinrich.

Hubbard pushed Rooney into his car. Heinrich jumped into the Corvette. I ran with my hand on the door until Heinrich stopped the car to let me in. He drove on Hubbard's bumper to the police station.

ALEXANDRA

Anthony and I are having sex in a red Corvette in front of high schoolers in 1950s' prom attire. The kids are gasping except four onlookers. There is a cop standing next to a petite olive skin woman and a blond man standing next to a plump brunette. The blond and his brunette have their eyes fixated on Anthony and me. The cop approaches us.

"Now, now, didn't my grandson talk to the both of you about this sort of thing?"

It can't be the late Father Hubbard! Of all the times to finally meet him, it had to be like this!

The brunette points to my stomach. "Charlotte Winnifred. You can call her Charlie."

I wake up. "Damn it! I am pregnant!"

The last time I dreamt Anthony and I were having sex among witnesses was when he returned from Iraq. As Nona mentioned last night, I jumped him anytime I could; it didn't matter if he was missing a leg as long as he returned breathing.

One night I dreamt we were having sex in the war fields of Vietnam. From the swap grass, my father-in-law emerged. He shook his head and said, "Let it be a girl."

The next day, I found out I was pregnant with Natalia.

Anthony is making huevos rancheros in the kitchen. He has poured me a large glass of orange juice, which he gives me with a kiss.

"I'll have Mom buy some decaf coffee from work today. No wine or caffeine for the next nine months for you."

"Joy," I mutter.

Caffeine and wine are the easiest things for me to give up when I'm pregnant. Still, I don't like it when I do.

Shona and I head to Limestone Manor for another interview with Heinrich Adolphson. We are still are nowhere to getting any substantial information from him. If I don't get any useful information today, I might just abandon the story. Being pregnant, I'll have to give up a job now that Nona is working. I might as well have the decision made for me instead of trying to make it myself.

Jenelle Hubbard is exiting Mr. Adolphson's room indignantly when we arrive. She leans back against the wall. She sees us and shakes her head.

"That is the most wretched man I ever met!"

"What's going on?" I asked.

"I was visiting this man as a favor for another doctor. He read my name tag and asked me if I was related to McKinley Hubbard. I told him I was and he made a remark that it was fitting for Papa Hubbard to have a Negro grandchild! Like I'm a lesser person than that frail bag of bone!"

"He's just a disgruntle ex-con," I say, "He's alluded your grandfather arrested him a while back."

"That's not all, Alex. He asked me if my grandmother was 'that shifty Itty'!"

"He did what!"

"Alex! Keep your voice down!" Shona hush.

"I won't!"

220

"He even claimed that Nana framed an innocent man in the name of Mussolini!"

"That man is dead!"

I open the door as Jenelle asks Shona, "What's gotten into her?"

I'll tell them about the baby later. Now, I am going to tell that yellowed leather bag of bones off!

"Hells fire!" swore Adolphson, "what's gotten into you?"

"Do you care to explain yourself why you felt the need to disrespect my family?"

"Your family?"

"Yes, Dr. Jenelle Hubbard is my family. So is her Nana. While I'm at it, so his her late grandfather even though I never met him."

"How are they your family?"

"I don't have to explain that to you! The only one who needs to explain anything is you!"

Adolphson snorted.

I sat down and took a breath. Shona walked into the room and stood near the doorway. I heard Jenelle's footsteps down the hall.

"Mr. Adolphson, I have been assigned to write a story about a man who tried to drive trucks off the road dressed as a skeleton…"

"I didn't dress up as a skeleton. It was an optical illusion. Look it up! It's called Pepper's Ghost!"

"Still, you became nothing but a good for nothing criminal. Show it to him, Shona."

Shona sighs and pulls out a filed from her notebook. "You spent three years in prison for attempted kidnapping and repeatedly arrested for vagrancy and unlawful encampment until the turn of the century."

"That was my child they claimed I kidnapped! They stuck me in prison so they could take the shop from under me! I was homeless when I got out!"

"Given that you are a racist mean spirited son of a bitch, why should I care?" I asked. "As far as I'm concerned, the Route 40 Phantom can remain a legend. You can die a faceless man who got the life he deserved."

I got up and turned to the door. Adolphson laughed until he started coughing. Shona ran to him. I turn to find her wiping phlegm from his lip. He patted her arm.

"You know, that 'bitch' I was the son of, she would have loved you, Shona. Of course, she would have loved your sister despite the hell she inflicts."

"What are you rambling about?" I asked.

"Do you ever wonder where you get your gumption?" Adolphson said as he turned to me. "Or the nerve you have that propels you to barrage in here and yell at a dying old man?"

"Not really," I reply. "Come on, Shona, let's get going."

Adolphson places his head on Shona's arm. "You see, Shona, you got Natalie's sense of inquiry. You have to read and explore stuff. Your sister, well, she got her knack for trouble. Susan got both."

"Susan?" Shona replies.

"Yeah, I met her in seventy-seven. She claimed she made a mistake and left."

"You are talking nonsense," I mutter.

"The guard told me who her name. I had to wait for twenty some years for the internet. By then I found out she was divorced with two daughters and a professor. I love the internet, don't you?"

Shona stepped back from the bed, "What are you saying?"

"You know exactly what I am saying, dear Shona. You were a good girl and looked up Natalie Studebaker, didn't you?"

"We did," I remark, "all we found out that she got pregnant and dropped out of school. There is nothing impressive about that. If she was alive, I don't think I would interview her."

"There's a photo in the top dresser drawer," Heinrich tells Shona. "Get it for your sister."

Shona walks to the small wooden dresser. She pulls out a small framed photo. Her eyes go wide. I walk over and lose my breath. It's the blond man and the brunette girl I saw in my dream last night. Shona stares intently until I realize she is staring at the mirror. Despite the plump cheeks, the brunette has the same pointed nose and sloping chin as Shona.

"That's Natalie and me. She was five months pregnant in that picture. Four months later, she died."

NATALIE

I spent prom night sleeping in the back of the Corvette in front of the police station. Heinrich came out at five in the morning.

"They're not letting him out! That Itty girl says that he tried to take advantage of her! Since she is so thick with Hubbard, the captain believes Mussolini's little bitch!"

"She has to have misunderstood," I said, "She's just a little girl."

Mariola, the baby girl two months my senior. I knew she was naïve to the ways of the world. Still, I would never dream that she would be making an accusation like that. Rooney got booked in the clink. There was no way the cops were going to let him out now.

Heinrich drove back to the shop. He walked wordlessly to the bedroom. I followed. Heinrich kicked off his shoes and gave me the iciest stare. I didn't dare enter the room although the early morning wind chilled my bare arms.

"The cops were about to question me about things that weren't their business, things that aren't nobody's business. They are looking for trouble. I got to lay low. You should too. Go wherever you want, just don't go home to your mother. She'll raise further trouble with the courts."

"I don't want to go anywhere."

"You would if you knew what was good for you."

I retreated to the outhouse and cried. Heinrich had to have heard me for I bawled so loudly. I bawled until my side ached. Suddenly, I felt a bubble burst in my abdomen. Then I felt another. The baby was kicking. I couldn't be retreating to tears. I stood up and exit from the outhouse. I

224

vowed not to cry again until the day I died.

I walked to the shack. Picking inside, I read the clock on the wall. It was 9 o'clock. Despite my absence, Mother would take Chester to church to save face. If I walked now, I would be to the house while she was away.

"I hope you didn't get into trouble with Mrs. Studebaker."

I arrived home to find McKinley Hubbard wearing plain clothes in the kitchen with Mariola. Mariola was at the table rolling dough into hollow tubes. She wore her work clothes. I stood in the doorway. Both her oblivious to my presence.

"She says there was no sense in punishing me. The realization that the outcome could be worse was the punishment that fit the crime."

"She right."

Mariola wiped flour from her hands with the dish rag.

"The cannoli will be ready in about an hour. You can stay if you would like."

"I would fear that would be seen as improper. I only came to call to see if you were okay from last night's ordeal."

"I am fine. Mrs. Studebaker insisted for me to stay home from church so I could get my rest. I couldn't, so I came down to bake you an apple pie for your troubles last night. I am just not good with the crust. Also, we don't have apples. Ms. Studebaker had the ingredients for me to make cannoli, but I bet she was hoping for lasagna when she bought the ricotta."

"I was only doing my duty, Ms. Chinecci."

"You can call me, Mariola, Officer Hubbard."

"If that is what you wish, then you can call me, McKinley."

Mariola put some dough tubes in a pot of boiling oil.

"I've been wondering, what kind of name is McKinley?"

Hubbards face lit up. "I was named after our 25th president, William McKinley. He was born in Ohio. My father's name was Harrison after Benjamin Harrison. He was our 23rd president. There have been eight Ohio presidents. I'll bet you a soda at Whittman's if you can name another Ohio president."

"I'll see you wager and raise you a sundae of you can name a Canadian Prime Minister."

"I forgot you are from Canada."

Mariola pulled the tube of the oil.

"To be honest, you could have named Woody Woodpecker as a Prime Minister and won the sundae. Better yet," Mariola turned to the stove, 'you could have called Daffy Duck to lead the country. I think a screwball duck would have done a better job in ruling Canada."

Hubbard leaned against the counter. "When your camp was arrested, I overheard rumors that you and your mother were kicked out of Canada due to your family's support for Mussolini."

"That was my father's business. It had nothing to do with Mother and me. And yet, "Mariola pretend to wiped flour off her face instead of a tear, "Mother had to pay continually for his crimes along after he died. She told me before the last arrest that if she ever endured that again, she would die."

Mariola walked a plate of fried tubes to the kitchen table. Quietly, she scooped what appeared to be a thick cream into them. Hubbard walked over to her and put his hand on the back of her chair.

"Mariola," he sighed. "I understand that this town can be prejudicial. It is not fair what happened to your mother, especially since she apparently raised you to be a good citizen despite your impoverish condition. You have proven yourself to be a value to the community for all you do to help Mrs. Studebaker with her son. I hope you will stay in Englewood after high school. Have you secured employment for when you graduate?"

"I haven't given it as much thought as I should. I have been busy helping out with Chester. I haven't dare look elsewhere."

Hubbard stood erect, "It is about time you think about your future employment. Mrs. Studebaker should certainly understand your need to earn a wage. I'll tell you what! My mother has worked at the switchboard since my father died. She is now the head operator. She usually loses some girls to marriage right around this time. I could put in a word about your character."

Mariola turned to Hubbard. "Thank you. I do need you to understand that if your mother somehow is pleased with me and offers me the position, I cannot leave Ms. Studebaker without her blessing. She has been good to me."

"I understand," Hubbard replied boastfully. "To be honest, it takes a long time to impress my mother. She is a woman of upstanding morals. She may consider that you being Italian means you are a Catholic and that may cause issues."

"To be honest, I am not sure if I even believe in God."

"Well, it is by the grace of God you are here today! I'll tell you what! I'll ask Mrs. Studebaker if you can accompany my family to church next week. That way my mother can get to know you. You have no problems with the Methodist faith, I assume.

"I guess not," Mariola stood up, "but before you vouch for my character, there is something I have to tell you."

"What is that?"

"I think I might be part of the Phantom's crime on my own ignorance."

I burst into the kitchen. "You know not what you speak of, Mariola!"

Mariola crossed her arms in an attempt to hide herself. "I do too, Natalie!"
"Officer Hubbard, I demand you leave my house. I apologize for Ms. Chinicci to have taken up so much of your time."

"Very well, Ms. Studebaker," Hubbard said. Then he leaned to Mariola. "I think it is a shame that half the town doesn't see your beauty. The biggest shame of all is that your one of them."

Hubbard walked out of the kitchen with a "Good Day, Ladies."

227

At the sound of the front door closing, I stomped over to Mariola and continuously slapped her across the face.

"You snitch! You dirty whore! You're nothing up a woodland savage that can never be domesticated. You're a fraud."

Mariola grabbed my wrist. "If I am what you say I am, why are you attacking me? It is you who doesn't know what she speaks of. There is only one whore in this room. It is because you are a whore that I don't strike you. I am civilized enough not to hurt a baby."

Mariola walked to the sink and turned on the faucet.

"You're an idiot! You are an undereducated moron. You should just go back to Canada or Sicily, wherever you came from!"

"I know what a pregnant woman looks like even when she tries to hide it," Mariola said in a flat voice. "Anglo men had an expectation of Italian women. When my mother became pregnant with my brother, Marco, she hung her head in shame. It was a blessing Marco was born dead so we could forget the matter."

Mariola turned off the faucet. "I don't understand how you can walk around as if you were a queen; especially when the only kingdom who could be the queen of is that of the junkyard. I pray for your baby to have Marco's fate for I can't bear for a child to be raised in lesser conditions than I was."

"You little bitch!"

I reached to grab Mariola's ponytail. She let how a scream.

"Girls! Stop this nonsense at once!"

Mother stood at the doorway with Chester. She entered the kitchen and grabbed me by the arm.

"Mariola, please fix lunch for Chester."

"I will, Ma'am."

Mother walked me to my bedroom with great force that I swore she intended to pull my arm out its socket. When we arrived at my room, she flung me to my bed.

"Is what Mariola saying is true?"

"That I am a whore?" I stammered, "Mother, I caught her in the kitchen with McKinley Hubbard!"

"McKinley Hubbard called and asked me if he could visit Mariola! I allowed it! I know his character to know nothing of the sort would happen! Unfortunately, I feel I know his character better than yours! Is what Mariola say is true? Are you with child?"

Mother didn't allow me to answer. She put her hand on my stomach. Once she removed it, she fell onto Mariola's bed in despair. She quickly gathered herself.

"There are places for girls like you to go. I will have to find one of them. Maybe I could say you found an opportunity elsewhere. But you are to stay in this room until I figure out what to do with you! Do I make myself clear?"

"Yes, ma'am."

The moment I heard Mother's footsteps down the stairs, I removed my prom dress. After dressing in my work shirt and Dungarees, I gather a few baggy clothes and whether else still fit into my suitcase. I pulled my sheets of the bed. I looped one over the suitcase handle. I tied the other sheet at the end. Opening my window, I gauged the fall. Two sheets should be able to get me down safely.

Quickly, I went through a box of Mariola's meager belongings of her gypsy life. Her kerchief was lying at the bottom of the box. I pulled it out and quickly shoved the box back under her bed. Not knowing how to tie a kerchief, I pinned the scarf to my head.

I tossed the suitcase to the window and tied the other end of the curtain rod. Remembering what I saw the boys do in the gym, I climbed down the sheet. No one was in their front yards yet; I had time to escape. With one tug, the sheet fell from the open window. I quickly shoved it behind the bushes. I took off my glasses and head towards Heinrich.

Cutting through a maze of lawns made my journey to Heinrich's longer. The stone pillows that were my feet ached. Finally, I had reached the bottom of the hill. Heinrich was blaring Rock-a-Billy music blaring from somewhere. At a distance, I saw Heinrich leaning against the Corvette, smoking. Another man danced around the Corvette like a fool. He stopped long enough to make me realized who he was.

"Rooney!" I squealed as I ran up the hill.

Rooney pushed his hand out.

"Don't come any closer to me, Lady! I don't need any more trouble from the likes of you!"

"AH, Rooney, why do you have to be like that?"

Heinrich stubbed his cigarette out onto the ground. He sneered at my suitcase. He turned and walked the shed. Placing my suitcase on the ground, I followed him. He leaned against the station wagon swinging the hand of the plastic skeleton that poked through the window. He looked at me with the stern look that was becoming too familiar to me.

"You didn't tell me the Itty was Hubbard's girlfriend."

"She's not. She doesn't date anyone."

Hubbard took drags from his cigarette. After watching five smoke rings float out the shed, I asked, "When they let Rooney out?"

"This afternoon. The bitch decided not to press charges. The judge would only determine that she was asking for it wearing a dress like that. The reason the cops didn't let him out last night is that they wanted to rough him up a bit. Try forcing him to give him information and make a false allegation. But Rooney is loyal. He betrays no one. There is no hope ever becoming right in the head after last night's beating. What do you got over there?"

Heinrich sneered at my suitcase.

"My mother found out about the baby," I answered, " she was going to place me in a home. I came here."

"Go back to your mama," Heinrich said, stubbing his cigarette. "I have enough heat on me. You stay here, and this will be the first place the cops look. They'll arrest me for harboring you then I lose everything!"

"I go back to my mom's, and we lose the baby! What's more important to protect than that?"

Heinrich jumped onto the front hood of the station wagon.

"This is my Kingdom! My Empire! It ain't much, but it is all I got!"

"What good is a kingdom if you have no heirs? Or an army to help you fight for it?"

Heinrich jumped off the car. "What do you mean?"

"My life has been nothing but crazy rules. People constantly told how to think and feel. I met you than the world finally made sense! You show me that we could live life on our own terms. You taught me what actually matters. I am not going back to my old life. I want to stay here and raise our child to be the heir the kingdom you built for us."

Heinrich embraced me. We kissed long and hard. Once we broke the embrace, Heinrich whistled. Rooney ran to the shed.

"When your mama sends the cops here, we better be gone. Let's ride tonight!"

Heinrich walked me over to my seat in the front. Rooney entered the back. Heinrich pulled out of the shed and onto the open road. I didn't know where we were going, and it excited me. I was in the chariot of my king!

ALEXANDRA

I pull up to the Marion's Pizza strip mall, parking near the hill at the end. We get out of the car. Shona steadies me up the hill towards the cemetery.

"Why did they put strip mall near a cemetery?" Shona asked.

"Englewood got landlocked by Clayton and Union sometime in the seventies I think," I answer. "Not much space to expand, I guess. Anyways, I think the earliest grave dug was in nineteen forty-two. If Heinrich Adolphson was telling the truth, we would find Natalie Studebaker's grave here."

Shona opens the gate, and we wander. I had visited this place only a few times when Mother Hubbard was visiting Lisa. I wish I brought flowers for Lisa's grave.

"Ouch!"

I stub my toe on a small gravestone. Damn, it is going to swell up good. I can't take ibuprofen! Looking down, I read the name, "Edmonson": "Chester and Winifred." Those must be Chip's relatives. I briefly fold my hands in prayer. I move on to the next grave. It reads: "Studebaker: Charles and Natalie."

"Shona, I found it!"

Shona peered over my shoulder. "She was married to a man name Charles?"

I read the dates. "No, Charles was born in nineteen nineteen and died in nineteen forty-three. Natalie was born in nineteen thirty-four and died in nineteen fifty-three. I guess Charles was her father. Maybe he died in World War Two."

"A picture was taken of Heinrich and Natalie when she was five months pregnant. Four months later she died. Natalie Studebaker died in childbirth! Mom was born in nineteen fifty-three!"

"December twenty-fifth nineteen thirty-five to September nineteenth fifty-three," I read with a sigh of relief. "Mom's birthday is September twenty-third."

"That was the day social services had your mother in their custody. Your great grandmother never had the birth certificate corrected in hopes that no one would know."

Shona and I turned around to find Mother Hubbard and Jenelle standing in front of us. Mother Hubbard bowed her head. Jenelle shook hers.

"I went home to calm down from what that awful man said to me. Nana told me there was some truth to what he said. We thought you were still at Limestone Manor until we saw you while we were driving."

"Let's go to my house, dearies," Mother Hubbard said. "I have a story to tell. Jenelle can make us some tea."

We follow Mother Hubbard and Jenelle out the cemetery. On the way, Shona picks a bunch of dandelions. She breaks her bundle in half and places one group on the Edmonson' grave and the rest on our grandmother's grave.

NATALIE

September nineteenth was reported to be chilly in nineteen fifty-three. My body was an oven. The pains started early in the morning. Heinrich was nowhere to be found. Rooney got into trouble at some bar the night before. He and Heinrich rode off into the night to evade cops. I hadn't seen him for a day. I needed to go to the hospital, but I couldn't drive. I sat on the porch hoping the breeze would cool me off. With each contraction, I grabbed the post to the entrance of the shack.

I saw headlights coming from town. I tried picking up myself up from the porch step to run inside. Another contraction came forcing me to remained sitting on the porch. The headlights stopped at the bottom of the hill. I saw a dark haired woman get out of the car. She started walking towards the shack. As she entered the glow of the porch light, I saw that she was Mariola.

Mariola looked different. Her hair was done in a chignon. She wore a black dress and a choker of pearls that rested on her collar. With my hair matted to my face and the only clothes that fit me being the coveralls of Heinrich's fat father, Mariola was the last person I wanted to see.

"Hello Natalie," Mariola said as she approached the porch.

"What are you doing here?" I seethed.

"Your mother is wondering how you are. She knows the baby is coming soon. McKinley and I were on our way to a wake in Arlington. I asked McKinley to stop so that I could call on you. He's waiting in the car."

"Who died?"

"Arther Meyer."

"Arther Meyer? Didn't he win the scholarship to Ohio State? I thought I read it in the paper."

"He declined it after his brother died in Korea. He decided to stay on the family farm. A tractor ran over him. Everyone is morose about his death. Joretta cries about it every time I run into in town; however, ever since Robert broke up with her for a girl at Loyola, she cries about everything."

I laughed. Lovely, perfect Joretta Barr dumped! She graduated without a ring! I laughed until I felt another piercing pain in lower back.

"She has men making daily deposits at the bank she works at; pennies they just find in the street so they can see her again. I got a job as a switchboard operator. McKinley made good on his promise."

"Is that how you bought the little black dress," I remarked.

"Yes, I had to buy a new wardrobe because I am a working woman for now."

"For now?"

"McKinley intends on asking me to marry him. He just needs to save up for a ring, and we both need to save up for a household. He still lives with his mother, and I am still with Aunt Winifred."

I snickered.

Mariola put her arms in akimbo.

"I never understood why you acted so superior over than me the moment you started working in this trash heap. Sure I am not creamy or dreamy; still, I am a good person. I got a good life here. I am sorry all you got is this junk and that I alone in these greasy coveralls."

"I don't need your pity. I got everything I need."

"Couldn't your baby's father buy you a maternity dress? Is he even around?"

"Needn't need to waste money on something I would only wear for a few months. That is a part of being a grown-up," I said, with the confidence

I had faltering with the next contraction. "You have to make practical financial choices."

"So you wear something that has a greasy stain on your bottom?"

I lean against the post. "I don't think that is grease."

Mariola ran to the car. A few moments later she ran up the hill. Hubbard's car made a U-turn back into town. Mariola attempted to lift me from the porch. I clung to the post.

"Get up!" she ordered. "We need to get you to your bed. McKinley is getting help right now. He might not make it back here in time. We can't wait! Where's your room?"

I pointed to the direction to Heinrich's bedroom before collapsing all my weight onto Mariola. Somehow, Mariola carried my weight to the room before gently lowering me to the mattress.

"You need to get undress," she said, "I need to get towels and boil water. Where is your kitchen?"

"Outside," I muttered, "we refer it as the fire pit."

"What about a bathroom?"

"It's called an outhouse."

Mariola sighed, "We'll have to make do with what we have. I wish things were more...Well, never mind! We need to get you out of that bloody thing."

I touched the zipper but hesitated.

"This is no time for modesty! Out of that thing now! We can cover you with this blanket!"

"I need help!"

Mariola unzipped me and helped me out of the coveralls. Immediately, she whipped the dirty blanket over my naked body. She lifted my head and propped it with pillows. She went to the foot of my bed. She peaked underneath the blanket.

"Natalie, the baby is crowning! You are going to need to push."

I push my knees into my chest immediately collapsing. Mariola ran to me and pushed my shoulders to my up. Never have I felt pain in my life!

Mariola propped me with pillows and clothes laying around on the ground. She ran back to my feet.

"Push as hard as you can, Natalie! If you can at least push the head out, maybe I could pull the baby out!"

For eternity, I pushed hard. Then I felt tugging underneath me. Suddenly I heard a sound of a whack followed by crying. Mariola gently placed the baby onto my stomach.

"Careful, she is still connected inside you. You are going to have to push the after birth."

I stroked the baby's hair. She is crying. I need to feed her, but I can't move.

Instead, I slipped away.

MARIOLA

"She was dead by the time McKinley got there with the doctors," I tell Natalie's granddaughters, "The doctors declared she died of sepsis."

We are all sitting in my living room with my granddaughter, Lisa Janelle, along with Anthony and his mother. Anthony was driving his mother home from work when they saw us enter my house. I motion them to come. This story affects them too, after all, it is one-quarter of their beloved Natalia's heritage.

"Natalie had no strength after the baby was bored. She tried to hold her. All she could manage was stroking the baby's red hair. Oh! Even during the worst of Lisa's cancer, I knew that there was no way I could feel as helpless as Natalie did after the baby was born!"

Anthony shifted uncomfortably on the couch. Nona told me despite dealing with seeing his leg blown off; he fainted when Alex gave birth to Natalia.

Shona looks at me from the armchair.

"So the cops came, and mom got sent to the orphanage?"

"Child, it was never our intention to take the baby to the orphanage. First, the baby needed care. Luckily, I knew of a woman who once served as a doctor's assistant."

"She is so beautiful," Aunt Winifred said as she walked the baby in the living room, now clean and dressed in Natalie's christening gown.

"She has your red hair," I commented.

"She does. She also has Natalie's nose. It was Charles nose too."

Aunt Winifred walked her granddaughter tightly clutched to her breast. I sat on the loveseat. McKinely stood next it. We watched Aunt Winifred holding the baby while wiping her silent tears in misshapen blanket Natalie knitted.

"Ma'am, I hate to bring this up during your time of grief," McKinley stated, "However if Heinrich Adolphson comes to the house and demands the baby, I have no choice but to hand the baby over to him. As the father, he has the legal right to her."

"He has no proof," I said. "The child looks nothing like him."

"Yet, when word gets out that Natalie Studebaker had a baby, the town will know figure it is his," McKinley remarked, "she made a stir with him going to prom together."

"Shhh," I hushed.

"I know I ought to be realistic about these things," Aunt Winifred said. "I certainly can't stay home and care for her if I am to provide for Chester as well. Still, I can't bear for the child to grow up in the filth that killed her mother."

"We can do it!" I blurted out from the seat.

Walking towards Aunt Winifred, "McKinley and I could take the baby. You will stay in the baby's life for you will always be my 'Aunt Winifred'."

McKinley stood erect. "It would be an honor for to take the baby in our charge. However, I can't see the possibility of it being feasible. We have no house, nor a marriage certificate. Even if in the rare event we could obtain those tonight, Heinrich Adolphson would harass us, maybe even kill us for his child."

"I know how to travel across the continent with only a knapsack. We can just take the baby and go. I know how to camp, hunt, and fish better than a Boy Scout. Nature provides for us if we allow it. Maybe we can stumble upon my God family while we as we travel. My godfather could even marry us."

"Our union would only be legal in the gypsy kingdom."

I walked over to McKinley, putting his hand in mine.

"I don't need a ring or a house. If you think I do, then you don't know me as well. What I do need is that baby. If you love me, please help me care for her and keep the Studebakers together. I can live with barely anything else."

"We will at least need to obtain a car," McKinley answered. "It is irresponsible to expose a baby to the elements. My sister lives in Indianapolis. I will get a car and send notice that we are staying with her until I can secure a position within a nearby department. We can find a justice of the peace on the way there to obtain our marriage certificate."

I embraced McKinley.

"I must make haste. We need to leave as soon as possible under the cloak of night. Please gather your things and the necessities for the baby. Be ready by ten o'clock tomorrow night."

With a parting kiss, McKinley left.

True to his word, McKinley was at the house at ten o'clock the next night with a station wagon. He wore a dark coat and a hat. I dressed in the same dress as yesterday. Thankfully, it the black sky couldn't illuminate the blood stains from the night before. Aunt Winifred gave the baby one final kiss before placing her in the traveling basket.

"God speed," she said to me with a kiss.

"I'll call you the moment we arrive. I'll write every day and send pictures when we can afford a camera."

"You just stay safe."

I went to the car and in the front passenger seat with the basket on my lap. McKinley pulled out of the driveway. Aunt Winifred waved at us at the front door as we drove down the street. Mrs. Kaiser peeked through her window. I sent her a little wave. She shook her head and retreated to her living room.

McKinley drove us now Main Street past Route 40. One mile out, a damaged truck laid in our path. With the street empty behind us, McKinley backed up to turn right. He turned to nearly collide with a busted car. We glance into the rearview mirror. Another vehicle laid in our path. McKinley sighed and backed up to the right. We would have to drive down Route 40. "The road is clear, maybe if we drive fast enough, no one can mess with us," McKinley said.

Despite his own pep talk, McKinley drove onto the bridge with apprehension. He picked up speed. I clutch the basket tightly. The bridge was only one mile long. Despite McKinley's speed, the drive seemed treacherously long. Halfway up the bridge, we see a station wagon parked horizontally in front us. A green glow illuminated from the windows. As we drove closer, we could see a skeleton.

McKinley backed up.

"I am not falling for the phantom decoy, Adolphson!"

McKinley sped towards the station wagon. The station wagon turned at an angle. Suddenly it jackknifed us!

"McKinley! McKinley!"

McKinley's body slumped over the steering wheel. He let out the faintest of groans. I leaned over. I saw blood dripping behind his ear.

All of a sudden, the passenger side window broke. A hand grabbed me by my hair from behind. To avoid being dragged out of the window, I wrapped my legs to brace myself around McKinley. A hand grabbed my throat. At the loss of air, my muscles went limp. The basket fell with a thud as my body was pulled through the window. The baby cried.

The moment my feet dragged onto the streets, my head was whipped to face a man with a painted skeleton face. He gave me an evil sneer.

241

"You Itty Bitch!" seethed Adolphson lifting his fist. "You are going to get what you deserved."

Adolphson punched me squared in the jaw then slapped me out of shock. He threw me down on the street. As I attempted to rise, he stomped my lower back. I tried not to let him win. After each stomp, I tried pushing myself up. It was no use. Adolphson stomped on my lower back each time. When I was unable to get up, he stomped the side of my face.

Unable to open my eyes, I laid helpless in the street. I heard the baby cries become faint as Adolphson footsteps walked away.

A week later, I sat on the couch in Aunt Winifred's living room. The swelling around my eye had gone down. Pillows were propping me from behind. My hips still hurt. Aunt Winifred looked out the window behind the television set, smoking a cigarette, a habit she chide us not to do because it was undignified. McKinley stood dressed in his uniform. Without his hat, you could see a long bruise snaking right below the hairline. He stood next to the couch in what would have been considered "at attention" if his hand wasn't on my shoulder.

"It was Riley Rooney who gave the station the tip of Adolphson's intent," McKinley stated. "His son, who we all know, got arrested for harassment again. He didn't bother to post bond for his son; Mr. Rooney quietly informed us that his son's arrest was a ruse to distract the cops. That is when the entire department drove through town. A squad found Mariola laying on Route 40 moments after Adolphson left us for dead."

I closed my eyes. It was my first night out of the hospital since that dreadful evening. I thought I was ready to know what happened, yet, my head throbbed as McKinley told us what he knew.

"The judge threw the book at him after he saw pictures of Mariola's injuries. Adolphson will be locked up for a while. However, the baby..."

Aunt Winifred turned around, "The baby is on the train to Upstate New York courtesy of Randolph Township social services on behalf of Englewood's Friendly Society. A good family will be waiting for her to give her a home. The good folks at Good Samaritan hospital claimed her as being born there a day ago. The younger the baby, the more appealing she is to the adoptive parents."

"My apologies, ma'am, I suppose you already know being you work in the courts," McKinley said. "If I may, it doesn't have to end up like this. You now have claim to the baby now that Adolphson is heading to prison. It's not right for the child to go to another family when her grandmother is a fine citizen of the county."

"Did you read the file, Officer Hubbard?" Aunt Winifred asked. "The Richards are an ideal family. She is a housewife from a wealthy family. He is an owner of a construction company. They could afford to buy her the diapers, a new christening gown, and all the formula she needs. Hell, they can send her to private schools and universities. They could give her the education Natalie always wanted."

"I don't mean to overstep my bounds..."

"Then don't!"

"But Mrs. Studebaker, a child needs her family more than the ability to attend fancy schools."

"Her mother didn't believe that," I remarked.

"Mariola, remember yourself!" McKinley hushed.

I grew angry at Natalie as I remember nights I slept in dirt thankful to be sleeping next to my mother instead of an orphanage. That night, all I could think of how Natalie turned her back on the people who did everything to give her a secure life only to die of the neglect of that scum, Adolphson. It wasn't until I had Lisa did I understand Natalie's sense of ire towards an unequal education system.

"Mariola is right," Aunt Winifred sighed, "I lost Natalie when she lost her collegiate dreams. If I take the child, I will only lose her as well."

"Mrs. Studebaker..."

"It's for the child's own good!" Aunt Winifred screamed. "She'll have a complete family. If she stays here, she'll just be an orphan bastard. She will have no standing here in this wretched, country town!"

McKinley and I shook our heads. Aunt Winifred was right. The child would be unfairly judged by the sins of her parents.
"

My apologies," Aunt Winifred said. "I didn't mean for that to come out as such."

"No offense taken," McKinley replied.

"I need to go to bed. Winifred said. "I can trust you to lock up once you retire. Office Hubbard, you may stay in you don't mind sleeping in Dr. Studebaker's office, you can stay the night."

Thus, Aunt Winifred walked up the steps dejectedly, as she did every night she remained in the house.

****

"Life quickly went back to normal, although it seemed like it oughtn't," I continue, "My body healed and I went back work as a switchboard operator. Two years later, McKinley and I were married. We were in a rush to have kids. After what happened to Natalie, we were afraid. Then Marcus arrived, and Lisa after that. Then the sixties happened, and I went on the pill."

Janelle and Anthony blush. I don't know why. Both ought to have knowledge about birth control at their age. Shona dabs tears with her sleeve. Anthony wraps his arm about Alexandra.

Alexandra draws in a breath. "I don't suppose my Great Grandmother is still alive."

"No child, she died in 1999."

"That was the year before I moved here!"

"Moved to Ohio, honey," Anthony corrects her, "You lived in Columbus for the first couple of years."

"I know that, Anthony! It's just...I can't believe it. I was nineteen when she died. I had ample chance in my childhood to know her and I didn't. The timing, it's all too close."

"Did she stay in Englewood?" Shona asks.

"Soon after Natalie died, her brother took her and her son, Chester, in his home in Cincinnati. The house held more bad memories than good. A girl who graduated with us-Jorretta Barr-moved in the house and raised her four daughters in there.

"The sixties, well they sparked the cause of civil liberties in all folk. Many parents were scared and shunned the children who didn't live the standard Christian life. Aunt Winifred was different. She couldn't bear to lose another child. When Chester declared he was heading for San Francisco to live as an openly gay man, she followed him."

"We have a gay uncle?" Shona askes.

"Unfortunately, Chester passed away in eighty-two. He died of AIDS despite having old fashion values. He was committed to his boyfriend, Chris Junior. They lived as husbands. Winifred married Chester's father-in-law. After the marriage, both Chester and Winifred took on Chris Senior's last name. Despite the commitment, Chris Junior liked to sample the flamboyant nightlife. Such a shame for they left a child behind. A woman Chester and Chris Junior went to school agree to serve as a surrogate mother to their baby. Chester and Chris Junior. Both claimed paternity of the boy. In essence, that was true. Yet, when I look at Chip, I know darn well that Chester is his biological father..."

"Chip!" exclaims Alexandra. "The grave next to my grandma's belongs to a Chester and Winifred Edmonson!"

"Yes," I answer, "Yes it does. Winifred was mad that she had to bury another child. She moved back to Englewood with Chip under the guise that it was only to bury Chester. I don't know what happened to the marriage between her and Chris Edmonson Senior. She moved back during Lisa's bout with cancer. She was a big help. During that time, Aunt Winifred refused to talk about her troubles. She lived out the remainder of her days here in Englewood. Chip went back to San Francisco for college, but couldn't bear to be away. He moved back to Englewood after graduation. Even though Chip is a rather odd duck, I think he wants to be in the town of his family heritage."

Anthony contemplates, "What I don't get is that everyone else seem to know that Alex and Shona were Natalie Studebaker's granddaughters. How could that be possible?"

I motion Jenelle to my chair. Once she leans over to me, I whisper, "There is a wooden box on the top shelf in my bedroom closet. Can you fetch it for me?"

With a pat on my shoulder, Janelle goes to retrieve my treasures. Amongst the beads, rocks, and calico scraps I obtained in my childhood is a picture from my year in high school. Natalie, Aunt Winifred, and I stand in front of the house on the first day of schools. Chester took the photo. He didn't want to be photograph because he hated the speckle of freckles on his nose. I hand the photo to Alexandra and Anthony.

"As you can see, Alexandra is the splitting image of her grandmother. With Natalie's profile Shona is a prettier version of Natalie with her thin face and Irish complexion."

Nona peers over behind the couch. She points at the photograph.

"That brick! It looks familiar."

"Of course, it does, the photo was taken over there, " I say pointing to the house across the street.

The Wilsons run to the window to look at their house. Janelle gasps.

"Nana, are you telling us Alex lives in the same house her grandmother grew up in?"

"It's impossible!" cries Shona.

"Not really," I sigh.

As my gypsy godfather always told me, the spirits always lead you home.

ALEXANDRA

"You think she'd be up?" I ask as I pull into Mom's driveway, "She doesn't know we're coming."

"She'll be up," Shona says, "But if she's not, we can raid the wine cellar!"

"I can't drink!"

"Perfect! That means more Pinot Noir for me!"

"Lush," I mutter.

Shona and I decided we need to celebrate publishing the article about our grandfather. Grandfather. It is still weird to think that crazy, old Heinrich Adolphson is our grandfather.

After we left Mother Hubbard's that fateful day, I immediately texted Chip, "You knew all this time!"

He didn't bother to ask what I meant. He replied, "Take all the time you need to finish that article."

Shona and I only needed two days. Mother Hubbard's story gave us our ending. We titled it: "Finding the Route 40 Phantom. A Story about our Long Lost Relative." Since then, the town as flocked us. They kept asking questions about what kind of daughter that crazy man could have. Some wondered how we could be so normal. A couple of the soccer moms mentioned snidely that the article explained a lot about me. The notoriety was fun for a day. The next day, we were planning our road trip.

After spending a day driving through Amish villages so Shona could start a quilt collection, we drove to the Finger Lakes. After driving Shona around area's wineries, she got the wild idea to visit Mother. We were only an hour from Rochester.

Mother is drinking tea at the kitchen table with a scrapbook in front of her. She stands up as Shona stumbles in the apartment.

"Hi Mom," Shona giggles. "Is my room still here? If it is, I am going to lay down."

Mother and I watch as Shona staggers to her room until we the thud of her collapsing onto her mattress.

"What has gotten into her?"

"Three liters of wine," I answer, "We stopped around Lake Seneca today."

"I wish you girls had called. I don't have any beds prepped for you. Shona fell on a bare mattress."

"There are five Amish quilts in my car. I can get a couple."

"You don't have to bother. Why don't you come to the kitchen with me? I can brew you some coffee. I have that Cinnamon Sugar Cookie flavored coffee Jolene loves."

Sniffing the air, I ask, "Is that peppermint tea you are having? I'd rather have that."

"I can quickly make you a cup. You have a seat."

"Thanks."

Mother goes to the cupboard to grab a mug and a teabag. I sit and notice a newspaper next to her scrapbook. It is a copy of the Englewood Herald with an article cut out. I see the date and notice it was the issue my article about Lisa Hubbard. I thumb through the pages backward. On the front is my only feature for OSU.

"You've been collecting my work since I graduated college?"

Mother put a mug in the microwave.

"Actually, I have been collecting your work before your article about Anthony's seven-inch emotional gamut. You have a talent for telling people stories. This scrapbook is the collection of your best work. I aspect it to be filled soon. Shona told me you are going to be a feature writer for your paper."

"Well, don't get too excited," I say as Mother places the mug in front of me. "I just found out I got the feature job out of nepotism."

"Nepotism?"

"It ends up that my editor, Chip Edmonson, is the nephew of the late Natalie Studebaker."

Mother's face becomes stone.

"The last assignment he had me write about was about some crazy guy who drove trucks off the road with a skeleton in his car in the 1950s. It was supposed to be some mystery, but those in the know directed me to Heinrich Adolphson."

Mother shakes her head and sighs.

"I take it you know that name, Mom?"

"I do. Did you ask for the assignment?"

"Nope," I answer, "those who knew my Grandmother, Winifred, were tired of waiting for me to figure out where I got my good looks." I pull out my phone to show here the picture I scanned from Mother Hubbard. "See, I am a splitting image of her. Shona looks like her daughter. Well, you're a mixture of them both."

"Where did you get that?"

I pointed to Mother Hubbard in the photo.

"That girl is Mariola Hubbard. Anthony and I call her Mother Hubbard. She lived with your mother's family after her mother died. She told me all about her. She would love to have you visit so she can tell you all about your family."

Mother sighs, "I came to terms that the Richards were my parents a long time ago. Rightfully so, they are the couple that raised me."

"Because you met Heinrich Adolphson while he was in prison?" I ask. "He alluded to that. He knows about us because he followed you once he had access to the internet. But not everyone in your family was crazy. Your grandfather was the county's doctor. He joined the Army and died in World War II. Your grandmother had a law degree. Both met at Ohio State where I went. The only reason she didn't keep you was because she wanted you to get a higher education she couldn't afford her daughter being a widow. And she would have accepted you as gay because she moved to California so she could be with her son in a homosexual community. She would have accepted you if only you got to meet her."

"The secret to my contentment is that I never thought of how things might have been."

"How so?"

"What do you mean?"

"Are you actually content?"

"Yes, I don't regret my life."

"Then, why all the barriers?"

"Excuse me?"

"Why didn't you tell me you were adopted? Why didn't you let me know you and dad were gay when I was growing up? The only thing we ever talked about were books you thought I should read. Also, Nona was quick to point out in an argument that I was the obligatory child and that the space between Shona and me means I didn't live up to our expectations."

Mother throws her head back. "Ha! You believe that? We had Shona because you begged for a sibling! You started reading 'The Babysitters Club' series. You were the youngest kid in our neighborhood at the time. You wanted a sibling to babysit. You begged so excessively that your father and

I figured 'what the hell?' A baby would be quieter than you, and I was dreading facing empty nest syndrome in the next decade."

I do not believe what I am hearing, nor will I believe what I am about to hear?

"Actually, Alexandra, you ended up exceeding my expectations for you."

"Come again?"

"You don't believe me? I thought we moved on years ago."

"I think you need to start from the beginning because I am missing something."

"Alright," Mom begins, "Since I can remember, I figured I was adopted. I looked nothing like either of my parents. Jo-Jo parented like Joan Crawford on steroids. She made sure I knew she was my savior, although she never did admit my adoption. She wished that I emulate her in every way; so, I made two vows. One, I was going to find my adoption certificate and my birth parents. Two, I was going to raise my child to be herself.

"At thirteen, I started snooping around the house when my parents left me home alone on Card Club nights. I found the certificate from Christian Family Services in Ohio. I made inquiries to the states and the agency that handled the adoption. My mother retrieved the mail one day to find a letter from the state addressed to me. She read the state's message advising me that I was not entitled to answers until I was eighteen. After that, Jo-Jo began manifesting Joan Crawford one hundred percent. My teenage years were a nightmare. The fact that I didn't pursue male companionship added fuel to the fire. She perpetuated the notion I was unlovable because I didn't date. She kept informing me that if it weren't for her, I wouldn't have a home. Still, nothing I did lived up to her unattainable standards. She wanted me the debutante I could never be.

"Even though my parents lived fifteen minutes from the University of Rochester campus, I never went to see them except on the obligatory holidays. The Lesbian and Gay community found me. I started cutting my hair in a pixie cut and secretly dated some of my dorm mates. I met your dad through the circle. We decided to each other's public boyfriend and girlfriend. The sixties and seventies broke many barriers, but gay rights weren't one of them. I didn't like living in the closeted life. Rationally, I knew there was no choice if I wanted to keep my life; however, I held the belief that when I found my birth parents, I would find the people who would let me be my true self.

"I made another round of inquiries to the agencies the handled my adoption. I received a copy of Natalie Studebaker's death certificate with an apology letter for my lost. There was nothing about my father. Your dad persuaded your Grandma Anna to give him extra money one month so I could hire a private investigator. Within a week, the man I hired came back with Heinrich Adolphson's name and address.

"I was aware I was heading to a prison to meet my father. I grew up in the sixties. I had this disillusion of grandeur that my father was a civil activist arrested in a big protest. As I went inside the tiny prison, I lowered my expectations to my father being a petty criminal. Either way, having a criminal father appealed to me more than my status quo maintaining mother.

"I never forget sitting in front of him. He was a tall skinny man with yellow leather for skin. He looked at me up and now. He asked, 'Are you the dyke Legal Aide sent me?'"

"I got up and told him I made a mistake. I took the next bus to back to Rochester. A couple of weeks later, friends of mine came out. A month later, they were raped and murdered in their apartment. Many of our friends paired off into seemingly heterosexual relationships. Your father and I both wanted to a family. We like each other enough, so we agreed to be married and allow each other to peruse our own romantic interest."

"A life of secrecy doesn't sound like a happy life.," I say.

"I was happy. By the time I was thirty I had my doctorate and my family. As I said, I don't regret my life."

"Still, you could have told me that you and dad were gay! I would have handled it. What I couldn't deal with was being blind sighted."

"I remember. You have to understand that when you were a child, the world was dangerous to homosexual people. If we told you as a little child that we were gay, you would have told the whole world. Whereas you would have thought to have gay parents as no big deal, the school district would have thought differently. Honesty would have resulted in social services taking you away. Aside from that, you were always free to be yourself. That was the one quality I wanted you to have, self-esteem. You exceeded my expectations."

"Come again?"

"Why are you scrunching your face at me like that? You don't believe me?"

"Well, I am just curious to know if you were happy that I exceeded your expectation in self-esteem as you say it."

"Why do you say that?"

"I don't know! It's just that growing up I always felt that I never met your expectations. You were always critical of me."

Mother draws in a breath.

"Alex, I am not a perfect person. Being raised by Jo-Jo constantly reminded of that. I decided that when I became a mother, I wasn't going to raise my daughter to live unattainable standards. Now quit giving me that face."

I don't realize I am twisting my face. It is becoming quite bothersome to maintain concertation on my facial expression and listen to what my mother is saying. '

"I'll admit, Alex, I became what I never intended to be: your judgmental mother. Jo-Jo was always quick to point out that the only commonality we have is our red hair. Her nagging made her hate that your self-esteem. I'm sorry, but that is the truth. Until you left for Ohio, it became a battle between us to convert you into our image. Thankfully, we failed. Now, will you quit staring at me in disbelief?"

I run my finger around the rim of my teacup.

"I can't believe it's just that. You never visited Englewood. Even if it is because of your crazy biological father is from there, you never had the respect to tell me. If Chip didn't send me on a wild goose chase to find the Route 40 Phantom, I wouldn't know I had an insane relative. Anything that could make yourself relatable you kept close to your chest. Look, I remember Jo-Jo, but you can't give her all the blame."

Mother shakes her head. "To be honest, Alex, your close relationship to your mother-in-law kills me. Angelina or what do you call her?"

"Nona."

"Nona has made it very clear that she is the matriarch of your house. If you have a problem, she solves it. If she can't, you call your dad."

"Dad has the money."

True. Still, with Nona caring for the three of you, there is no room for me."

"That's not true."

"You never invite me."

"I never invited Shona. She's been at my house for a month. We made room for her. You shouldn't have to wait for an invitation to visit the home your family built. You have more claim to my house than she does."

"My life is here."

"And your family history is in Englewood. It is available to you if you want. Now, the shack you were born in became a strip mall turn gas station. It is an excellent place to get ice cream. Not only will Mother Hubbard be happy to tell you about your family history, but she can also do it sitting in your grandparents' kitchen as we serve dinner."

"Would the owners of that house mind?"

"Well, I am not one to cook, but no Anthony and I won't care."

Now Mother's face twist in disbelief.

"Yes, the house Anthony and I bought is the house your grandparents built."

"This is all unbelievable."

"Now, you have been invited to my house."

Mother stares into her empty teacup. For five minutes she blinks her eyes, wipes her face with her bare hands, then shakes her head. "This is all too much to sink in. I severed my biological ties, and now they are thicker knots."

"Well, you at least have nine months to make peace with it. Don't worry about Nona. Once Charlie is born, she'll appreciate your help. So will Anthony."

"You're pregnant?"

"One month along."

"That is too soon to know your baby is a boy."

"Grandma Natalie told me it is a girl. I am naming her Charlotte Winifred after her parents. She also inspired Natalia's name. It is no coincidence that Natalia Loraine is similar to Natalie Lauren. She whispered the name in my sleep."

"That's interesting."

"She'll whisper dreams to you when you stay in our house. You need to come to Englewood and often. Jolene needs to come too. I never lied about my parents."

"Sounds like I have many reasons to visit Englewood."

"You do."

Suddenly the lights flicker on and off.

"It's the damn fuse," Mother says, "I'll check it."

Out of the corner of my eye, I see a white cloud of a girl near the light switches. I look at my Grandma Natalie, and we both laugh.

NATALIE

"What's so funny?" my daughter, Susan says.

"It's not the fuse," Alexandra replies.

Susan walks back to the table. "Whatever."

My spirit has been commonplace in Susan's life. She doesn't acknowledge my presence, she just accepts it. I stood by her side her entire childhood. I never approved how her adopted mother treated her. I stay in hopes she could feel my strength. She became the beautiful, independent woman she was destined to be.

When Susan had kids, I split my time between her and her daughters, whoever needed comforting the most. With Alexandra and my great granddaughter Natalia in my old house, I am there more often. I appreciate Alexandra's proximity to Mariola Chinecci-Hubbard as well.

After I had died, I held ambivalent feelings towards Mariola. She attempted to keep Susan and my mother united. She also led Heinrich's arrest. As the years past, I realize that Heinrich wasn't the love of my life. He destroyed my life. I got swept away in the romance of my own mind; as a result, I fooled myself that there was love between Heinrich and I. I feel he remembers me fondly. I don't visit him. I just don't like to admit I was wrong. Because of him, I died of my own pride.

I didn't need to visit Mariola much in the beginning. She had McKinley's steadfast love and their two beautiful children. I didn't visit much until Lisa Hubbard had cancer. I hate to say this, but one of the best moments of my afterlife was when Lisa died. I witnessed her passing peacefully with family around her. Lisa's first words in the afterlife were, "Aunt Natalie? Hello!"

I knew Mariola held me dear all those years despite how awfully I treated her. Sometimes I feel sad that it will be awhile before we are reunited. She has another decade before she reunites with Lisa and me. She will see Lincoln's baby. That will be years down the road. Its name won't be Obama.

Chester and my mother followed. At times one of them will join me as I observe my family with pride. Susan, my lovely daughter, achieved more than I had dared dream of when she broke through academic, professional, and political barriers to become an openly gay college professor. Alexandra is a perfect blend of my mother and me: weaving practicality and whimsy in all that she does. Shona, my dear ambitious yet directionless granddaughter. She'll find her way. My nephew Chip is going to point her towards San Francisco where he has contacts at newspapers and graduate schools. The rest will be up to her.

Then my great-granddaughter, Natalia, she is a fun one too watch. She has all of the favorable traits of her father. She is charming and funny. Sometimes she sees me. I could never talk to her, but now the next time she holds one of her parlor trick séance for the neighbor kids, she'll know who I am.

A green glow illuminates the room. Susan and Alexandra are oblivious to it. From behind, I hear a car horn honk. I turn around and walk through the apartment into the street.

There is Heinrich, parked in a red Chevrolet Corvette. His wrinkled face's painted as a skeleton. He wears a black suit with glowing painted bones.

"Get in."

"Are you freshly dead?"

"I ain't all dead," Heinrich says, "but I sure ain't alive."

"Get back in your body! Susan is coming back to Ohio! She can visit you! You'll get closure!"

"Closure is overrated," Heinrich remarks as he revs his engine.

"Where do you think you are going? Especially with the sins you committed?"

"Heaven. I found Jesus in prison. Now are you finally going to leave the sphere trap and expand your horizon?"

"No! Alex is pregnant! I want to see the baby. Shona is going to build her writing career and Susan is going to strive to be a better grandmother. I want to see these things!"

"Why? I was alive! They left me to rot!"

"You dug your own grave when you let me fall into mine!"

I feel the tingle. I feel it with Natalia whenever she sees me. I look up. Shona is staring at us through the window.

"What about her?" I ask. "She respects you."

"I left something," Heinrich answers, "the family copy of 'the Town and the City".

He drives away. It's all I can expect from him. I walk through the brick into Susan's apartment. Shona walks into the kitchen.

"I have this feeling something happened…"

Alexandra asks, "What are you talking about Shone?"

"I think Grandpa Adolphson just died."

"Okay…."

Susan chimes, "Grandpa Adolphson?"

Alexandra laugh, "Yeah, if you weren't adopted, your name would have been Adolphson. Another bullet you dodged, Mom!"

I laugh with my girls.

These are the moments that keep me on Earth. I didn't choose to die and leave my child motherless. In spirit, I decided to live. In my family, I find so much for my spirit to continue living.

Dear Reader,

The Route 40 Phantom is a legend from my parents' hometown of Englewood Ohio. My mother recounted the legend when we were out to dinner one night, not knowing I use what she tells me in my novels. In the 1950s, an unidentified man tried to drive people off the Englewood Dam on Route 40 wearing a skeleton mask and an illuminated suit. Most articles claimed the "Phantom" was a mentally ill young man. Whoever he was, the unknown prankster left his mark in Ohio History. Musician Jim Colegrove wrote a song about him. Many supernatural experts include the Phantom in their haunted history despite him not being an actual ghost.

A real ghost I experienced while writing this novel was that of my grandmother, Joretta Barr Weimer. I finished my first novel, "Answered" coming home from her funeral. During that trip, I visited the Randolph Township Historical Society with my grandfather. There I learned more about the Route 40 Phantom. I started the novel immediately when I returned to Minnesota. For a few months, unexplainable things happened.

Weeks after my "Gram's" death, I was talking to my "Pops" on the phone. I had placed a glass of on the table when my partner came in the door. As I went to hug him, my Pops cracked a joke about my Grams' particular nature in decorating. The moment I laugh, the wine glass was thrown across the room.

During the following Christmas, my daughter had a bunch of star balloons from her birthday resting on the ceiling. A red star lowered itself and started floating around the entire apartment. When I saw it dip itself to enter the kitchen, I knew any source of air flow moved the balloon!

My Grams never cared for by love of ghost stories, yet she bought me my first copy of "A Christmas Carol" and tolerated my playing with the Ouija board in her house. Had she hated my honest portrayal of her complex persona in my supernatural novel, her ghost would have hacked my computer. Instead, I wrote the book without the hurdles that I jumped through in writing "Answered." Grams propelled me in spirit to achieved what she couldn't witness in life.

Sincerely,

S. Collin Ellsworth

ABOUT THE AUTHOR

S.Collin Ellsworth is the author of the novel, "Answered" and the host of the podcast, "10,000 Lakes, 10,000,000 Books: Conversations with Minnesota Authors." She was born in Dayton, OH. She moved to Eden Prairie, MN as a child and is an alumnus of Minnesota State University Moorhead. She is the daughter, niece, and cousin of Northmont High School Alumni. Her maternal grandparents were charter members of the Randolph Township Historical Society. Ms. Ellsworth currently resides in Bloomington, MN with her family.

www.ingramcontent.com/pod-product-compliance
Lightning Source LLC
Chambersburg PA
CBHW071132170626
46809CB00002B/590